SNIFF

BOOK 1 IN THE SNIFF, SMOKE, SHOOT SERIES

GC BROWN

STORY MERCHANT BOOKS
LOS ANGELES

SNIFF

ISBN-13: 978-1-970157-47-5

Story Merchant Books
400 S. Burnside Avenue, #11B
Los Angeles, CA 90036
www.storymerchantbooks.com

www.529bookdesign.com

www.gcbrownbooks.com

SNIFF

GC BROWN

This book is dedicated to anyone who's ever had the balls to change who they were.

SNIFF

BANK ROBBIN' DAVE

The End!

That's what this looks like.

Some of the worst of the worst type of shit.

I'm sitting in my Aston Martin Vanquish, all the way in the back of a public park in Pompano Beach, Florida, minding my own business. There's a gun under the passenger seat, a needle hanging out of my arm, and a bag of cash on the floorboard, which technically doesn't belong to me.

And cops are closing in from all directions.

Smart money says I'm fucked.

And to think, I thought I got away with it.

The first two banks went off without a hitch. I walked in through the front doors wearin' a ski mask, wavin' a note around. Both times, I left carrying a sack of cash to the collective tune of two hundred and eighty-six thousand dollars.

I needed sixty-four thousand more, and I was hangin' up my cleats.

One more job.

I got the sixty-four thousand…and then some.

The "then some" is the cash on the floorboard. It's about forty thousand. It's slated to go to a guy named Paper. Paper sells China White—the good shit. Because of it, a few weeks back, I was almost dead. Like *murdered* dead. I was in a garage, kneeling on a piece of plastic with a gun to my head. If I hadn't confessed to robbing banks, Paper would've had his enforcer, Link, pull the trigger.

I owe Paper seventy-five grand.

And he wants it like right off the bat.

I'm still short, but he'll have to be okay with the forty for now.

Thankfully, I stopped off at the house first and dropped off the sixty-four thousand—what I needed to be done robbing banks. It's now stashed with the other cash in a lead-lined bag in the ceiling above my garage, giving me a grand total of three hundred and fifty thousand. Or, as I refer to it, the amount my wife's cancer doctor is blackmailing me for.

This is after already giving him close to two million dollars.

For the record, that two mil didn't come from robbing banks.

I took it from a Russian gangster named Yakhov. Pronounced *Yak-off*, if you're the guy who took the money. I agreed to pay it back. Even pinky swore. Starting out, I had good intentions. I made the first couple of weekly vig payments, like four months ago.

It's been "get fucked!" ever since.

This makes Yack-off very angry. He keeps sending guys around to break my legs. I keep sending 'em back. Hasn't helped our relationship. I suppose the heroin addiction hasn't exactly helped either.

If you only knew the whole story....

I used to be somewhat of a big deal.

A professional Money Maker, livin' the dream.

I took my helicopter back 'n' forth to work every day. I dealt with billions of dollars. Movin' and shakin'. It was my grind. And I was lucky enough to do it while living with the love of my life and l'il Tom in a Swiss chateau right outside Zurich.

Things changed.

I lost it all.

It started with an arms deal in Yemen and spiraled into doctors telling me my wife would be dead within six months. Now, here I am, surrounded by cops. They seem to be pouring in from every direction. They've moved in closer now, pointing service weapons at me from behind the safety of their open car doors. There's a helicopter circling somewhere above. Someone's screaming at me over a loudspeaker. It's pandemonium.

I need more time.

I grab the gun from beneath the passenger seat and put it to my head.

This gives the cops pause and me time to scroll through the contacts on my phone. I'm calling a retired hooker who used to work for me. She's the only person I know who can help at this point. I find her number, hit dial, and put it on speaker.

The cops are screamin' again to lower the weapon.

The curve ball didn't work for long.

It's finally ringing. *C'mon, pick up. Pick up. Please.*

"Hello…."

PART 1

1

CHARGE IT!

Dubai
Three Years Ago

It's 10:00 a.m.

At least that's what I think the clock says.

One of my arms is still tied to the bed, and I'm trying to focus around a nipple. The nipple belongs to a hooker. To which hooker, I have no earthly idea. I seem to recall several of them hanging around last night.

Fuck, my head hurts.

It takes me a couple of tries, but I get myself untied. I sit up, swing my feet over the side of the bed, and step on another hooker passed out on the floor. She doesn't even move. I wish I could tell you the whole story, but I was halfway in on a bender when they showed up. I will tell you this—although I'm super fucking annoyed I'm stuck in Dubai, I'm happy to have at least made it back to my hotel.

There have been other occasions where I've come to on the other side of the world.

It's the main reason I rarely do cocaine.

We don't get along, cocaine and me.

The problem is we keep trying to work it out. You know how it is, some days you have to just step over a hooker to start your day, and others, you wake up and just have to figure out where the fuck you are.

Whaddaya gonna do?

I throw on a hotel robe and go off to find my phone. The hotel suite runs right around seventeen grand a night, so the robe is posh. Same with the view. I'm forty-five floors up in the world's only self-proclaimed seven-star hotel, staring out at the Persian Gulf.

I know what some of you are thinking: *What's this jerk off bitching about?*

Well, for starters, fuck off.

You come over here and deal with these Hezbollahs.

Plus, I'm hungover as hell, my phone is MIA, there are hookers lying around like wet beach towels, and this place is a fucking mess. I've been holed up here in the Sandbox for the last five days...waiting on a fucking phone call. Not to mention, I've got sand wedged into places my mother's never seen.

To top it all off, I'm *supposed* to be in Greece on a three-week vacation.

Do you have any idea what the hookers are like in Mykonos this time of year?

It's the height of the season there. Hookers from every nook and cranny on the planet. The place is crawling with 'em. Exotic hookers. Crazy hookers. High-class hookers.

Low-class hookers. Hookers with a friend. Hookers I might never see again. It's hookers and hookers and hookers.

Again, whaddaya gonna do?

Before you and I can go any further, we need to get something straight. I don't need to pay for sex, by any stretch of the imagination. I'm six five, two hundred and thirty pounds, and work out like my life depends on it. My mother's Puerto Rican, like J.Lo. My dad's six five, Belgian with dark hair and blue eyes. I have his height and coloring and Mom's olive skin. Plus, I read, write, and speak four languages—French, English, Spanish, and Russian.

And if all that's not enough to make you puke or want to punch me, I'm paid.

I mean like *paid* paid.

Honestly, I only pay for sex because I can. Plus, I have a hooker fetish.

I'm not talking about hookers you find on Main Street. I'm talking about *Pretty Woman*-type hookers. Hookers who run two and three thousand dollars a night. Hookers who'll earn you a smack from wifey for trying to cop a second peek. I parade 'em around town. It's dinner. It's dancing. She tells me the lies I wanna hear. Then it's back to my place for anything I like.

Poof! She's gone in the morning.

Simple.

It's my pop's fault. He bought me my first hooker. I was fifteen. Shy. He said it was easier than trying to explain the birds and the bees. Two weeks later, it was a lot harder to explain the rash to my mother. She called her priest back in San Juan while Dad went out of town on business.

Anyway, I finally find my phone under a couch cushion and walk out onto my balcony, while it's still almost bearable outside. I've missed several calls and texts from Mikale. He's my business partner back in Zurich. We've been best friends since we were kids. He's at his sister's wedding in Lake Geneva.

I've known Maggie her entire life. I was supposed to attend the wedding. I'm basically part of the family. The problem is, I very recently had a "thing" with Maggie's maid of honor, Kennedy. And Kennedy's married to a dickweed billionaire who runs in their father's inner circle.

Hence, the thing.

Two months back, a glass just missed my head at one of the umpteen social events leading up to Maggie's wedding. A short time later, their family decided it might be better for everyone if I sat it out. Mikale didn't have the *couilles* to tell me to my face. Instead, a few days ago, he left a first-class ticket to Greece on my desk, with the note: *Sorry, Buddy. Get some R&R. You deserve it. See ya in three weeks.*

As I was cheerfully packing, the phone rang.

Ten minutes later, Mikale and I were on a video conference with Dubai. The landowners were ready to sign the deal on our next build site. This is Mikale's end. I close the deals, he signs them. This is a fairly good size deal for us. We've been waiting on the call for months. Fucking Mikale tells them he can't make it over because of the wedding. Doesn't even try to ease it in.

It was crickets on the call.

I jumped in.

I figured, fuck it, guess I gotta go. No problem. I'll drop into Dubai for a day or two, do a little schmoozing, grab the check for two hundred million dollars, then it's hookers here I come.

Shit never works out like that, though.

Ever!

The next day, I flew here. When I arrived, the front desk handed me a note from the landowners: *Enjoy Dubai. We'll be in contact soon.* And nothing since. I've been telling Mikale their panties are in a wad because he ducked out on being here. He says I'm being irrational.

Go figure.

I'm calling his ass right now. He's not picking up, of course. Oh well, I reckon it's as good a time as any to break the news to him. So, at the beep, I leave a message. "Dick-face, I put another round of hookers on the credit card. I'm not going to stop until there's a check in my hand."

Charging pussy to the business account is my go-to.

Even more so when I want to get even with Mikale.

Last year about this time, Eva, Mikale's wife, went all Sherlock Holmes on our credit card statements and uncovered my sins. The line item didn't exactly say *Pussy for Sale*, but it didn't take a professional dick either.

Eva gives Mikale all kinds of hell over it, which gives me the warm fuzzies. Eva and I don't see eye to eye on anything. She thinks I'm a total dick. I'm not expecting the relationship to get better anytime soon. Truthfully, I couldn't care less if she discovers my indiscretions. I'm not trying to score points with her. However, Mikale thinks she'll eventually spill the beans to one of our investors. It's a fucking crock. I've never professed to be an altar boy. I agreed to make our investors money. And make money, we all have.

Mikale and I manage some serious loot.

Wall Street-type loot.

Valtara Enterprises is our company.

We've got a handful of investors with Batman money who've kicked into our fund. All of it goes toward condominium development projects around the world. We've been at it for a few years now. Boca Raton, Florida, was the site of our first project. Dubai's going to be our second…if the fuckers would just call and bring me the check.

I need to get back inside, get rid of the hookers, and get on with this day.

2

FUCKING DUBAI

Exotic Entertainment: $11,856.00

I told ya it doesn't exactly say *Pussy for Sale.*

I just got an email alert from our business credit card. Means Mikale did too. Wouldn't even surprise me if Eva got one. Dollars to doughnuts, he brings it up the next time we speak.

Oh well.

So, today, I'll probably just hang around the hotel, smoke some hashish, do a few laps in the pool, lunch on the veranda, and maybe grab a massage. That's about it, though. I'm still sore from yesterday. I went skiing from like nine in the morning until running into the hookers around four in the afternoon.

The day turned into a marathon from there.

You know about the hookers, so let me tell you about the skiing.

Most would assume, since I'm in the desert next to an ocean, I'm referring to some type of water skiing. Well, no. I went snow skiing…right up the block from my hotel. These people have so much money, they've built a mountain on top of the sand, enclosed it, and made it snow.

I'm not talking about a little hill where you wait your turn to ski down either.

Try some real-life, Aspen-type shit.

And talk about fuckin' you in the drive-thru. They don't even advertise the skiing 'til you get off the plane. After all, how would Burberry, Hermes, Gucci, and Prada sell enough winter clothes to afford the commercial rent they're paying here in town? It ended up costing me twenty-five grand for the day just to keep warm.

I said these fuckers had a lot of bread.

I didn't say they were stupid.

You don't build the most outlandish city in the world with shit for brains. When Mikale and I told our investors we were headed here next, and that the same project we'd just built in Boca Raton, Florida, was now going to cost them double, no one batted an eye. Who wouldn't want a condo in Dubai, right?

"You ain't made it 'til you've done it in Dubai!"

I was going to put the slogan on a red hat.

Look what it did for 45.

Anyway, these guys I'm waiting on are brothers, the Khaleed brothers. They're rumored to be related to the Royal Family in Saudi Arabia. The problem is, everyone over here with a few more camels than his neighbor says the same thing. So, who knows? I don't put stock in any of it. I will tell you this—these brothers are flush.

Like "rollin' in it" flush.

They own a ton of sand here.

The brothers are said to have strong-armed their way into town when it became apparent the place was about to go bananas. Timing is everything. We met them through one of Mikale's contacts, a Jack Hassan. Jack is old, old money that goes all the way back to the turn of the last century.

Mikale has all kinds of contacts like this. That's because Mikale's daddy, Mr. Lars Van den Broeck, is a VIP. And VIPs send their kids off to boarding schools. For his seventh birthday, Daddy sent his little boy off packin' to a school in Switzerland—an all-male boarding school that's been ranked in the top three in the world for the last hundred years.

Mikale graduated from there with a Rolodex of *Who's Who.*

Some real silver spoon-type shit.

One night about a year and a half back, Mikale and I were out celebrating the recent success of our Boca Raton project in my favorite nightclub in Zurich. Naturally, high-class hookers and cocaine were present. For me, anyway. Mikale crushed up a Ritalin and had a glass of wine.

So, we're sittin' there shootin' the shit, and Mikale gets a call from our contact in Cabo San Lucas, Mexico. Cabo was supposed to be the site of our next development following Boca Raton. Turned out, someone stepped in at the last minute and outbid us on the land. At the time, construction in Boca was more than 50 percent complete. In order to keep our investors happy, we needed to find a new build site and *rapido.*

Mikale began to hyperventilate. He left and went home to hammer the phones. I went to the restroom, did a rail of coke. Figured I'd get to the office late the next day and do what I do, which is close deals.

Things changed.

I woke up four days later at the Four Seasons Hotel in Maui.

By the time I rolled back into Zurich, Mikale had arranged a meeting in Dubai with this Jack Hassan. We brought along our construction plans from Boca and told him we wanted to replicate the condominium development here. Jack took our plans and said he'd see what he could do. He called back a month later to say he had just the guys for us—the Khaleed brothers.

Seven months later, here we are.

I walk back out onto the balcony to have a smoke. As soon as I pull from the hookah, someone buzzes the door at the front of the suite. *Putain de merde! Can't a guy just smoke a little hash in peace?* It's probably just housekeeping. I walk back inside and fling the door open.

Fuck.

It's two Arab mercenary-lookin' dudes…with attitude. *Can they smell the hash?* I shit my pants. The penalty for drug use over here is a firing squad…if you're lucky. A super-speedy trial too.

"Get dressed, Mr. Liecht," one of them says, barging his way in.

Get dressed? What the fuck?

They seem to be looking around, like they're making sure I'm alone.

"Care to tell me where we're going?"

"The Khaleed brothers are prepared to meet with you," the pushy one says.

"*Yalla imshi!*" the other one at the door adds.

That loosely translates to "get the fuck moving!" like I'm the one holding them up.

Mikale is so dead.

3

THE MIDDLE OF FUCKING NOWHERE

Things seem a tad off.

Could it be the hash?

I'd gotten dressed and followed the Khaleed brothers' henchmen out of my suite and into the service elevators at the far end of my hotel floor. The whole time they appeared to be looking over their shoulders, without trying to appear to be looking over their shoulders.

Seemed a little strange, but I didn't object.

They hustled me through the kitchen and out the back emergency exit of the hotel. Again, not so crazy enough for me to speak up. A white Range Rover was waiting, motor running. Two more flunkies were standing there with the doors open. Before I had the time to express my concerns, I was wedged in the back seat between the Middle East's version of Hobbs and Shaw. Now, it's too late. There are more pressing issues to be concerned about.

Like trying to make it out of this vehicle alive.

If you've never driven in the Middle East…don't.

There are no set rules, only mere suggestions. This guy behind the wheel's got the speedometer pegged, and he's more interested in blabbing away to his buddies than keeping his eyes on the road. The four of them haven't shut up since we left the hotel. The conversation seems normal enough, but Arabic is not one of my four languages, so….

We left the city limits of Dubai a while ago. It's now down to two lanes. Every five or ten kilometers, we pass another hovel with penned-up goats, camels and sand. Spades in all three. I've rung Mikale, over and over, right up to the point of losing reception. Of course, he didn't pick up. His text messages are now full of caps and f-bombs. In so many words, if I end up on a milk carton, he'd better hope no one ever finds me.

I told you, Mikale and I have known each other forever. He was my first friend in Brussels. When I was fourteen, my parents sold our home in Yonkers, New York, and we moved there. Mikale's family's estate was a couple of miles up the road. When he'd come home from boarding school "on holiday" and summer vacation, we'd hang out.

We were total opposites.

Heads and tails.

Still are.

Mikale is stuffy dinner parties, where he consumes no more than two glasses of wine, wearing starchy shirts and creased pants. Home and in bed by 10:00 p.m. To work every day, he's Dapper Dan with his custom suits and straitlaced wingtips. He was born into money.

Not me.

I'm a craps table in Monaco, a hundred grand on the line, blow in my pocket, and a dime on my arm who cost me four racks for the evening. And to work…forget about it. I'm usually late, rushing through the door in sweaty gym clothes or still dressed from the night before.

Mikale says I'm undignified.

He came looking for me, so….

Six years ago, I was bouncing back and forth between Wall Street and the Intercontinental Exchange in London. I'd been working the trade desk for one of these venture capital firms. Because I have the gift, I made my bones early in the game. I was already sitting on a cushy, green mountain of success.

In walks Mikale with a business proposal.

Now, he's always been a bit shady in my opinion, but a friend nonetheless, so I listened to his pitch.

At the time, he was Senior Vice President of Development for the Four Seasons Hotel chain. But he wasn't getting along with upper management and wanted to branch out on his own. He needed a wheeler-dealer. Someone slick with the lingo.

In walks *moi* with his solution.

I came with a list of demands—the least of which was that the home office needed to be in Zurich so I could ski. Three months later, with views of the mountains in Uetliberg off in the distance, we were putting together deals.

Been doin' it ever since.

Holy shit, it seems like we've been driving forever.

We're finally exiting the highway in the middle of fucking nowhere. There's a man at the corner of the off-ramp, wearing the Muslim costume. The sheet looks like it's been slept in. The turban's seen better days. He's leaning against a camel, smoking a cigarette, scrolling through his smartphone. Doesn't even bother to look up.

Fucking guy's probably on TikTok.

I'm basically being held hostage, and I can't get a signal to save my life.

We're now headed in the opposite direction of the paved highway…across sand. Kilometers and kilometers of the shit. Doesn't keep Ali Baba from continuing to drive like a bat out of hell, though. And he's still blabbing away. It's another twenty-five minutes and an end doesn't seem forthcoming.

And just so you know, phone-totting camel jockeys aren't even an anomaly over here.

They're fucking everywhere.

We finally reach the top of another dune and, off in the distance, something's reflecting the sun. This must be where we're headed. Up and down more dunes and we run into four armed men, standing in front of an old Land Cruiser. All of 'em smoking. All of 'em wearing the sheets and turbans. We stop. The windows go down. Turns out they're all buddies.

Hehe-ing and *haha*-ing…for like ten minutes already.

You believe this shit?

I lean forward and smack the back of the driver's arm. "Hey! You think you and Makmood here can talk about blowing something up later? I need to be somewhere this afternoon…back there in civilization," I say, pointing over my shoulder.

I'm not sure how many of them understand English, but everyone goes silent for a second before picking right back up where they left off. Like I'm not even here.

I'm contemplating saying something a little more offensive, but I'm not sure exactly how far I can push the envelope with these types. You think Mikale's going to be mad about the hookers on the credit card, try returning home two hundred million dollars short.

I'd never hear the end of it.

We're moving again.

Two more crests of sand and there's a huge purple-and-gold tent set up in a valley. Think Old Testament, only the tent's much bigger and a helluva lot nicer. I'm positive the biblical camels are close by, but I'm betting the Khaleed brothers arrived in one of the four Range Rovers parked out front.

We pull to a stop, and everyone gets out.

In this corner of the globe, individuals continue to reside under the control of figures not unlike these brothers. It's still slaves and masters. And I'm sure when the slaves are delivering their captives to their masters, certain protocols are expected to be followed. Like walking the kidnapped through the front doors, possibly even forcing them to their knees to bow to the master.

Not today, fellas.

I'm not following anyone, especially out here.

Plus, I've vowed to only kneel to God and pussy.

I run around the back of the Rovers and come out in front of the tent...unescorted. Like I said, the tent is big. The two panels at the front are being held open with thick burgundy ropes, with two six-foot stone flowerpots flanking each side, probably weighing close to a metric ton each.

It's sheer Muslim audacity.

The good thing is the place looks too nice to behead anyone.

I step out of my loafers and leave them outside in the sand. When I walk through the open panels, it's dim. Doesn't keep me from noticing the two guards right inside. They're wearing matching sheets with expensive-looking jewels on their turbans and in the hilts of the scimitars on their sides.

Two of my kidnappers tried following me in but were dismissed in harsh Arabic.

They'll probably lose some fingers and shit shortly.

C'est la vie.

A carpet covers the sand from one end of the tent to the other, and there are a handful of servants moving around. The brothers are at the back, sitting on giant pillows, smoking from hookahs. They stare me down as I cross the tent, finally standing when I stop in front of their little picnic.

The older of the two, Mohammed, reaches out his hand first. "David," he says, with a slight bow. "We are sorry to have kept you waiting. We hope your stay in Dubai has been pleasant."

"What the fuck, Mohammed? Why the kidnapping?"

"We've had some recent threats. Until they are settled, we are staying outside of the city and taking precautions. Please, let us sit. We have much to discuss."

As Mohammed shouts several commands in his native tongue, Akmed, the other brother, bows and says, "Good afternoon, Mr. Liecht."

From thin air, two extremely gorgeous women appear, dressed as Disney's bad Jasmine. One has a large pillow, which she sets down. The other one is carrying a hookah. Everyone waits for me to sit.

"Hashish, I hope," I say half joking as I pull from the water bong.

Neither of them responds, like they're suddenly the pope.

It's not hash, by the way. It's flavored tobacco. Tastes like bad goat. Hookahs are part of a long tradition over here, so…. Truth be told, hash is the way to go. If you're going. I take one more pull, pretending I give a shit about their customs. Getting down to business is really all I'm interested in. If we hurry, I can still catch the late flight out to Mykonos. A few *zzz's* on the plane and I'll hit the party runnin'.

"Let me just say, on behalf of both Mikale and me, we are looking forward to a long and prosperous relationship with you here in the Middle East."

"Ah, well…yes, let us talk," Mohammed says, all serious. *Meirda.*

Here it comes. It's always something. Can't ever just hand over the fucking check and sit back. They must think I'm going to sit here and listen to some sob story or reassure them they're making the right decision. Not today. Not me. I know from past experiences the deal wagon will come around again tomorrow. They can hand over the check or not. I don't care. I've been kidnapped, crammed between five hundred pounds of smelly hummus, and brought all the way out to the middle of fucking nowhere.

I don't have the patience to deal with this today.

These boys have the wrong partner.

"Gentlemen, if I may speak frankly," I begin. "I'm not going to sell you on this deal again. It's take it or leave it. I can have a backup for the money by this evening. And we can certainly find another piece of sand to build on. We've only kept the door open for this long as a courtesy to Mikale's contact here."

Mohammed does the slight-bow thing again. "We are most grateful for the opportunity. We are not looking to back out of the deal. In fact, quite the opposite. We have brought the money with us," he says, happily.

There's something more coming, I can see it on Akmed's face.

"Please follow me outside," Mohammed says.

I follow him out the tent and over to the Range Rovers. Mohammed walks around to the driver's side and opens the door. He motions for me to look inside. Stacked on the passenger seat and floorboard are black duffel bags. He gives me a nudge and says, "Look all the way inside."

A wall of bags fills the vehicle from one end to the other. "What's in them?" I ask, praying he's not going to say what I think he's going to say.

"Two hundred and thirty million dollars."

Thought so.

"Can't be mine. This is not what we discussed. The funds need to be wired to our business account in Switzerland. Plus, there's an extra thirty million here."

"The extra thirty is for your troubles, David. You can figure out how to get it wherever you need," Mohammed says. There's something in his voice, like I don't have a choice in the matter.

"Maybe before 9/11, but not today. It'd be easier to get a camel through the eye of a needle."

"It is possible. My contacts tell me you and Mikale are the guys to get it done. The thirty million dollars is a great incentive."

I can't spend it from a jail cell, you daft cunt.

By now, some of the brothers' muscle have moved in closer, and Akmed's whispering to their two private guards at the entrance to the tent.

All right, all right, I get the point. Everyone just keep their hands where I can see 'em.

I take another second to consider my options. Fine! Yes, I can probably get it done. And the extra thirty million dollars does help.

"I will do my best to make it work," I tell Mohammed.

"*Inshallah,*" he says. "God willing."

Suddenly, there's no undercurrent threat, and he's Allah's man again. It's fucking bullshit.

So much for Greece.

4

TALK ABOUT RIDIN' DIRTY

I feel like I'm in a low-budget hip-hop video.

No drugs. No guns. No homies.

It's all about the Benjamins, baby....

Two hundred and thirty million dollars' worth. Plus the Range Rover, which the Khaleed brothers told me to keep, before pointing me in the right direction. I've been driving for forty minutes, and I'm still in the fucking sand. The GPS shows 6.4 kilometers more until I hit pavement.

I can't wait to get Mikale on the fucking phone.

His ass, I gotta hear about this wedding bullshit. Who the fuck throws a wedding for ten days anyway? This cock-sucking phone—how is it I still have no reception? I've passed two separate caravans of Bedouins on camelback, and most of them were on their phones, blabbin' away.

Fucking third world bullshit.

It takes me another twenty minutes, but I finally get a signal. I can't dial Mikale's phone fast enough. It's just fucking ringing and ringing, though. No answer. This ass-lick dickface! This is the shit I'm talking about, and he's worried about me showing up to the office in sweaty gym clothes and charging pussy to the credit card? Fuck him.

He's left me no choice.

I dial Kennedy, Maggie's maid of honor. We haven't spoken since she decided to stay with her husband.

She answers. "I thought you might never speak to me again," she says, almost in a whisper.

"How's vanilla?"

She laughs. "Boring."

"Want me to record a few of my best moves? I can send them to his phone…like a dick pic."

Another laugh.

That laugh. I still hear it all the time. "How's he treating you?"

"You know, we're trying to do the counseling thing."

"Remember what I told you about a turd."

"Hard to polish."

"Bingo. Listen, as much as I love keeping you from him, I need to speak with Mikale. It's kind of an emergency, and he's not picking up."

"He hasn't left his daddy's side for the past three days. Every time I see them, they're whispering about something. I'll go find Mikale and tell him to call you right back."

"I'm here in the Sandbox. Reception is super shitty. Tell him to keep trying."

"I thought you were in Greece."

"Yeah, no."

"Okay, let me go find him. I miss you," she hurries and says, then disconnects. Like she had to say it but didn't want to chance me not saying it back.

I would have. Not that I wanted to, but I would have.

The "thing" I was telling you about with Kennedy, it went for over a year. No one knew. Not Mikale. Not even Maggie, and she and Kennedy have been best friends their entire lives. They met when they were in diapers. Mikale and I are more than a decade older than them. Maggie was an accident. By the time they were running off to their first day of school, Mikale was studying International Business at Oxford, and I was at NYU in the United States, studying Finance.

After graduating, I started rippin' and runnin'. I'd seen Kennedy a handful of times over the years, but it had been at least seven or eight before we both ended up at one of these "My Dad's Bigger Than Your Dad" parties. This particular one was being thrown by Mikale's father.

Kennedy showed up…married.

In my defense, she didn't exactly bring this up right away. In fact, she never said anything about it until my hand was already in the cookie jar. And some things you just can't take back. If I'm being totally honest, I'd heard she'd married a few years earlier, but….

I didn't have intentions of attending the party. Ironically, I purposively planned not to attend. It was in Brussels for one. And two, I've always hated this type of crowd. My plan was to get out of Zurich for the weekend and head to my flat in London for a few days, reacquaint myself with the Queen's hookers. Mikale wouldn't let the fucking thing go, though. Kept insisting I attend, whining, "There'll be more than a hundred billion dollars in the room."

"So fucking what," I'd said.

Mikale doesn't get it, never has, never will.

Biggie said it best: "*Mo money, mo problems.*"

I'm pulling in six to eight mil a year. In my sleep. Easy peasy. I'm not trying to grow the business any bigger than a forty- sometimes fifty-hour workweek. That's it. I'm living this thing they call the American Dream, but overseas. Mikale's trying to land in *Forbes'* Foreign Billionaires next to his old man.

All the same, I eventually let Mikale talk me into going to the party. I did put my foot down, though. "I'll go, but I'm doing it baked," I told him.

Two hours into the party, I was bored out of my mind. If I had to listen to another "on my yacht in the South of France," or "at my Swiss chalet" story, I was going to blow a fucking gasket. I snuck out back. Fired up a spliff.

Twenty minutes into imagining myself anywhere but there, Kennedy plopped down next to me and invited herself to the other half of the joint. She took a big pull. Held it like a man. "If I ever throw one of these lame-ass parties, punch me in the vag," she said, exhaling.

"Deal."

We locked it in with a fist bump.

"Let's get out of here," she said.

I figured, what the hell? Run it up the flagpole. See what happens.

Well, I ended up falling. Hard. Head over heels. I even stopped hookers, cold turkey. She kept telling me she was going to leave her billionaire hubby—they weren't shaggin'.

Then she ended up pregnant. It was his. She broke the news to me a few weeks before one of Maggie's many wedding shindigs.

"We're going to try and work things out."

She told him she'd been having an affair but never disclosed with whom.

Fast-forward to the party. *Hors d'oeuvres.* I'd been drinking. Heavily. "Toast! I've got a toast," I slurred. Even clinked a champagne glass a couple of times with a spoon. Got everyone's attention.

Dead silence.

After two minutes of slobbering, there were no secrets left in the room. I finished with, "And Kennedy says you're a boring fuck. Vanilla."

Mic drop.

Her husband was the one who threw the glass at my head.

I lied, telling myself I was starting to crave hookers again anyway.

It's taken fifteen minutes, but Mikale's calling now. I answer. Before I can unload on him, he says, *"Enculer!"* (It's French. Literally translates to *ass-fuck*. Slang for jerk-off, shithead, ass-munch, dickface—names you'd call your buddies.)

"Asshole. I've been calling you all day."

"I sent you a text telling you I'd be unavailable. It's Mother. She makes Father and I hand over our phones every morning. We don't get them back until the end of the day's festivities. I just had to go explain to her that it was an emergency. She's been planning this wedding since Maggie turned four."

"How do you manage to swing from Mommy's nipple to polishing Daddy's knob so seamlessly?"

"Lots of practice. Now, what's the emergency?"

"Have you bothered to even check your texts or voicemail?"

"Not yet."

"I've got the money. I'm driving it back to the hotel now."

"What do you mean?"

"It means your terrorist buddies paid in cash."

"Cash? The whole two hundred million?"

"No, they gave me five twenty-dollar bills and the rest in food vouchers. What the fuck do you think?"

"I think you're a dick. How are you going to get that much cash into the bank?"

"No idea. They gave us an extra thirty million to help figure it out."

"Well, if there was ever a guy to figure it out. Money needs to get to the contractors in London, though. There's zero chance they'll take cash. You'll have to be very careful cleaning it. You won't make a good prison bitch."

"Why do you assume it would be me going to jail?"

"Mommy's nipple, Daddy's knob."

Good point.

"I'm going to get the money up to the hotel room. We'll go from there."

"Do you think that's safe?"

"Well, I'm not going to advertise it. Got any better ideas?"

"Not at the moment. I'll pull Father aside, see what he thinks we should do."

"I'll be back at the hotel in about an hour. Call me back, Mikale. I fucking mean it," I say and disconnect.

Before I get to the hotel, I receive a text from him saying we need to talk about the hookers.

Did he miss the part about the Rover stuffed with dough?

5

HOOKUPS

I've been thinking.

I need a guy.

Someone who knows their way around. Someone who can keep their mouth shut. Gotta have some *cajones* too. Why not a bellhop? Everyone, the world over, knows they're the hookups in town. Especially at these "seven"-star gigs. Drugs. Hookers. Underground fight clubs. Illegal gambling. Cock fighting. Dogfighting. You name it, they got it…for a price.

I'm back at my hotel.

Instead of pulling all the way up to the valet in front of the lobby, I park half a football field away to assess the situation. I'm staring at the bellhops. I'm about to ask one of them to help me move two hundred and thirty million dollars without telling them it's *two hundred and thirty million dollars*.

If I'm going to be killed over this money, I'd like to at least pick my own poison.

I thought about moving the money myself, but how am I going to get forty-odd duffel bags up to my room without drawing attention? No one carries their own luggage to their rooms. Especially here.

Guess it's now or never.

I pull up and stop in front of the bellhops. Half a dozen of them are standing next to luggage carts, waiting to pounce on the next big tipper. I lower my window and point to one. He strolls over. His name is Zachariah, says so on his name badge. "I've got some bags I need to get up to my room," I tell him, covertly handing him a hundred-dollar bill. "I don't want to walk them through the lobby."

He leans forward and spies the bags in the passenger seat. I roll down the rear window. He takes in the full scene and quickly tabulates a big tip. "Go around to the back of the hotel. I will bring a helper," he says.

As I'm driving around back, Mikale calls.

"Tell me something good, cretin."

"Father made some calls. These Khaleed brothers are into some bad shit. Suspected of being in the opium trade. Dangerous guys, he says."

"A little late to start playing investigator. These are your friends. We met them through your contact."

"Maybe give the money back while you're still there."

"Lemme get this straight. You want me to go and tell a couple of dangerous guys, 'I'm sorry. I no longer want your drug money,' in a place where chopping off heads is just another day at the office? Do me a solid, blow it out yours and your daddy's asses."

"Well, when you put it like that. What are you thinking then?"

"I'm thinking of calling Bundu."

"What for? He's in Morocco."

"No way his father could've gotten rid of all those diamonds he stole, right?"

"No way. He took billions' worth. Got to have them stashed somewhere," Mikale says.

"I have a friend in the Diamond District in New York. If I bring him the stones, he'll send a wire transfer wherever we need it to go."

"Are you thinking of doing the whole two hundred million like that?"

"I don't want all our eggs in one basket."

"What with the rest then?"

"I'm calling Kennedy."

"What the hell for? Are you out of your rabid-ass mind? Do you know what I've had to endure over the past week, because of you and Kennedy? My father blames me for not controlling you. Like I have any say-so over where you put your little dick."

"That hurts. I'm dealing with Hezbollah cell leaders over here, and you're worried about Daddy. Now, do you remember Sam, the little dude who followed Maggie and Kennedy around when they were in high school?"

"Vaguely."

"Well, Sam turned out to be LGBTQ or some shit. I'm not sure which letter applies, but it's Sasha now. He's like some big-time gay. Reps his district and shit. Owns a chain of art galleries around the world. Art's just like diamonds, instant cash. I can get him to send a wire transfer too."

"Tell me you'll keep it strictly business with Kennedy," he says.

"I'll keep it strictly business with Kennedy."

"Ah, fuck you, David. I can hear the smug look on your face."

"Gotta run. Give Daddy my best."

Right as I hang up, Zachariah and his helper are pushing luggage carts through the same exit I came out of this morning. I pull right up to them and unlock the doors. It takes about ten minutes to get all the duffel bags transferred from the Rover to the carts. There are forty-six of them in all. Five million in each bag. If I had to guess, I'd say each one weighs right around fifty kilos.

That's like a hearty nine-year-old.

Try stacking forty-six of them.

We're in the service elevator now. This is what it takes to get both luggage carts in the same elevator with the three of us. The two bellhops are sweating like Trump on election night.

The other bellhop, whose name is Ivan, called me a dickeater in Russian. It wasn't to my face, so I let it slide. He was in the middle of trying to position one of the nine-year-olds on top of the stack. "*Trakhni menya! Chto u etogo chlenoyeda v etikh sumkakh?*" he mumbled to himself. "Fuck me! What's this dickeater got in these bags?"

Ivan doesn't know I'm fluent in his native tongue. Not yet.

I just looked at him…hmm. Then I glanced at Zachariah to see if he understood Russian too. He did not. I told you I need a guy. Ivan might just work. Depends. He needs to pass the test. Starts with him throwing a punch at me…or not.

Don't worry—I'm not going to be sticking around, waiting on it. Not for nothing, people have been taking shots at me my whole life. I've been told I'm a smart ass. Tends to get me in shit. But I'm something of a ninja, and the shots rarely land.

Okay, maybe not a ninja, but I do have a fifth-degree black belt in karate. I've been practicing since my dad took me to a dojo when I was four. He did it to get away from my nagging mother. There was a bar right next to the dojo. Billy the Kid's Karate on one side, Billy the Kid's Buds & Suds on the other.

Same owner: Sum Li.

Went by Billy.

It was circa 1970s in fucking Yonkers. I don't know what to tell you. I didn't learn until years later, in the middle of sparring with Sensei Billy, that "Billy the Kid" was the only reference to American pop culture he could remember from his childhood growing up in Tokyo.

Sum Li moved to the Land of Little Big Dreams with his family when he was twelve. Started calling himself Billy. He ended up owning half the town. On top of the bar and dojo, Sum "Billy" Li owned Billy the Kid's Toss & Tumble for Kids, Billy the Kid's Laundromat, Billy the Kid's Hot Dogs & Chips, Billy the Kid's Pawn Shop, and Billy the Kid's Travel Agency.

Billy was kickin' the shit out of Yonkers.

For like ten years, Pops drank at Billy the Kid's Buds & Suds five days a week, while I trained with Sensei Billy next door. When we moved to Brussels, Pops found me a karate school around the corner from our house. I went here and there, but it wasn't the same. When I moved back to New York for college, I started training again at Billy's place. After graduating, every time I went back to New York, I'd go by the dojo to work out.

I attended Billy's funeral about six years ago.

He owned that place too: Billy the Kid's Dead and Gone Funeral Services.

I open the doors to my suite and direct the bellhops to leave the carts in front of the piano. "I'll empty them and call the front desk when I finish." I give each of them a three-hundred-dollar tip. I'm sure that's their hourly rate anyway. Especially here.

They turn to leave.

"Ivan, your mother takes it up the ass from camels," I say in Russian.

He turns with fire in his eyes.

"Yeah, I know her. Best blowjobs in all of Russia."

He takes a second, then charges me and takes a big swing. I casually step to the side, avoiding the Deontay Wilder haymaker. He went right on by. It takes him a second to regain his balance. I see him considering coming at me from a different angle.

Karate, like most martial arts, teaches you to not fight. Teaches you to walk away. Most times, I do. This Russian charges me again, though. He's going to need vodka for the headache.

I hold up my hands. "In all fairness, you called me a dickeater first," I tell him in Russian.

He considers this. Relaxes.

33

"Now, I got a job for you if you want it. Alone, and you cannot tell anyone. That includes your buddy here," I say, chin-pointing to Zachariah.

"What's it pay?" he asks. Not *What kind of job?*

"*Dve tysyachi dollarov v den.*"

Basically, two stacks a day. I'm sure it's more than he's ever made. He'll be back. I walk over to the door and hold it open. "Be back here this evening at *shest' chasov*. Don't be late."

He nods, and they leave.

I hang the *Do Not Disturb* sign from the doorknob. Engage the lock. Clasp the chain. Head for the patio. I need to think. The hash will help. I'm halfway through a huge pull when my phone rings. Mikale.

I hit the speakerphone but can't say anything.

"David…. Asshole! You there?" He pauses. "Hellooo."

I finally exhale for as long as I can, then cough. "Yeah, I'm here."

"Are you getting high? Now?"

"Nah, it's just hash."

"A drug?!"

"Nah, it isn't even as strong as mid-grade weed."

"I hope they shoot you in the nuts."

"That's fucked up, dude."

"It's confirmed, these brothers are the bomb diggity—no pun intended—in the opium business. It's not widely known, but my contact Jack Hassan was able to do a little more diggin' and confirmed. The Khaleeds have covered most of it up over the last ten years, but all their money stems from drug sales."

"Too late to turn back now. We've got thirty million reasons to make it work."

The door buzzes.

"I gotta go. Someone's here. Keep your phone on."

So much for the *Do Not Disturb* sign. I take another pull from the hookah. Quick hold. Exhale. Fan the air a few times. Go to the door. It's the Russian. Early. I let him in. *Shest' chasov,* means 6:00 p.m. I look at him, like, *what gives?*

"My shift finish. Nowhere to be," Ivan says.

He's still wearing the uniform.

"Stay here," I tell him and walk over to the bags of cash. I reach in and peel off seventy-five hundred dollars in crisp bills. "Get rid of the monkey suit. Go buy yourself three black suits, white-collared shirts. The tie is up to you. I don't give a rat's ass either way." I hand him the money. "Know any more Russians looking for work?"

"Da."

"Bring four of them here. Rotate them round the clock outside the door. Get back here as quick as you can. You're on my time now." I pass him my phone. "Put your number in here."

"Da, Boss."

I've got to hide this money somewhere.

6

BLOODY DIAMONDS

The phone hasn't left my ear.

It's been close to three hours.

It's taken me this long to track down Bundu. Excuse me, "Prince" Bundu now. I've known Bundu as long as I've known Mikale. He moved to Brussels at the same time as me. We were the new kids. I never had to call him Prince. No one did. He was just Bundu.

Technically, he is royalty.

His uncle was the king of Zaire, now called the Democratic Republic of Congo, in Central Africa. Bundu's father, the king's only brother, was the hand to the king. Together, they caused so much bloodshed, the country eventually broke out in a civil war. Bundu's family—and I mean from the king down—were overthrown and asked to leave the country by an angry mob, chasing them on foot with sticks and stones.

Three decades later, they still appear to be having difficulty accepting the defeat.

Because Zaire was always war-torn and famished, the privileged kids were sent to different schools around the world for their education, which is how Bundu and I wound up at the same international school and became friends.

Bundu lived in a palace his parents built for him.

I used to stay over for days on end.

The place had like nineteen bedrooms, twenty-five baths, a movie theater, and so on. Bundu had dozens of servants, all dressed in Central African-type clothing, running around doing everything but wiping his teenage ass.

One time, I opened a back bedroom door, looking for Bundu, and stacked from floor to ceiling, front to back, were hundred-dollar bills. Bundu said there were several more rooms just like it in several other palaces around the globe. I believed him. BBC News said that, while in power, his uncle and father stole billions in cash and diamonds from the country.

These people were loaded.

When Bundu's family was finally banished from Zaire, and war-crime fingers pointed, Belgium turned its back too. In our junior year of high school, Belgium officials seized the palace in Brussels. I talked my mom and dad into letting Bundu stay with us so he could graduate.

Bundu's family stayed on the run for a little more than a year, until some Moroccan officials could be bought off. They settled in Casablanca. Two days after we graduated, Bundu hightailed it to Morocco. I couldn't really blame the guy. We stayed in contact for a while, but life is life.

It's probably been three or four years since we last spoke.

It took a circus of phone calls to reach him.

When I did, a servant answered and told me his "Prince" Bundu was napping. I cursed him in everything but Chinese and swore I'd have Bundu cut his balls off if he didn't immediately go and tell him I was on the phone.

I hear him trying to wake Bundu now.

"My prince, someone is demanding to speak with you."

Bundu is screaming something in Swahili. I don't understand the language, but I catch the drift. "Who is this?" Bundu finally screams into the phone.

"Ricky Martin, muddafukka!"

"Anus!" Pronounced *a-noose.*

French for, well, you guessed it.

"It took me almost three hours to track your black ass down, then your manservant said "his Prince" was getting his beauty sleep. What the fuck, man?"

"Sorry. My father insists the staff call me Prince. My uncle and all his sons are dead."

"So, you're next in line to be king...of what?"

"Exactly."

"My father is off his rocker."

"How is the serial killer these days?"

"Scared shitless. Thinks Morocco is going to give him up any time. I tell him he's probably right, and that he should just stay in his room. I have him convinced Morocco's Directorate for External Security is right outside the front door."

"You're a psychiatrist's wet dream."

"Fuck him. He's guilty of killing half the population of my country. What's the harm in mind-fucking him a little now? He's got dementia anyway. Plus, it's not like I got him hiding under the bed. So, what's up with your cracker-ass?"

"I'm half Latino, you know?"

"Yeah, but you act and look super-white."

"In some places, you'd be considered racist."

"Not here. White lives don't matter."

"For sheezy, my neezy."

For the record, Bundu and I, along with our whole gang of friends in Brussels, grew up on Snoop Dogg, Dr. Dre, and NWA. That wasn't just West Coast hip-hop. That shit was everywhere. We seen *Friday* in the theaters, too, just like you, so don't get shit twisted.

"Hey, did I hear you and Kennedy were bangin' behind her hubby's back? Fucking lover boy. You never could keep your dick to yourself. You better not fuck up the Nova Terra deal."

"Nova-what?"

"Her husband's big multi-billion-dollar deal. I figured you and Mikale would be involved."

"Oh, yeah, that deal. Of course. I thought you said something else. Anyway, Kennedy dumped me a few months back. In other news, listen, I need your help. Your dad still have all those stolen diamonds lying around?"

"Some. We've sold a lot. It's not cheap to live on the run."

"I'll give you top dollar. Cash."

"How much are we talking here?"

"A hundred million dollars' worth."

"Whoa! What are you wrapped up in now?"

"I've got to wash some cash, then get it into an account in London."

"I can scrape together about half that without telling the old man."

"Any of the stones legal, by chance?"

"Legal? They're blood diamonds."

"Worth a try."

"I can get some origination certificates for you. I've got a guy right here in Morocco. The paperwork will be good enough to get past Customs in most countries."

"The United States?"

"You would say there. I'll make sure he goes the extra mile."

"What's it going to cost me?"

"A parcel that big, the family discount, of course, probably talking five million."

"Fine. Can you set it up?"

"No problem. When do you need them?"

"Twenty minutes ago."

"Where are you? You'll have to come to me. Because of the death threats, I haven't been able to leave Morocco in the last two years."

"Shit. Sorry, buddy. I'm in Dubai. I'll have to line up a private plane for tomorrow. I'm bringing the cash, so I won't be able to fly commercial."

"Don't worry about lining up a flight. I'll send my plane. We bought a brand new G6 that's just sitting around. It needs to be flown. You're staying for my birthday party tomorrow night too."

"That's right, happy birthday, man. But, no, I cannot stay. I know how your parties turn out. I have to return to Dubai. I'm deep in the shit right now, dude."

"Lots and lots of women will be there." He says it like he's dangling the carrot. "You still like women, right?"

"Is this your clever way of trying to get me in the sack?"

He laughs. "Who the fuck knows these days? This gay shit's everywhere."

"Right? How big was this closet these people were hiding in?"

"You're tellin' me. All right, my manservant will text you the details for the flight. We'll talk about the party when you get here."

"Bundu, I'm not staying. I mean it. I know your stupid ass."

He laughs as we disconnect.

I still have to figure out where I'm going to hide the money.

And what the fuck this Nova Terra deal is.

7

DIRTY MONEY

When I said seven-star hotel, I meant seven fucking stars.

Like I've said, 'bout seventeen grand a night.

I've got three master bedroom suites, a full kitchen with a private butler—I told him to beat it the first day—my own patio with a pool facing the ocean, a piano, pool table, living room, dining, and two powder baths. Prices only go up from here. Almost a hundred grand a night for the penthouse.

I'm not sure what they could possibly have up there.

I'd look and tell you, if I thought I could get past the security guards protecting the private elevators to those floors. And don't be thinking it's a couple of fat guys with whistles and pepper spray. I'd walk right past those clowns. No, these guys look like they're daring someone to try and get past them.

"Over my dead body! I'll blow us to smithereens!"

In Arabic, of course.

I'm not racial profiling here, either.

I'm in the shower in my bathroom. Settle the fuck down. It's not that kind of story. This is where I've decided to stash the cash until I figure some shit out. I get the last bag stacked inside and shut the glass doors. Funny thing is, even with the two hundred and thirty million in cash, there's still room to take a Puerto Rican bath.

Before stacking the money, I called the front desk and told them I'd be staying here for at least another week, and nobody goes in my room for the duration of my stay. The request is not at all unusual in places like this. Believe me. Rich men from all over the world show up to rent the higher floors for their wives, their jewels, cash, et cetera, then put the mistresses and girlfriends under lock and key in the rooms below. Nobody in, nobody out. Period. Secrecy is a must. It could be the single difference in a costly divorce versus just a run-of-the-mill nasty one. Nobody wants to give up half their fortune—and still have to take the kids every other weekend.

Some of my friends have the li'l fuckers.

They just run around all day, making messes. I'd like to wet their lips, stick 'em to the window. Fifteen, sixteen years later pull 'em down, teach 'em to take over the world. I mean, imagine not having to watch *Dora the Explorer* or *Barney* four thousand times a day.

If I see purple dinosaurs, it's because I've smoked some killer shit.

Now, where's this fuckin' Russian? I find his number in my phone. Fucking jerk-off doesn't pick up. The first day on the job, he's already ignoring my calls. I'm getting ready to leave a "friendly" message when Mikale calls.

"Awe, Mummy let you use the phone. That's cute. Now whaddaya want?"

"Listen, *conard,* Father has a way to clean a hundred million or so of your dirty money."

"You've got a lot of nerve, *my* fuckin' money. You got me wrapped up in this bullshit. And since when does Mr. Tight Ass want to get his hands dirty with anything?"

"Not him exactly. One of his friends. Some big shot lawyer to the king of Belgium. I've met him once or twice before. His name's Jargons. He's a giant slob, always wears white suits. He's here at the wedding." He pauses, expecting me to say something.

"I'm listening, asshole."

"I don't have all the particulars, but Father said Jargons asked him for a hundred million in cash three or four weeks back. Told him he needs it for some kind of arms deal. Said he'd send a bank wire within a month with an extra ten million on top. Father said he was considering doing it."

"The balls on you. First, you get me wrapped up with Middle East drug lords. Now you want to get us involved in some arms deal? Are you trying to get me killed?"

"Get ahold of yourself. The deal must be on the up and up for my father to even consider doing it."

"And I suppose Daddy still wants the ten mil?"

"Half. You know how he is."

"Well, at least it covers the cost for the diamonds. I have to give five million to our black friend for the paperwork to get the stones into the United States."

"How is Bundu?"

"Confined to Morocco. Asked me if I was involved in some Nova deal with Kennedy's husband. Somehow, he knew about us. You hear anything about this deal? Pretty strange Bundu knows about it clear in Morocco."

"No. Nothing. The guy's a billionaire. I'm sure there are lots of deals we haven't heard about."

"Yeah, you're probably right. Anyway, Bundu's sending a plane for me in the morning. Trying to get me to stay for his birthday party."

"No way. You'd be crazy to. I said I'd never go to another one of his parties again as long as I live. You remember last time? Someone put something in my drink. I woke up to an Asian prostitute trying to stick her fingers up my ass."

"She told us you likey likey."

"Fuck you. That shit's not funny. I've never been the same."

"Save it for your shrink. Let me know what's up with Daddy and go find Kennedy. Tell her to sneak away and call me. Tell her I need to get in contact with her homo friend Sasha."

"It better be for Sasha. Her husband's going to have your balls severed. Send Bundu my best. Later."

Might as well enjoy Dubai for the night. I'll pop a couple Xannies on the plane tomorrow, wake up in Morocco. I googled the flight time. I'm going to be stuck in the air for like nine hours.

Someone's buzzing the door. I squint through the peep-hole. It's Ivan and his friends, I think. Looks like Jersey Shore meets Putin. Ivan's in a suit. His four friends are in jogging suits and jewelry. Two of 'em with toothpicks dangling from the corners of their mouth.

I make Ivan's friends wait in the hall.

45

"Where'd you get these guys, a movie set?" I ask when the door closes behind him. He starts to answer, but I cut him off. "Never mind. Pay each of them a grand a day. Rotate two of them round the clock outside the door. No one gets in unless I say so. Understood?"

"*Da.*"

"And go to the front desk, tell them you quit. I'm going to need you for at least a week. I'm giving you twenty-five thousand dollars flat. That'll hold you over 'til you can find another job after I leave." I stare at him, expecting him to argue. Truthfully, it might make it easier coming and going with him still employed here, but I can't chance him gossiping about things he might see.

"*Da,*" he finally says.

"Is *da* all you know?"

"For twenty-five thousand dollars? *Da.*"

"Good point. I need to blow off some steam tonight. Know any high-class Russian hookers?"

"No." He looks at me seriously, then laughs. "*Da!* Of course. The very best."

"Well get to it then."

8

A-MUSE-ING

Ocean is this one's name.

It's actually *Ocianna*.

Her friends call her Ocean. Apparently, so do her johns. Either way, she's Russian, twenty-eight years old, and the hottest chick in the room. She's also fluent in several languages. Been in Dubai for a couple of years now, on break from putting herself through law school in Paris.

Technically, at her rate, I'm paying for her law degree.

I don't bring this up.

We're out to dinner for sushi at The Naked Fish, located on the 154th floor of the tallest building in the world. It's the place to be tonight. From where we're seated, I see sheiks, sultans, an Egyptian pop star, and diplomats from around the globe. The only reason I was able to get a table is because of Ivan. And, on top of getting us in, there was a complimentary bottle of expensive wine on the table when we sat down.

I told you, bellhops are the hookups. Ivan's probably recommended this place to his hotel guests a hundred times
over. The owner knows it, so when Ivan calls and asks for
something, he gets it.

The waiter's pouring each of us a glass of wine.

"Tell me, *Da-veed*," (This is the way Ocean pronounces
my name—from her eyes to her chest. Like I'm exotic or
something.) "What brings you to the UAE, business or
pleasure?"

"Business, I'm afraid. I find no pleasure in the desert."

"Is there a wife or girlfriend back in Switzerland?"

"I'm recently single. I was involved with a married
woman."

"Not something I hear men admit to every day."

"She chose to stay with him. I got to meet you. Case
closed."

"Did the husband find out?"

"He did."

"And?"

"He launched a champagne glass at me."

"Scandalous. Do you miss her?"

"Sometimes."

"If she walked in the room right now?"

"You're my secretary."

"And if she's still sleeping with her husband?"

"Secretary with benefits."

"You're funny. Do you gamble, Da-veed?"

"I play craps and blackjack sometimes. I love Monaco."

"Oh, yeah? Would you like to play tonight?"

I shrug. "Could be fun."

"Give me your phone," she says, holding out her hand.

She's having a conversation with someone in a language I don't understand. Gives me the time to set a few things straight. I know some of you are under the impression there's no gambling over here in Muslim country. Sharia Law, they call it. That's just what the fanatics want us to believe. Fake news. Everyone sins. And the bigger the money, the bigger the sins.

Probably worse here in Dubai than most places.

Think Las Vegas. The extravagance. The dazzle. The shock. The mind-blowing excitement of the place. Well, Dubai bends Las Vegas over the desk. For three straight days. Goes to town. Not even spit. *Bam! Bam! Bam!* Seventy-two hours, zero breaks.

What happens in Dubai, stays in Vegas's ass.

Someone should put that on a T-shirt.

Ocean finishes her conversation and hands my phone back. We finish eating. She goes to powder something while I pay the tab. Raw fish for two, cold sake, free wine, and wasabi ice cream for dessert; comes to the monthly electric bill for my London flat.

Not complaining.

Just painting a picture.

We leave and board the elevator outside the restaurant. I'm expecting to go down, in more ways than you can imagine, but Ocean has other plans. "The helipad," she tells the porter, and up we go.

Ten minutes later, we're in the back of a private, eight-to ten-person helicopter, the interior decked out in Louis Vuitton. Easily twenty million dollars. Ocean's sitting across from me. Legs crossed at the knees. Dress just covering the parts I'm thinking about. She's taking me to Abu Dhabi to

49

a private party being thrown by some sultan. "It's about a thirty-minute flight," she tells me.

We arrive at an all-white oasis, out in the middle of the desert. It's lit up like New York City. The palace looks like the Taj Mahal. We're hovering over the top of the helipad now. There are four more helicopters the same as this one, all grounded below.

This guy is soaking in the mullah.

We're driven in golf carts to the front entrance of the palace. On the way, we pass a motor court with sports cars galore, and at least four separate motorcades of limos. I've counted at least two dozen paramilitary dudes scattered around, too. All of 'em heavily armed.

I'm not sure if it makes me feel safe or not.

The giant doors behind two more guards at the front entrance peel open. Talk about iced-out or turnt up. Oh, not familiar with hip-hop terms? Try opulent then. I've never seen anything like this, and I've been in my share of lavish properties all over the world. This guy has managed to find the fat in all this sand…and raked it in, hand over fist.

Believe me, he's got it.

And wifey must not be home because she'd never go for this, unless she's into this kind of thing.

There are fifty to sixty people in this room. Probably two to one, women to men. People from all over the map. All of them fawning. The room smells of anticipated sex. I get a look out at the pool area and there's at least as many people there too. Same odds. And all the twos look like dimes, with only four cents' worth left of their bathing suits.

It's pure, unadulterated hedonism.

The deluxe package.

Again, don't believe the hype. All the women over here are not covered from head to toe in the black sheet. It's more fake news. And, believe me, there's not a single man here complaining about it. Funny, no prayer rugs in sight either.

Pussy wins again.

The motherfucker's undefeated.

Before we can get across the room, someone's screeching, "Ocean! Darling!"

I glance around and spot this guy sashaying toward us. He's wearing a white linen suit and a hot-pink boa.

Ocean leans over and whispers, "That's Marty. He owns the place."

Are you fucking kidding me?

The sultan and Ocean do the French-kiss thing—cheek to cheek, cheek to cheek. He gives me the once-over, mm-hmms to Ocean, then leans into me for the kiss. I mean all the way in. Like possibly trying for tongue.

He's met by my hand, three fingers to his forehead. "Easy, Elton," I tell him.

Ocean laughs. "Not this one, darling."

"A travesty." He bites his lip, then shakes my hand, turns, and spreads his arms. "My home is your home. Anything you should desire, I will have arranged." Before I can even respond, Marty pats me on the ass *à la* "*good game!*" then leaves to go fondle someone else.

Ocean thinks it's hilarious.

As we make our way across the room, conversations stop. Everyone knows Ocean. The ones who don't, look like they want to. It has nothing to do with casual sex either. Goes way beyond. It's painted across their faces. She works the room. A cheek kiss here. A whisper there. A pat on the chest. Even a pair of high-fives. More languages than I care to count. It's like she's a muse or something.

She introduces me as Da-veed to her friends.

The last person left in the direction we're headed turns and catches sight of us. Well, he sees her if I'm being honest. A military man. Not a grunt either. This guy's ranking. Razor-pleated blue slacks, red jacket drippin' brass and ribbons. As we get a little closer, I recognize him from billboards around Dubai.

Ocean walks right up, leans in. French-kiss thing again. "This is General Alsheri, Da-veed," she says. "Commander of UAE Special Forces."

"General." I shake his hand. "Shit goes down, I'm following you."

He laughs. "I've got a tank parked out back."

"Good. We can pull one of those helicopters. I'd like to have one back in Zurich."

"Oh, Zurich. A banker then?"

"Kind of, I guess. I manage a fund for some friends."

"Don't be modest. If you're at this party, with this lovely woman, then they must be very rich friends."

Ocean butts in. "Not tonight, my loves. No boring business. Let's have fun." She locks her arm through mine again and drags me away from the general, as he chuckles.

Who the fuck is this woman?

We walk through the palace. Round a corner. Bend a couple of hallways. Pass rooms you can't imagine. End up in front of a pair of closed doors. There are two huge Africans—black as the color purple—out front. They're both wearing floor-length, white fur coats, bright-red, knee-high leather boots, Marky Mark underwear, which are also red, and no pants or shirts, with the fur coats wide open.

Fuckin' Marty.

One of them opens the doors.

It's the adult version of Mandalay Bay. The room is two stories with a glass catwalk halfway up that goes all the way around the room. A dozen or so women are dancing to house music in their birthday suits. That's not totally true, two of them have Albino Boas slithering around their necks and bodies.

I'm not talking about boas from Marty's closet either.

Everyone's clear on the type of party and people here, right? Then let me explain some of the other sins, at least according to Sharia Law, in my eyeline: slot machines to card tables—baccarat, craps, roulette––and scantily clad waitresses serving the alcohol of your choice.

One of them is standing in front of us right now, holding a tray of cigars, Monte Cristos to Macanudos. I decline. Ocean chooses a Cuban. She runs it under her nose, then hands it to the waitress for her to clip and light. "You don't know what you're missing," Ocean tells me, pulling on the cigar.

Seriously? I love this hooker.

If I find out she watches football on Sundays and occasionally farts—"Mom, Dad, there's someone I'd like you to meet…."

I follow Ocean to the back of the room to the blackjack table. I take the only open seat, considered to be first base.

Ocean stands behind me, her arms resting across my shoulders. She leans in, her breath touching my ear, "Good luck, love," she says just loud enough for me to hear.

53

9

FUCKIN' ACES

The blackjack dealer is shuffling the decks.

I'm still at first base.

I'm down a little over a million bucks. Not sure I even care. I've had a few and have come to realize this is all Mikale's fault. I'm billing everything to my expense account. It's "pussy and gambling." Figure out a way to write it off. It can be done.

Call Trump.

It's down to the four of us now, plus Ocean, and the prick dealing the cards. The guy to my left has spent more time paying attention to Ocean than he has his cards. He hasn't shut up since he sat down, blabbin' away to her in Spanish. Neither of them knows I speak the language.

Comes in handy.

We're in a private palace in Abu Dhabi, on the other side of anywhere considered Latino. He assumes it's just the two of them in some far-off land. Like, "What are the chances?"

He's told Ocean about his whole life. Says his friends call him Sobe.

Sobe reminds me of the James Bond type, just a tad older. He's sporting an expensive tuxedo, wavy, salt-and-pepper hair, and bright-white teeth. He hasn't said, "Shaken not stirred," but looks like he could at any moment.

Sobe's a pilot. He's confessed to Ocean that he's done some time for flying cocaine out of Colombia back in the day. He's here now, flying privately for someone else. Doesn't take a big leap to assume he's still smugglin'. Just do the math. He's here, hangin' with a bunch of fat cats with big wads, and Abu Dhabi happens to be smack dab in the middle of the world's opium trade. Not to mention he's been playing between fifty and hundred thousand dollars per hand and doesn't seem to mind that he's losing.

Two plus two equals four.

On Sobe's left is "Toe."

That's what the guy said to call him when he sat down. I didn't ask him why. He's some kind of music mogul from Atlanta, Georgia. There's an act here in the UAE he's somehow affiliated with. He's giving tickets away to people who come around to say hello.

Toe's had pretty good luck tonight. He can certainly afford to spend some of his winnings on the couple of tarts standing right behind him.

To his left is an Algerian Jew.

I know, doesn't make sense to me either. His name is Uri. He didn't tell us this. He hasn't said much, in fact. Mum's the word. Ocean whispered his name in my ear. Said they've been acquainted in the past.

Mm-hmm. "Acquainted."

I bet.

Anyway, can't really blame the guy for keeping his mouth shut. Uri's wife is here. Wowzers. You should see this one. She's a Parisian hotel heiress. She's at the next table over, trying her luck at poker. I've seen her over the years in the London tabloids.

I examine this Jew a little closer. What's this lucky motherfucker have? Is it the nouveau, pretty-boy beard? The slick suit? He looks like he works out breakfast, lunch, and dinner. Can this be it? Maybe he fucks like a rabbit. Who knows? The last shoe was good to him, though. He's up a half-million dollars at least.

The last seat, third base, is occupied by some local prince. Ocean told me his name, but I couldn't pronounce it if you promised me tickets to the World Cup. I do know the guy has A-RAB money. He's wearing the Muslim sheik wrap thing. The headpiece too. And sunglasses…inside! His security team is within spitting distance, and there are enough women around to be considered a harem.

Money's not a problem.

He's an annoying shithead.

He's been playing a million dollars a hand. Aloof. Clueless. A couple of hands ago the dealer was showing an eight, eighteen you have to figure. The wankjob had fourteen. The book says to hit and hope for the best. It certainly doesn't say to double down with another million bucks. Obviously, he didn't read the book. He slid the million dollars across the felt. Took one card: queen of hearts. Busted. Could've done it for free. Instead, another two million dollars out the window. He said something in Arabic. Everyone but me laughed. He slid another million out for the next hand.

Lost that too.

The dealer's done shuffling.

It's the first hand of the new shoe. I push two hundred thousand dollars' worth of chips out. I always bet heavy on the first hand of a new shoe. I have no idea why. It rarely works. The dealer buries the first card, then turns up a nine of diamonds for me. He comes back around and puts a king on top of the nine: nineteen. He's showing a five of spades. A lot of blackjack players play this as a bust hand.

Everyone at the table stays.

The dealer busts. Everyone wins.

I've got five hundred thousand and some change in front of me now. I leave two hundred thousand out for the next hand. I get an ace of diamonds for my first card. I need the dealer to paint it for Blackjack. That means any ten, jack, queen, or king. There are sixteen of those in every deck. We're playing with six decks, three hundred and twelve cards. Ninety-six of the ones I need. 'Bout one to every three. Pays two to one, if I get one. I'll walk out of here down less than two hundred thousand dollars—one of my wrist watches.

Mikale won't even bitch.

The dealer gives himself a six of spades—the worst card he could have drawn. He slides my second card out and flips it over, another ace. The book says to split them. Make two hands. Fuck it. I slide out another two hundred grand in chips. The dealer completes the second round of cards to the other players.

He's back to me.

He slides out the second card for my first ace. It's a nine of clubs for twenty. An excellent hand facing the dealer's sixteen. The next card for my second ace is another ace. Shit.

I've obviously got to split 'em again. Another two hundred grand. I don't have that much left in front of me. I have to get another marker. I'm into Marty for a million-plus already. He's holding my Black Card hostage.

I told him I have the cash back at my hotel.

The dealer calls the pit boss over, whispers. The pit boss nods. The dealer pushes the chips out, then gives me a seven of hearts for eighteen. One hand left. He slides the next card out of the shoe. It's a four of diamonds, five or fifteen. I'm facing the dealer's sixteen. What the hell? Double down. I call for another marker. Pit boss again. More whispers. Another nod. Two hundred thousand dollars more on my bill. One card.

It's a six for twenty-one.

I'm hot as fish grease!

I've got eight hundred thousand smackeroos on the line with a twenty, eighteen, and a twenty-one...facing a bust. Almost impossible to lose. I'll leave with money in my pocket. The dealer congratulates me, moves on to Sobe. He's got seventeen. Stands. Toe has nineteen. He's happy with it. Mossad's got blackjack. Looks like he's got about eighty thousand out in chips. First hand all night he's played more than fifty thousand dollars.

I told you the motherfucker's lucky.

Third base to go. Prince Wankjob has sixteen. Definitely a stand. Let the dealer bust out. Not this clown. He pushes out another million dollars and fucking doubles down. Insanity! Even the dealer pauses to make sure he heard him right. No one at the table is happy. The dealer slides the card across the felt and turns it over, revealing a jack of clubs. He busts.

Another two million dollars gone.

He doesn't care.

The dealer turns over his hidden card. It's a ten of hearts. He's got sixteen! The House would've busted if this daft cunt hadn't taken a card. I'm holding my breath, not on purpose, it just won't come. The dealer slides the next card to the front of him, turns it over. It's a fucking five of clubs.

He's got twenty-one!

I lose every hand, even the push goes to the House.

The dealer rakes everyone's chips. The pilot tells Ocean he's had enough blackjack, going to try poker instead. Toe's muttering "Parental Advisory" lyrics, and the Jew's just happy he won…again. Lucky for me, my phone vibrates in my suit jacket. It's Mikale. I tell Ocean to play with the few chips left over and excuse myself from the table.

I find my way out of Marty's palace.

10

PROS AND CONS

Of all fucking things.

I'm driving to Yemen.

Not right now. In three days.

This is what Mikale was calling about. Now I have to meet this arms deal guy, Jargons, there. Red flags are popping up in my brain. I mentioned them to Mikale. He pooh-poohed them away. Easy for him—it's not his ass on the line. Everything in me says walk away. The fuck do I know about an arms deal in Terrorist Town?

I'm a fucking banker, not some *Mission Impossible* dude.

Things don't add up.

One, this Jargons is supposed to be some kind of an attorney to the king of Belgium. So what the fuck is he doing involved in an arms deal? In fucking Yemen to boot. Two, he's looking for cash…a lot of it. Why not just go to the bank? Three, why's he not doing it in his own country, where he has immunity or at least the king's protection?

Four, and the worst of the reasons, he can't come to Dubai to pick the money up on the way to Yemen. I have to drive it there.

It's always something.

I let Mikale rattle off the nine thousand reasons why it wasn't safe to take the cash by plane before I finally hung up on his dumb ass. I then sent him a text: *You just lost a million and a half dollars playing blackjack. And you can bet your balls there are going to be lots more hookers. I'll call you back from the chopper, dickbag.*

Let him wrap his mind around all that.

The more time I have to think, the more I realize I'm way in over my head. Yeah, I do a few drugs here and there, and I listen to gangsta rap. So fucking what. Doesn't mean I'm comfortable with shootin' up the block or cookin' up a batch of crack…or driving a truckload of cash through fucking terrorist training camps.

I need to figure out how to keep all this together, without being kidnapped or killed.

Shit like this, I gotta keep updating my pros and cons.

I immediately started doing just that when the Khaleed brothers basically forced the two hundred and thirty million dollars on me in the middle of the desert. Cons: One, I had to drive the cash back to my hotel. Two, I was going to have to figure out a couple of quick deals to wash the money. I couldn't really come up with a third.

It was easy to find three pros.

One, the hotel was only right up the road. Two, I've been doing deals my entire life. And, three—*ka-ching!*— *thirty mil.*

Simple enough.

Let's go, ya chicken shit!

Ten minutes later, I was driving the cash-packed Range Rover across the desert.

Again, I find myself in a very similar situation—driving cash across the desert—albeit there's a different set of pros and cons. We'll start with the cons again. Like last time, there are only two. One, I have to road-trip the cash roughly twelve hundred miles through the Hilton-free Middle East. Two, there are rumors of actual terrorist training camps existing all along the way.

Now the pros.

I could only come up with two. One, if I wear a nice bedsheet, the turban, and a pair of dark sunglasses, I'll pass as a wealthy sheik. And, two, with the money we'll make from the diamonds, art, and the five million from this arms deal, Mikale and I will pocket close to forty million fat ones.

Two cons. Two pros.

Tie goes to the money.

Guess I'll be driving to Yemen.

Let's go, ya chicken shit!

I'd walked outside Marty's palace to talk to Mikale in private. When I stroll back inside, Ocean's still in my seat at the blackjack table. I need to get out of here, so I can figure some shit out. I tell Ocean I need to find Marty. I owe him a bunch of money. I should dine and dash on his ass, like back in Yonkers. However, he has the credit card. Plus, there's the small matter of needing one of the helicopters to get back to Dubai.

I tip the dealer ten grand, and we excuse ourselves from the table.

SNIFF

Ocean says she needs to use the ladies' room before we leave. I'm waiting right outside and up walks this Toe guy from earlier. "Ello, Chap," he says, faking a British accent and shaking my hand. When he lets go, he leaves a small, glass vial in my palm. "Egyptian Viagra. Cheerio," he says, winking as he walks off.

Hmm.

Not sure what to make of this.

The Viagra might be useful, though.

Ocean's back. Now, where in the fuck is this little fruitcake, Marty? We find him outside on the veranda. We walk up as he's finishing his story. "Ocean darling," he says, all lips and hips, "meet my new friends Ryan and Bryan. They're brothers." The three of them do the French kiss thing.

It's my turn. Marty introduces his new friends to me. "Don't go in for the kiss," he tells them, then giggles. In turn, they giggle. Everyone all lips and hips.

I thank Marty for the evening and tell him we must be getting along. He snaps his fingers. One of the Africans in the fur coat walks over, his red boots clicking on the marble. They have a conversation in a language I don't understand. I get the gist, though. The African's coming with us to get the cash.

If changing into something more appropriate has crossed anyone's mind, no one bothers to mention it.

An hour later, we're walking through the lobby of my hotel. It's after 2:00 a.m. Thankfully, there aren't many people around at this hour. The ones who are here, can't take their eyes off us. *A hotel guest with a striking call girl and a massive African man, wearing matching red boots and panties...draped in chinchilla.*

They probably think I'm some kind of freak.

Same thing goes for Ivan's guys upstairs.

Two of them are posted up in front of my suite. They're starin' at me when we walk up.

"Take it easy, assholes," I say to them in Russian. "The African's just here to pick something up. Keep him here with you. I'll be right back."

Ocean and I pass through the doors alone. The quicker I get rid of the streaker, the quicker I can get the hooker in the sack. I leave her in the living room to get comfortable and run off to my bedroom. I remove one of the pillowcases from the bed and fill it with 1.4 million dollars from the shower.

Mikale's going to have something to say about this, I'm sure.

11

TRIPPIN' BALLS

I was just hangin' from the base of the toilet.

A zebra-striped rhinoceros was chasin' me.

Some serious shit!

I did a line. The Toe guy said, "Egyptian Viagra." Bullshit. I've done my share and the next guy's share of Viagra. This ain't Viagra. It may have Viagra in it, but there's unquestionably something more. Feels like Ecstasy and Peruvian Mushroom Dust are in an all-out fistfight. One second, I couldn't wait to get this hooker in the sack. The next, I was in an office building, tryin' to outrun a rhino.

Like, WTF?

Maybe I did too much.

I crushed up four of the little pills on the bathroom sink, rolled up a hundred-dollar bill, and went to town. I checked myself in the mirror. As I turned to walk out of the bathroom, something felt off. Like "oh shit!" off. I turned the door handle, and the entire wall melted away. I looked down and I was in an elevator, still holding the handle.

When the elevator door slid open, I was staring at a dirt path, running through the middle of *Jurassic Park*-type leafy foliage. In surround sound, birds and monkeys were squawking and screeching, like they knew some shit was about to happen.

I stepped out of the elevator, and they began screaming louder and louder, to the point I had to cover my ears and do a 360 to check for 'em. What I found, instead, was a fucking rhinoceros, dressed like a zebra, starin' me down. He did the bull-snort thing, shook his enormous head, hoofed at the dirt, and barreled toward me.

I took off running, screaming like a bitch.

As I came around a bend, a waterfall appeared. I jumped, and as I was getting ready to hit the water, I ended up in a hallway of some office building. I glanced over my shoulder to check if the beast was still on my ass. And he was. I took off running again. I looked up, and the ceiling was gone. I could see all the way through to the top floor of the building. In front of me, up ahead, a fire escape ladder awaited.

I climbed as fast as I could.

Without warning, I snapped out of it.

I was lying on the bathroom floor, holding onto the base of the toilet. I stood up and studied my reflection in the mirror. "Did that really just happen?" I splashed cold water on my face until my heartbeat went back down into the double digits. I tried to shake off the crippling anxiety and headed into the living room. The hooker was standing at the piano, staring out through the patio doors toward the

Persian Gulf. I walked across the room to the bar to make us a drink.

That's what I'm trying to do right now.

It's not working, though.

I'm spilling the champagne everywhere, trying to pour it in the flutes. Out of nowhere, it feels like it's nine thousand degrees in here. *Who the fuck turned up the heat?* I'm sweating my balls off. *Oh shit, something's happening again....*

Bam! I've got a raging hard-on.

A "not good" raging hard-on.

I gaze down at my crotch. It's cartoon-throbbing in 3D. It fucking hurts. And it's getting harder and harder. Like it's gonna break. I can't touch it. Can't even get near it. I tried unzipping my pants, but it hurt so bad I had to stop. I move behind one of the pillars and slide to the floor.

It hurts so bad, I have to get on all fours.

I'm trying to imagine anything that will make the pain go away. I've tried a number of things. I'm now picturing my grandfather goin' down on Granny. Ugh! I know, like how'd we get to this point? Believe me, nothing else worked and this seems to be...if Gramps can just hold out for another minute or two....

Ugh! Again.

Finally, the throbbing stops.

I get myself together and stand back up. I slide out from behind the pillar. The hooker's starin' at me with a peculiar expression. Like I've done something weird. I grab the half-filled flutes and walk over to her.

She looks me up and down. "Why are you sweating like that?"

I hand her the flute and examine the front of me. My shirt's soaked all the way through, as if I ran here from the blackjack table. "I don't really have an answer for you."

She gives me that peculiar look again. "You took the Egyptian Viagra."

"Uh, what? No. Wait! How do you know this?"

She laughs. "I gave it to Toe to give to you."

"What the hell's in it?"

"No one knows. It's extra-strength, though. You only need one."

"One? The guy gave me a vial full."

She rushes over to her purse and glances inside. "Shit! I gave him the wrong bottle. How many did you take?"

"Uh…three…four."

"Eto ne mozhet byt'!" she says. *This can't be!* She pauses then adds, *"Kruto!"*—which means *cool* or *awesome*.

Hmmph.

"How do you feel?"

"Completely fine now, like I never even snorted them." As soon as I say this, the walls disappear. Ocean and I are standing in the desert. It's after dark. City lights glimmer in the distance. Somewhere nearby, an engine is winding. It's getting closer and closer. Headlights appear at the top of the sand dune behind us. The driver flicks the lights at us. I wave like I'm flaggin' them down. They floor it down the dune, heading right for us, with no intention of slowing. I shove Ocean out of the way as a Toyota Land Cruiser barely misses creaming us. I grab her arm as they make a looping turn to come back around.

We make a run for it.

I snap out of it.

I have Ocean by the arm, dragging her toward the bedroom. She's trying to get out of her shoes and dress on the way, laughing. Like she can't wait. "You should hydrate first," she says as we pass the bathroom.

"No time!"

I don't bother to unbutton my shirt. I'll buy a new one later. I try balancing on one foot to untie my shoes. Doesn't work. I must sit on the floor at the end of the bed.

"I'm so excited," she says.

Talk about loving what you do for a living. "Do you normally drug your clients?"

"No. Normally, it's fat and sweaty old men. I want to get it done as fast as possible."

"How'd you know I'd take them?"

"Puh-lease."

She tackles me on the floor. Three minutes later, it's over. I'm trying to catch my breath to explain this never happens when she jumps up like she's twelve—wait! Bad example. She jumps up like she's a gymnast who's just won the gold. "Let's get on the bed," she says. "You'll be ready again in sixty seconds."

Huh?

Before I even stand up, something is going on down there, a tingling.

Twenty-five minutes later, there are no covers or sheets left on the bed. I was trying to keep you in the loop. I lost the pen, though. I just found it when we changed positions. It was under her knee the whole time. I barely had time to grab it before she threw me down on my back.

She's now riding me like Seabiscuit coming out of a curve. She turns her head to the side like she's possessed.

Something seems off. She starts screaming obscenities, "Fuck, cunt, bitch, shit! Fuck, cunt, dick, shit!" She stops. Starts again, "Fuck, fuck! Fuck, cunt! Ass-dick! You motherfucker!"

Am I trippin' again?

I start to pull away.

"Ne fucking dvigaysya!" she says. Don't fucking move!

She locks me in with her hips, leans over, and punches me in the face. Hard.

I taste blood on my lip but do as I'm told.

She picks up the pace. Forty-five seconds more, and she's back to calling me everything but a white man. Her fists are raining down on my chest, leaving bruises. I'm not sure what's going on, but I'm putting all my effort into it now. I'm trying to push my hips to the ceiling and still hold on at the same time. It works until I have to let go a few minutes later with a hamstring cramp.

Ocean's trying to catch her breath. Doesn't dismount, though. Smiles. "Sorry, I have a mild case of Tourette's. Only comes out when I orgasm," she says.

"Mild?! How long's it been?"

"Eight months."

Her bangs are matted to her forehead, and her skin's clammy. Mine too.

She finally gets up. "I'm going to get us some ice water. It'll take three or four minutes this time," she says, walking out of the room.

There's no way I'm leaving this place without a kilo of this shit.

12

MILE HIGH CLUB...ALMOST

Have you ever come to on the bathroom floor and felt weird?

Yeah, me too.

Just now, in fact. My head's pounding. My vision's blurred. My mouth tastes like I've been out licking crotch all night. And things feel weird. Like, *different* weird. *I don't want to talk about it* weird.

I'm lying face down on the marble next to the tub, 'bout four feet from the shower. The one with the two hundred and thirty million dollars inside. Like I said, my vision's blurred, but I can still see the bags. Thank God. I could've woken to a completely different situation, a worst-case scenario for sure. This hooker, Ocean, could've grabbed the bags and stepped right over me. *Poof!* I would've been out of a whole bunch of money that doesn't belong to me.

And that's exactly why you sleep with classy hookers.

Speaking of classy hookers, what the fuck was that?

I've been with crazy women before but fuck me. Who drugs their clients like that? I manage to get to my knees and brace myself as I chance a peek at the mirror. I've got a black eye and busted lip. My entire body feels bruised when I stand upright. I walk to the sink, and it hurts…back there. I already told you, something's different. Like *different* weird. I'm pretty sure I've been ass-raped by a Russian hooker. In fact, I'm positive.

I can't stop thinking about it.

I can't even file a police report. I paid the chick, then took drugs.

I'm in the middle of splashing water on my face when someone buzzes the doorbell…and they're laying into it too. "Fuck me. All right already. I'm coming!" It hurts to yell.

I make it to the door and glare through the peephole. It's Ivan. Two of his guys are behind him. I crack it open, holding my finger to my lips. "Shh." I point to the *Do Not Disturb* sign on the handle.

Ivan opens his mouth, "Boss—"

"Whisper!"

"Boss, there's a pilot downstairs. Says his prince sent him here from Morocco to pick you up."

Oh shit. "What time is it?"

"Ten thirty."

Shit. Shit. Shit. I'm three hours late for my flight. Bundu's manservant sent me the text last night while we were still at The Naked Fish. I open the door all the way to let Ivan in. I'm naked…with a black eye and busted lip, and I'm not having a very good hair day either. Doesn't keep him from walking right past me. Nor does it keep his guys from smirking as I shut the door on them.

"Call the front desk, tell them to inform the pilot I'll be down shortly. And have a pot of coffee sent up right away," I say.

"Rough night?" He laughs.

"Yeah, asshole. It was a rough night. Where'd you find that woman? Did you know she drugs her clients and then does unthinkable things to them?"

"*Da*. You should have never called my mother a whore."

"My coffee, now. And have a luggage cart sent up. You're dropping me off at the airport."

In the bedroom, I find a note on the pillow: *Thank you for a wonderful evening. Heart, Ocean.* I start thinking back to last night. Ocean fighting her way out of her dress, then tackling me. I don't get any further before I'm dealing with pressure from down below. I don't understand how I can still get a boner. I guess I can take care of it really quick in the shower.

Two birds, one stone.

Ten minutes later, I'm getting nowhere. This fucking Egyptian Viagra bullshit! I've tried everything but suffocation. I give up. Now I gotta walk around all day with a black eye and a hard-on.

I'm wearing a TB12 ball cap—pulled down low—dark sunglasses, blue jeans, a vintage tee, and my Ferragamo's. I look like one of these "low-key" douchebags. I slam the rest of the coffee. It's not helping with the soreness, though, but at least I can count again. I need twelve of the black duffel bags from the shower, sixty million dollars in total. Fifty for the stones. Five to Bundu's guy for the "legal" paperwork, and the extra five, just in case.

Ivan loads the bags on top of the luggage cart. "What the fuck's in these, Boss?"

"Nine-year-olds."

He just looks at me. I hand his guys four thousand dollars and remind them that no one gets in the room. At the front desk, I tell the same thing to the clerk, while Bundu's pilot helps Ivan transfer the bags to the Range Rover. I toss the keys to Ivan and tell the pilot to ride shotgun.

I need to lie across the back seat.

I don't feel so well.

Ivan keeps pushing me to do a little bump of cocaine—that I'll feel much better. I told him the whole story, the parts I remember, anyway.

He died laughing. "In all seriousness, do a little bump. It'll straighten you right out. Like when you drink too much vodka the night before. One shot the next morning, shazam! Back to strong like bull."

Russians for ya.

Fuck it. Maybe the coke'll help. I sniff an itsy-bitsy bump off the Rover key.

Twenty minutes later, I'm on Bundu's Gulfstream. A seventy-five-million-dollar jet. Holds twenty-plus people. There are four of us: two pilots, me, and a stewardess. The stewardess is *ooh-la-la* by the way. She just served me a drink and gave me an icepack for my headache.

An hour later, I do have to admit I'm feeling much better. I return my recliner to the upright position and press the button for the stewardess. She appears from behind me.

"Feeling better?" she asks.

"Definitely. Thank you, *cheri*."

"What can I do for you?" she asks, and if I didn't know any better, I'd say she was being flirtatious. *Must be the remains of the Egyptian sex drug.*

"Would you put on some Ahmet Kilic, please? I'd like to hear some music. Maybe another drink too."

"Ahmet is one of my favorites. I'll be right back with your drink."

"Where are you from, *cheri*?"

"Chile."

"You're very beautiful."

She giggles and walks off.

When she returns, she hands me my glass. "You can control the lighting, volume, and the window shades with this," she says, holding out a remote control. She kind of holds onto it when I grab it. Dare I say, flirtatious again?

"Are you sure there's nothing more I can do for you?" she asks, biting her lip.

This time, I'm sure it's not the funny pill. "Are you flirting with me, *mi amor*?"

"Everyone calls me Izzy. And yes."

"What would your boss say?"

"Prince Bundu? He's the one who paid me."

I look at her sideways. "A hooker?"

She smiles. "Prince Bundu says you love them."

"No strings."

"I hate strings too," she says, sitting on my lap. "Would you mind helping me out of mine?" She turns and pulls her hair to the side. The top of her dress is tied in a bow…made of strings. "There's a bedroom in the back."

I untie the bow, and the top half of her dress falls to her waist. "Can we just stay here? I have no desire to move right now."

She removes her bra, and I'm staring at doctor-made tatas. A full-C for sure. Pear-shaped. Little pink nipples.

Remind me to thank Bundu later. She presses the button on my chair, and it turns into a bed. I dim the lights, close the window shades, and push Ahmet Kilic to five on the volume.

I'm rounding second base.

She still has the bottom half of her dress on. I'm down to what I was born in. I hit third base standing up. I need to slow down and catch my breath. It's not time to bring it home just yet. I run my hands up the sides of her legs, pull her panties down, and run back to second. A little more making out. Kisses for the twins. Some nipple play.

Time to get back to third.

I slip my hand back up her dress, run my fingers up the inside her leg, and stop when something doesn't feel right. I hit the outside corner of home plate, and there are balls. A pair of them. I'm not talking about the pitch-count balls either. This chick has balls, real ones. And a bat!

"What the fuck?" I say, jumping up and grabbing my clothes.

She, him, them, whatever, hurries to cover their…tits, I guess?

"I'm sorry, Prince Bundu said you'd like me," she says.

"You have a dick!"

"Yeah, but it doesn't work."

"What the fuck does that mean?"

"I'm a woman trapped in a man's body. I just haven't had the surgery. Prince Bundu said he'd pay for it if I did this."

"You'd better get the money from him as fast as possible because I'm going to kill Prince Bundu when I see him."

"Do you think he will still pay for the surgery?"

"You just let me take care of Prince Bundu. I promise if you never speak of this, I'll pay for the damn surgery myself."

"Oh, thank you. Thank you. Would you like to finish? I promise I won't tell anyone."

"Aah, no. Thank you just the same. Please wake me when we land."

Six more hours before I can get my hands around "Prince" Bundu's neck.

13

AFRICAN BUSH ANYONE?

Have you ever been deep in the African Bush?

I mean, in so far the white man has never been there?

Yeah, me either.

Well, that's where Bundu's people are from. The men are out all day, barefoot, hunting lions with a spear, while the women stay back at camp stewing elephant soup, washing laundry in the Congo River.

Some real-life tribe shit.

Like I said, Bundu's family ruled Zaire. Back when Zaire was Zaire and not the Democratic Republic of Congo. His uncle was the crackpot king who waged war on his own country. He pillaged, starved, and murdered his people. If you dared to step out of line, you didn't make it back to your mud hut that night. He'd take your oxen, rape your wife, and order your children to become slaves.

Bundu's father, the hand to the king, did all the king's dirty work.

Imagine dinner with these two schizos at the table.

Growing up, Bundu lived behind the walls of the Royal Palace in Zaire, until moving to his own palace in Belgium. If you were to judge a book by its cover, you'd use words like bombastic, piggish, self-indulgent, even braggadocio to describe Bundu. He's not any of those things, though. Yeah, he's only ever lived in palaces—except the year and a half he lived with me—and yeah, he thinks Mitsubishis and Kias are only to be driven by servants, but that's all beside the point.

At best, Bundu's *non compos mentis*.

Latin for a little whacky.

Good whacky, but whacky no less.

While living in Belgium throughout his teen years, his parents never once dropped in for a visit. Instead, they sent more servants and cash. For his fifteenth birthday, I stayed over the night before. There were no cards, no cake, no party. The parents didn't even call. But when we woke up the next morning, there were two Lamborghini Aventadors in the driveway—one yellow, one green. Bundu couldn't have cared less about the cars. He wanted a party with his friends and family. The next year, and every year after, he threw his own birthday smash.

The Ta Dus have grown too outlandish.

I've attended a few and heard stories of the others.

We landed in Casablanca thirty minutes ago and taxied to Bundu's private hangar. When we "pulled in," Bundu was out front, laid out on the hood of his midnight-blue Bugatti Veyron Super Sport. A shit-eatin' grin on his face. Before I could even reach the bottom of the steps, he was on the ground, dying laughing.

The second he saw the look on my face, he knew he got me with the tranny.

It just tickled him pink.

Currently, Bundu's in the passenger seat of his three-point-five-million-dollar sports car, no longer grinning. He's been around exotic cars his whole life but has never had the stomach for danger. High speeds scare the shit out of him.

Nothing's changed.

We're screaming down one of the runways, with me behind the wheel. He's gripping the armrest and seat belt like they could essentially save him. The speedometer just passed three hundred and seventy-eight kilometers. Roughly two hundred and thirty-five miles per hour. And we're going to run out of pavement before I run out of pedal. It's why he's growing more pale by the millisecond.

Not so funny when the rabbit's got the gun, is it Prince Bundu?

I whip my gaze over to him. "Swear you'll never tell a soul."

"Bundu swear! Bundu promise! Please! Bundu beg friend to look to road!"

Normally, Bundu sounds like Obama…until I pull shit like this. His African tribe accent then comes out. I'm probably going to Hell for it, but the shit's hilarious. I back off to ninety miles per hour, slam the brakes, and cut the wheel hard to the right. When we come out of the drift, Bundu's gone as white as Martha Stewart…before Snoop Dogg. "And this doesn't make us even either," I tell him. "Not even close."

"Oh, thank the Jesus. Oh, thank the Jesus. Oh, thank the Jesus." He just keeps muttering. Like he wants to get out and kiss the pavement.

I'm still laughing.

He should've known better than to hand me the keys.

I turn onto the airport perimeter road. We're headed back to the hangar. We're taking Bundu's helicopter up around the bend to his weekend getaway. It's in Marrakesh. Another palace, by the way. He says this is where he keeps the stash of diamonds.

I pull the Bugatti inside the hangar and park next to the Gulfstream I arrived in.

The helicopter is just landing out front to pick us up. It's a Sikorsky S-92 Executive. Looks like it's fresh off *Pimp My Ride*. The red blades are still spinning. The rest of the bird is blacked-out. Badass. Another cool twenty or twenty-five million bucks.

I told you, these people ain't fakin'.

They got it.

And Bundu ain't scared to spend it.

Let me do this really quick for the nine people without a smartphone. Morocco is in Africa. Top left. To the west is the Atlantic Ocean. To the east is Algeria. South is the Western Sahara. And a hop, skip, and a jump north, you land in Spain.

We're now moving at right around one hundred and thirty miles per hour over the top of Casablanca—a port city and commercial hub of Morocco. There are roughly four million inhabitants scattered around the city. We just flew over Bundu's main palace in the northwest part of the city. The estate falls off into the Atlantic Ocean. Something right out of a movie.

"Wait a minute, jerk off!" I tell him. "You said your party's tonight. There was none of your typical birthday chaos going on back there at your castle."

"The party is in Marrakesh, homie," he says.

"I told you, I'm not staying."

"Relax. You must trust your old friend Bundu. We do our business, you return to Dubai. Promise. I can send Izzy along for the ride if you'd like," he says, obviously tickled pink again.

"You're lucky I don't know how to fly this chopper."

We skirt the coastline, then bank hard to the east to cross over the Atlas Mountains. Marrakesh is out in front of us now. It's a major economic center for Morocco with about a million people densely packed into the medieval city, which dates to the Berber Empire.

We come out of the mountain range, and the first thing I notice is approximately twenty hot air balloons up ahead, all grounded and equally spaced apart. I glance over at Bundu. He raises his eyebrows. "What? They're just balloons!"

"Let me ask you a question, schmuck. What time does your party start?"

"Umm, actually we're late," he says, laughing.

I fucking knew it.

We bank hard around the back of the balloons, approaching the pool area of Bundu's palace. I'm not going to waste time explaining what the place looks like. It's a fucking palace built by a line of kings. Figure it out. I'd rather tell you about the other things I see. Like the fact there are at least six or seven hundred people in his backyard, all staring up, waiting for us to land. And check this out....

Marshmello, costume and all, is suspended above the pool, doing his thing for the crowd.

None of this is so astonishing as to be extraordinary.

How 'bout this? There's a petting zoo down there, roaming around.

The fucking Serengeti!

Elephants, giraffes, gazelles, flamingos, and there's a flock of snow-white lambs being herded around. Who knows what else? We make a pass over the party at probably a buck ten, not fifty feet off the ground. Marshmello is fist-pumping the air. The pilot makes a big, hard-banking loop and passes over everyone one more time before landing.

Bundu opens the rear door of the chopper.

"I'm going to kill your black ass!" I yell over the roar of the blades.

I follow Bundu through the crowd. Everyone's stopping him to say happy birthday. He's introducing me to one beautiful woman after another. He knows them all. I'm not paying much attention, though. I know me. I don't even want to get started. I'm keeping my eye on the prize—get the diamonds and get out. But there's some other shocking shit going on that's pulling my interest.

I've counted a dozen giraffes already, walking around on super-long leashes.

Again, hold onto your socks, that's not even the shocking part.

The giraffes are being led around by naked midgets wearing animal-print body paint.

I believe I tried to tell you…whacky.

I follow Bundu inside.

The palace ain't shit. You should see the art. Bundu's a collector. The collection is rumored to be worth more than some countries' annual GDP. Part of the collection are heads. They're on the walls of his home office. Lions, rhinos, and crocks, oh my!

PETA would have a field day.

On each side of his gigantic desk are massive lions, killed by Bundu on a tribe hunt. Their manes are so enormous, I can't stretch my arms around them. Behind the desk, mounted to the wall, are a pair of ivory tusks, so big you could swing from them. The head belonging to the elephant is there too.

Bundu walks to the opposite side of the room and stops in front of an African buffalo head. "Watch this," he says, staring down the animal. I hear a couple of clicks, and the head swings to the side. There's a wall safe behind.

"How safe is that? Someone just has to have your eyeballs."

"Not true, my friend. The retinal scan also measures my heart rate. If it registers higher than normal, a satellite is triggered, and all kinds of shit starts to happen. We'd be locked in the room until the Rock shows up."

"Ahh, I see you still have a crush on the guy."

He flips me the bird…means the same in African.

Bundu reaches in the safe and pulls out a black velvet bag, 'bout the size of a softball. Presumably, the blood diamonds. He tosses it to me, shuts the safe, walks behind his desk, and pulls open one of the drawers. Out comes a mirror, just big enough for four good-sized lines of cocaine. I shake my head no three times, then walk over and take a sniff.

Instantaneously, Bundu and I start reminiscing. We each tell a story or two, and we both take another sniff before one of his staff comes looking for him. They were visibly upset, ranting and raving in African about someone doing something. It's one of Bundu's parties, which means it could be anything.

"I'm going to use the long drop," I tell him.

It's what they call the loo in Africa.

Bundu heads out to the party. I watch him walk all the way down the hall before I close myself inside his office. I need to have a look-see around. I can't stop wondering about this Nova Terra deal Bundu mentioned and Mikale denied knowing about. Doesn't add up for me…yet. Bundu said it was Kennedy's husband's deal. Bundu is involved. The chances of Kennedy's husband knowing Bundu are almost nil. Of course, people who are stupid rich know other stupid rich people.

It's a small circle jerk.

I search through a couple of the desk drawers. Rifle through some of the folders. Feel along the wall for a secret button. Hell, I even tug on both lion heads, looking for a hidden safe. Nothing jumps out. It's not the movies.

Bundu had to mention this deal to me for a reason. He knows me. He's ruffling my feathers for a reason.

Well, I can't find any intel on this deal.

Bundu left the tray of coke on the desk.

He also knows I hate to see things go to waste.

Fuck me.

14

THE NAKED TRUTH

What happened?

Shit's not good.

Can't be.

I'm staring at a rather large, naked black man on the floor. There are others too. For all I know they could all be dead. And that's not even the worst of it. I'm in fucking Egypt. Not like Bumfuck Egypt. I mean like King Tut's tomb is right up the block Egypt.

I have no idea how I got here, so don't go asking a bunch of stupid questions.

I've only beaten you here by like three minutes.

Here's what's gone down so far. I came alive three minutes ago, sprawled out naked across an unfamiliar bed. I sat up and waited for my eyes to focus. When they did, I realized I was in some high-end hotel room. The patio doors were open, and I was staring at the tops of mosques and the pyramids of Giza.

Seemed clear enough.

Now, how the fuck did I get here?

I was in the middle of trying to figure out how far Morocco is from Egypt, when a woman walked in the room. She was fresh out of the shower, wearing nothing but a grin—and complete with the correct plumbing this time.

"Um, hello," I said. "Did we...uh?"

"Shag, you mean?" she answered with a cool British accent. "A bloody blunder had we not."

"How'd we meet?"

"You tapped me on the shoulder last night at a club in Cairo, asked if I was a hooker."

You know I wanted to ask again right then.

Apparently, she was not a hooker. I apologized and bought her a drink.

"Long story short," she said, "my friends and I followed you and your friend back to the hotel."

My friend?

I was still drawing blanks. She nodded toward the other room, to the naked black guy sprawled out on the floor. My "friend."

I now scan the rest of the room and spot her naked friends lying on the furniture, passed out like they own the place. I walk over to the guy for a closer inspection. Yep, positive he's black. Positive he's not my friend. Wait a minute...he seems vaguely familiar. I need to go put on pants or at least my boxers. I wouldn't want some dude standing over me with morning wood, trying to nudge me awake.

Yes, ladies, I hear ya. It's why I brought it up.

The Brit babe is in the middle of getting dressed, trying to find one of her shoes when I waltz in and ask if she's seen my clothes.

"Try the balcony."

I don't ask questions. I told you…this is why I rarely do cocaine. It leads to unfamiliar hotels with unfamiliar women in unfamiliar lands. The problem is it's been around lately. A lot. I head out onto the balcony to search for my clothes, and I get clobbered with a wake-up call.

The diamonds!

Bundu's party!

Wait a minute, that's where I've seen the naked black guy before. He's one of Bundu's security operatives. His name's…Jenny. I remember him telling me this last night. Yes, Jenny. That's what he said to call him. Jenny's like some kind of real-life assassin. If he'd told me to call him Birthday Cake, Birthday Cake it would've been.

Can we move on?

I need to start eliminating possibilities, starting with the Brit and her friends.

My clothes are nowhere to be found. Chances are they're nineteen stories down, floating in the Nile River. Apparently, I undressed on the balcony and was swinging my pants above my head like an American cowboy.

Fucking cocaine.

I wrap a towel around my waist. Without being rude, I tell the woman I have to be somewhere. She gets the point and goes to wake her friends. I'm watching the three of them like a hawk. There aren't many places they can be hiding a bag of diamonds—not in those dresses. At the door, I give each of them a slightly creepy, slightly frisky hug.

They're clean.

Now how am I going to hug this G.I. Joe motherfucker?

I turn back around, and Jenny's finished dressing. His clothes were neatly assassin-folded on a chair. I call down to the front desk and tell them to send up a bellhop. I need to send someone out for clothes, and I need to get some answers.

"Do you have any idea how we got here, Jenny?"

"You spiked my drink."

What? ...That's right!

Jenny was on duty. It was like 10:00 p.m. Figured I stick around 'til midnight or one. I was pretty buzzed but still managing. The vial of Egyptian Viagras was in my pocket, burning a hole.

Why not pop one?

There was a table tucked away in an alcove right behind Jenny's post. A glass of something dark sat atop. I was drinking Courvoisier Erte de Napoléon. A dark cognac. I set my glass next to the other, covertly dropped in the sex pill and a couple of mollies Bundu gave me.

Twenty minutes later, I should've felt a freightliner rolling through my core and trying to escape through my pants. I didn't feel a thing.

I decided to up the dose.

I snuck off to the bathroom, crushed up the last of the Egyptian Viagra—I think there were five—and three mollies. Enough to choke a horse. I came out of the bathroom, and immediately, who do I see? Jenny. He's hiding behind a plant, acting strange.

I walk over. "What's up, buddy?"

"People are shooting at me. I think someone put something in my drink."

Putains! Quesque j'ai fait?

Sounds elegant in French, right?

In English, not so much: *Fuck! What have I done?*

Then things really started to dawn on me. Things like, *oh shit, I just took enough drugs to kill an elephant.* The next thing I know, I'm waking up in Cairo with no diamonds, talking to you.

I'm back in the bedroom now. I've flipped the mattress. I open all the dresser drawers and toss them on the floor. I turn the whole room upside down. Jenny's made the same mess in the rest of the suite. The bag of diamonds is nowhere to be found. Jenny looks worried.

This could land him anywhere between a simple firing and a firing squad.

For me, it's not quite as serious. Mikale's not going to be happy about it, but he'll eventually get over it. He knows I'll figure out a way to save the day. I might as well FaceTime him now. Nineteen of my missed calls are from him anyway.

He picks up on the first ring. "Where the fuck have you been?"

"What, are we dating now?"

"You posted those pictures on the company's social media!"

"What pictures?"

"What pictures? The pictures of you and the naked midgets."

Uh-oh. "Umm, so what's the big deal? They're just midgets."

"They're painted like zoo animals. You have them on leashes, smiling, like you're in a fucking gum commercial!"

"It was for charity. The li'l guys were half price."

"You're not funny, dickhead. Where the fuck are you?"

"I don't see any pharaohs, but the pyramids of Giza are off in the distance."

"Cairo. You're in fucking Egypt?!"

"All things considered."

"What the fuck are you doing there? And who gave you a black eye?"

"I was in Morocco. Someone must've spiked my drink. The black eye came from a hooker."

"Spiked your drink, my ass."

"Are you finished? I need to go find the bag of diamonds."

"Bundu's diamonds?"

"You're asking a lot of dumb questions today. More than usual."

"Where are the fucking diamonds, David? Black bag. You sent me a picture of them last night," he says, like I should know this.

"Can you see anything in the background?"

"Yeah, fucking midgets!"

"I'll call you back," I say and hang up. "Jenny! Jenny!" I burst into the living room. "The fucking midgets have them!"

"That's right. I remember midgets," he says.

I'm scrolling through my phone. There are twenty-one incriminating images saved in my Gallery. A new personal best. A variety of poses, too, I might add. Some with the li'l people standing at my legs, naked, smiling up for the camera, their li'l thumbs up in the air. Others? Well…. I'm holding two of them upside down by their ankles in one. The bag of diamonds hanging from one of their mouths. Like a bone.

And I posted all of them to the company's social media…hmm.

Good thing the only people following us are family, friends, and everyone who sends us money. It's going to be a minute before this is forgotten. I'm sticking to my story. "It was for charity."

Let me call Bundu, see what he knows. A few of the missed calls are from him, anyway.

"Well, if it isn't Mr. Party Boy," he answers, laughing.

"Bundu, what the hell happened?"

He laughs again. "A sniff here. A sniff there. We were dancing all night long. Like Lionel Richie." He starts butchering the song.

I interrupt him, "Bundu, I lost the diamonds."

"Not so, my friend."

"You have them?"

"In my safe as we speak. You left them by the pool. One of my staff found them."

"And they turned them in?"

"Consequences are extreme."

"You saved my ass, Bundu. Again."

"Not sure about your ass. Have you seen social media?"

"I guess I posted some pics."

"Everyone from all over the world posted them." He laughs hysterically.

Shit.

"Fuck it. I guess it's street cred now. I'll figure out how to use it later on. "Somehow, I'm in Cairo. I need to get back to Dubai and get my hands on the diamonds."

"You have my plane and Creole," he says.

"Creole?"

"The black guy."

"Oh. Yeah, he's here with me. I need to get back to Dubai, Bundu. I'm driving to Yemen tomorrow. Can you DHL the stones?"

"Always into something crazy. I envy you, my friend," he says. "Fuck driving to Yemen, you have the keys to my plane and one of my best men. They're both yours for as long as you need 'em."

"I have to carry a substantial amount of cash. Mikale says it's not safe to fly it because I'll have to report the cash to Customs. Better to drive it, he says."

"Hell no. They won't even board a private plane in Yemen. Customs is a joke there. Trust me, take my plane. If you have any problems, call me. I have people there."

"Bundu, thank you. I love your black ass, man."

"Yeah, yeah. Save it for your boyfriend. Text me an address, and I'll ship the diamonds."

Man, I have to quit getting myself into this kind of shit.

15

A BAD JOKE

A day and a half later....

Three dudes are driving across Yemen in taxis, carrying one hundred million dollars in cash. One of them's Haitian. One's Russian. The last one's half a spic....

Sounds like the beginning of a bad joke, right?

If only it were.

It's us: me, Ivan, and Bundu's man, Creole (Jenny). We've been in Yemen for the longest six hours of my life. We're driving across—surprise!—another fucking desert. We landed by plane in the capital city of Sanaa six hours ago. Unfortunately, the "X marks the spot" on our map is in the port city of Aden, a two-hundred-mile trek south, across nothing but more sand.

The travel options were limited to a caravan of camels, requiring a month of travel time, an old rusted-out Russian helicopter on its last wing, and a Yemen Uber, which is really just a taxi. We chose the taxi. Three of them.

It was the only way the money would fit.

There are twenty duffel bags crammed into the trunks and stacked on the back seats. And just so we're all on the same page, taxis in the Middle East are not like taxis in say, the Upper Eastside. My side mirror is held on with duct tape, the air doesn't work, neither does my window, and the engine knocks. There's no customary license on the dash with a picture of Habibi and that stupid-ass, I'm-glad-to-be-in-America grin either. However, my driver did have a sack. Asked if I minded. I did not.

"Puff. Puff. Pass," I told him, and he did.

It's Afghani weed. Shit's the bomb.

Speaking of bombs, I found out Yemen is the hub of the Middle East for arms deals, illegal and otherwise. Basically, you've got an Arab out front dressed as Bin Laden, spinning one of those spinny signs, yelling, "Step right up! Step right up! *As-salamu alaykum*. RPGs up front. Tanks out back. If you're paying with cash, go around to the side door."

No shirt, no shoes, no problem.

You don't even need ID.

Yeah, it's some serious shit.

So, we're headed to the Sheba Hotel on the backside of the city to meet this lawyer, Jargons. My driver says we'll be there in about thirty minutes. We're going to be early. Jenny wants to scope the place out on the down-low.

Yeah, right, on the down-low.

Three dudes walk in the lobby of a deserted hotel in Yemen: a jacked Haitian in aviator shades and a skin-tight T-shirt that says *Vote for Kamala*; a nervous Russian in a wrinkled black suit, sweating his *pirogues* off; and, obviously, I'm the spic, high as balls, not sure I'm wearing anything at all.

95

Trust me when I tell you, there's no "on the down-low."

When we walk in this hotel, the cat's out of the bag.

Meanwhile, the fucking pictures with the leopard-spotted midgets and me have circled the globe. *TMZ*'s called twice already for a comment. I'm not even allowed to talk about it. I've been instructed to keep my fat mouth shut until it all blows over. Mikale has hired a public relations firm to deal with our "public image."

Blew a million bucks on the guy.

Thinks it's coming out of my end of the deal.

Fat chance.

I've done some crazy shit before, but this arms deal tops the cake. I haven't unclenched my ass cheeks since we landed in Sanaa this afternoon. If I hadn't smoked, I'd be shitting my pants right now. I keep running the plan over in my head. This Jargons has directed me to leave a coded message at the front desk of the Sheba Hotel: *"Three beers for my friends and me."*

Yeah, I get it, it's not Hollywood. I'm not Ethan Fucking Hunt either…I'm a fucking banker. I live in the suburbs of an all-white country. I wrestle with naked midgets for fuck's sake. Just look at social media.

We finally make it to the hotel.

It's a shithole at the end of a shitty street.

There are three Arab men working under the hood of a car right out front. We pull in and get out. They all look up. There's no bellhop to hold the door open as the three of us, and our drivers, make trips back and forth trucking the twenty duffel bags inside.

Ivan and Jenny drag the cash over to the seating area—a single couch, missing one of the cushions, underneath a ceiling fan, missing one of the blades. I take a deep breath and approach the front desk. There's no one at the counter. I tap the little bell, *ding-ding*.

A guy comes out from the back. He's wearing the sheet thing. It's dingy. He's got the matching pillowcase on his head with a red rope wound around, holding it in place. He looks over to Ivan and Jenny, then back to me. Nods like.

"Three beers for my friends and me," I tell him.

This time it's a double nod. Like, *gotcha, wink-wink.*

He disappears to the back again.

I stand there like a dumbass for eleven minutes.

Out of nowhere, five Mercedes AMG G Wagons pull to a fast stop in front of the hotel. All of them are silver, and all of them have limo tint covering the windows. After the dust storm clears, heavily armed soldier types exit the SUVs and form a perimeter around the front of the hotel. They're all wearing dark shades and have the earpiece-thingies.

Holy fuck.

I feel like I'm in an action movie where everyone dies.

Even the guys working on the car out front look nervous, and they see this shit every day.

The rear door of one of the G Wagons opens. Out steps a fat version of Ric Flair, same all-white suit and white cowboy hat. Mikale already told me Jargons is fat and always wears a white suit. Chances are that would make the guy behind the lawyer the American.

I'm told his name's Kyle. Probably an alias. He looks like Eminem. The guy's covered in tats, from his ankles to his neck. He's wearing cargo shorts, a T-shirt that says *UpCup Koffee Company*, and tennis shoes. The two of them enter the hotel. Three of the "soldier dudes" stay at the front door.

Kyle and Jargons stride over to the seating area. Jargons reaches out his hand to introduce himself. The American doesn't say anything, doesn't extend his hand. Up close, I notice he has a diamond tattooed on his neck, the word *Savage* slicing through the middle of it. He gives me the once-over, then snaps his fingers.

The soldiers swirl over and cart the duffel bags of cash away. He still doesn't say a word, turns, and walks back out of the hotel.

Ungrateful prick.

Jargons says he'll be in touch, then leaves.

All's well that ends well, I guess.

It's been a long day. The last thing I feel like doing right now is cramming back in a 1980-something, bootleg Nissan Sentra to drive the six-plus hours back to Bundu's plane. I decide we'll stay the night, check out the sites here in Taliban Town.

Maybe I'll be able to find a hooker.

Yeah, right.

They sell guns and bombs, but pussy crosses a moral line.

Strange, but true.

16

"FLAVA FLAV" SHAKEDOWN

I woke up pretty much fucked.

I probably went to bed that way.

Who the fuck knows? We're about to find out. We're entering Dubai airspace now. Ocean is picking us up on the tarmac. Yes, the hooker who kicked the shit out of me. This was who Ivan 911'd for me. His guys—the ones I pay to stand outside my hotel suite—aren't taking his calls.

They haven't been since yesterday evening.

I was not made privy to this information 'til this morning.

Call me pessimistic, but I'm real big on the 2+2 equaling the obvious. Which is, they've blown town and taken the rest of my loot with them.

Ivan says there's no chance of this being the case, as he knows these guys. All of them left Russia together and moved to Dubai six months ago. One of them is Ivan's brother, two are first cousins, the other's Ivan's best friend. "They'd never do this!" he says.

I'm waiting to see.

What I didn't wait for was the Yemen Uber to take us to Bundu's plane. I hired a rust-bucket with a propeller. The pilot said the chopper served in WWII. I believed him. The side door didn't close, and we sat on milk crates, but we made it to the Gulfstream in one piece. Bundu's pilot then vamoosed our asses, lickety-split like, right back to Dubai.

We're taxiing to the private hangars at the Dubai airport now.

We pull in, and Ocean's on the tarmac, standing in front of a Toyota 4Runner. I take shotgun. As soon as she gets in the driver's side, I'm on her in *Española*. I'm not giving her any room to breathe. It's one question after another: *¿Qiuén? ¿Qué? ¿Dondé? ¿Cuándo? ¿Por qué?*

She's the only one of the three who understands Spanish.

She has all the right answers.

She could still be in on it, though. Who the fuck knows? I'm not a detective, and it's not like I can call one to help me out. I direct Ocean to pull up to the valet of my hotel. I take the valet stub when we get out. Far as I'm concerned, these two Russians aren't leaving my sight until I can figure some shit out. We exit the elevator on my floor and bend the corner. My suite's at the end of the hallway. There's no one standing outside. The *Do Not Disturb* sign is right where I left it yesterday.

I slide my key card through the reader and wait for it to turn green.

Click.

I open the door. There's a guy right inside. He's not Russian, way too dark. Not a friendly either. He's pointing a pistol at us. Well, at me, really.

"All of you get in here," he says. "Stand against the wall and do it quietly."

I have no idea what I'm up against yet, so I do what I'm told. I walk through the doorway with Ocean behind me, then Ivan and Jenny. When the door closes, the guy, who-ever he is, shuffles us through the suite. There are three more guys in the living room. Two of them are also pointing guns in our direction.

All four of the Russians are gagged and tied to the barstools.

Ocean grabs onto my arm, scared.

The one guy not pointing a gun—apparently, the guy in charge—is playing himself in a game of pool. He's zeroed in on a shot. Doesn't bother to look up. He's black and dressed in head-to-toe green and bling. Lots of green. Lots of bling.

I'm not kidding. His fedora's green, the Gucci suit's green, the Prada loafers, they're green too. And he's wearing enough rings to be Tom Brady incognito. All he's missing is his li'l John's crunk cup and a gold pimp cane.

He triple banks the cue and splits the nine and three balls—both of them find a pocket. He lays the cue stick on the table and struts over. "Do you know who I am, Mr. Li-etch?"

"Um, the pimp?"

It's hard to tell if he thinks I'm amusing or not.

Ocean squeezes my arm. It's a "not" for her.

The guy hands me a business card, also green, by the way. It's thick and feels like felt. Two raised, gold-leafed letters rest dead center: *NR*. No address. No contact info. No job title. Doesn't tell me anything. Just the two letters.

To be honest, it's the "pimp-ist" business card I've ever seen.

"My name is Naba Raheem. I'll give you three guesses as to what I do, Mr. Lietch," he says, starin' at me.

"Besides breaking and entering and tying up Russian kids?"

He doesn't answer and looks like he means it.

"What about the pimp thing? You really didn't give me a one way or the other." Is *madder* a word? He certainly looks it. No worries. It's all part of my plan.

"I was warned you were mouthy," he says, peering past me to one of his guys.

All I hear is "*pfft*," then commotion. I turn and glance back at the Russians. One of them is resisting his restraints with everything he has. Veins are bulging from his neck. Blood's oozing from the bullet hole in his shoulder.

This was not part of my plan.

"I'm paid, Mr. Lietch," he goes on, "to make sure plans go accordingly."

"Some plan," I mumble.

"Pardon?"

"Nothing. Now finish telling me this brilliant plan of yours."

He just stares at me for a second. "When the Khaleed brothers made their investment with you and your partner, they were not expecting you to hire kids to protect it—"

"So they paid you to break into my hotel room and tie them up?"

"No. You're paying me. The Khaleed brothers pay me to stay in the shadows and watch. When I have to come out of the shadows, expenses are incurred. Those are paid by you."

"And what's the going rate these days for shooting a kid?"

"In this instance, you owe me two million dollars."

"It's a flesh wound. He's not even dead!"

Again, he gives the same look to his guy behind me. By the time I turn around, his guy has his gun out, pointing it at the Russians. "All right! I'll pay. Don't shoot."

"Very wise, Mr. Lietch." His shooter lowers his gun. "Consider yourself lucky, you still have twenty-eight million left to cover your expenses."

I count out the two million dollars, while Ocean and Jenny bandage up the Russian. They both said they had experience with that sort of thing. I didn't inquire further.

Twenty minutes later, Flava Flav is gone, along with his thugs and my two million dollars. The Russian kid doesn't look so good. The pimp gave Ocean a number to a doctor in town who deals with this sort of thing. Ocean and Jenny are going to drive him there.

I'm going to get Mikale's ass on the phone, right now.

He doesn't pick up.

I fire off a text message. *Homo! Call me. I just got shook down for two million dollars by an all-green pimp. That's after he shot one of the Russians. And the guy works for your Khaleed creeps.*

Mikale calls back within seconds. "I just talked to you yesterday," he says before I can say anything. "You were going to sleep in Yemen."

"Things took a turn."

GC BROWN

"They always do with you."

"You want to trade places?"

"Not on your life. What happened?"

"I got back to Dubai and your terrorist friend's hitmen were in my hotel room. I hired a few Russians to stand outside the room. They were tied up and being held at gunpoint. A guy dressed like a pimp shook me down for the cash, but not before making his point clear by having one of his guys shoot one of the Russians in the shoulder."

"Is he all right?"

"Yeah, he'll be okay."

"I'm glad you're safe. Fuck the money. I'll call you in a few hours. I'm at the wedding rehearsal dinner. I'm in the bathroom hiding from Mother."

"You're such a vagina. Tell Kennedy to check her secret email right away." I disconnect before he can make a comment.

17

A BANANA OR JUST HAPPY TO SEE ME?

I'm now besties with a hooker.

I took Ocean to breakfast this morning and to dinner last night. Nothing in between, though. She says we can't and never will again. Says after going through our ordeal together, we are now friends. And, as my luck would have it, this is the one cardinal rule she refuses to break. I told her it's the dumbest of the cardinal rules.

I offered to pay double.

It was still a no.

She did manage to get me a dozen more Egyptian Viagras, so it wasn't a total loss. I'm thinking of adding her to the payroll. That's what breakfast was about. I'll discuss it with Mikale when I get home tomorrow. Right now, I'm heading to the only country in Europe shaped like a boot.

Italy looks like a boot Beyoncé might rock.

Right around Beyoncé's kneecap is Milan. That's where I'm headed. Home to three and a half million, dressed to impress dagos. The place has as many famous fashion designers as it has exquisite restaurants and art galleries. Sasha, Kennedy's gay friend, owns one of the galleries. He's who I'm flying in to meet. I'm going to hand Sasha fifty million dollars in cash for art painted by a nobody.

Sasha's then going to leak the news of a private collector dumping big money into this So-and-So nobody. So-and-So is going to turn into a celebrity overnight. His work is going to be to die for.

On Wall Street, it's called a "pump and dump."

It's illegal.

Not so in the art world. Sasha says we'll make between six and eight million dollars in the next ninety days. Have I mentioned I love the little fag? Full disclosure, he's grown on me. I've gotten to know him over the last year or so. He has residences around the globe. We've used them to hide out. Kennedy would tell the hubby she was off to spend the weekend with Sasha for hair, nails, and shopping—girl stuff.

I'd fly in.

We'd do other stuff.

If Sasha happened to be in town, we'd meet up for dinner, drinks, hair, nails, shopping—girl stuff. Didn't matter to me, if I got to be with Kennedy. I've talked shop with Sasha. He's told me about some of the "loopholes" in the art world. I had Kennedy call him last night to tell him I needed one of those loopholes. He was in Milan. Said to swing by. He had something right away we could do.

I called Kennedy back to say thank you.

She was still at the wedding rehearsal dinner and snuck away. We spent forty-five minutes on FaceTime, laughing and playing. She was hiding in the back of a coat closet at the resort, trying not to be loud. Felt just like old times. Neither of us wanted to hang up. After we did, I had a hard time falling asleep. When I finally dozed off, the front desk rang with my wake-up call. I grabbed the rest of the duffel bags of cash, had breakfast with Ocean, then met Bundu's operative, Jenny, at the hangar.

We hit the road again forty thousand feet up in Bundu's Gulfstream.

I'm happy to finally be out of the Sandbox. Now I understand why these fuckers are so excited to beat feet out of here. Guess I'd drive a cab and never shut the fuck up either. I'm just sayin'.

I'm high.

What did you expect?

It's an eight-hour flight from Dubai. I wasn't doing it sober. In the back of the taxi, on the way to the airport, I smoked enough hash to choke a camel. The driver kept sticking his head out the window. I told him I was American. He cursed me and spat.

My plan was to drop off the cash and keep going. My flat in Zurich is a gymnastic tumble from Milan. I was already thinking about dinner at my favorite sushi restaurant. Sasha has other plans, though. He's managed to peer pressure me into staying for one night. He promises I'll thank him later. The guy's doing me a fifty-million-dollar solid. What was I gonna say? Plus, if there's one thing I know about wealthy, gay men, there are always a ton of beautiful women around them. All lookin' for a little *penis*.

Pronounced "*pee-niece*."

French, for the obvious.

So, tonight I'm going with Sasha as his plus-one to some famous designer's fashion show. The fashionista is one of Sasha's good friends. Probably takes it up the can too. Just do the math. Normally, I'd spell out the algebra for you in black and white, but I've gone way too many rounds with Kennedy over this *who's gay and who's not gay* bullshit.

"You can't tell Sasha's gay unless he tells you," Kennedy claims.

Trust me, straight men, this is not an argument we can ever win.

I've learned to keep my opinions to myself and rely on my gaydar. If it walks like a duck, quacks like a duck, well, then, the motherfucker's prolly gay. And I don't give a shit one way or the other. I love shoes too! Fuck who you wanna fuck. Be happy. But, please, shut up about it. Quit rubbing our noses in it.

We get it, you like dick.

And since we're on the subject, let me also say that I want to be able to call my perfectly straight friend a fag or homo, if the mood strikes. And it does. Often. It's just heterosexual humor. Like you guys don't call your super-duper gay friends "straight" just to get a rise out of them. I know that shit happens. One of my really close friends is gay. Like super-duper gay. He earns his living from gay porn. Goes by Rocky Hendricks. Rocky tells everyone he's a bottom.

Not sure what that means? Find a gay guy and ask.

So, anyway, back to this fag I'm flyin' in to meet.

We've landed at the airport in Milan and are taxiing to the private hangars. Jenny's dropping me off and heading back to Morocco with Bundu's jet. A Customs agent clears me, and I follow her to the *Restricted Area* right outside the perimeter fence. Sasha's leaned up against a candy-cane-colored Wraith, talking on the phone. He sees me and squeals, then hangs up on whoever and walks over.

I reach out to shake his hand.

He pushes right past my arm, plants a French kiss on both my cheeks, and finishes with a groping hug…laughing.

On the way to his gallery, he tells me all about his new man. I tell him about Ocean and the Egyptian Viagra. He thinks it's the funniest thing he's ever heard. We pull up to his newest gallery twenty minutes later. It took him two years to build the place. The front of the two-story building is all glass. I can see all the way through to the inside back wall. There's a giant oil painting of some half-dressed dude with an eight-pack. His hair's blowing, hands are on his hips, his lips are puckered, and he's giving me the bedroom eyes.

No, Kennedy, nothing about Sasha screams gay.

Before we even exit the SUV, Sasha's people sashay their way outside to help. All dudes wearing all-skinny-everything. Once inside, Sasha shows me around and takes me to the back storage area. There's a shipping crate in the middle of the floor. Sasha does some kind of gay snap, and two of his helpers appear out of thin air.

They unpack seven different paintings from the crate.

They're what I'm getting for my fifty million dollars.

I'm not an art guy, per se. I like what I like. I don't give a shit about other people's work, but I can tell you this: I wouldn't trade nosebleed seats to a WNBA game for the seven paintings I just spent fifty million dollars on. To me, they look like a fourth grader wearing a helmet painted them. But, hey, what do I know?

Well, that's the last of it. The two hundred-plus million dollars has been cleaned, at least for right now. I just have to sit back and wait. I'll take the leftover cash, add a little to my hidden stash at my flat and walk the rest of it through the front doors of our Swiss bank over the next four months. If everything goes well, I can catch the last eight-to-ten days of the season in Mykonos.

Hello, hookers! Have I got a surprise for you: Egyptian Viagra. Hope your cardio's up because this shit's got some serious hangtime.

18

MIND BLOWIN'

Talk about Life takin' a left.

A lot of shit's gone down.

I came out on top, with a raucous cackle.

Let me start at the beginning, so I don't leave anything out. So, I hung out at Sasha's bachelor manor, waiting on this fashion show to roll around. The plan was to meet Sasha out in front of the place so he could walk me in. He sent a limo to pick me up. I threw on a Hugo Boss suit, Tom Ford shirt, and my Yves Saint Laurent loafers. When I exited the limo, there were lights, cameras, and red carpet for miles.

I walked up like I knew the owner.

Flashbulbs flashed. People asked who I was wearing. I made it to the front doors. There was a guest list. I wasn't on it. Sasha was nowhere to be found, and the security guard would not accept my bribe. Sasha wasn't picking up his phone. I was asked to step aside.

More flashbulbs, different set of questions.

I nodded and smiled. Didn't even care.

I was about to head home to Zurich. I was dying to get there. I turned to walk away, and Sasha came flouncing out the front doors. His phone had been on silent. He'd been in makeup, getting touched up for the show.

Kennedy, c'mon. The dude's a duck.

We walked in, and Sasha left to go play with the boys. I went to the bar. There was *chatte* everywhere. And I'm not just talking about on the runway either. I mean, it was *everywhere!* Here a *chatte*, there a *chatte*, everywhere a *chatte-chatte*. The place was crawlin' with it.

It's actually pronounced "*shh-at.*"

It's French, means, well…pussy.

So, I'm at the bar. *Chatte* and flamin' homos everywhere. It was like shooting fish in a barrel. I spotted this Brazilian model across the room, walked over, said something clever, and she followed me back to the bar. We were in the middle of choppin' it up. I'd just finished telling her my funny story about Egyptian Viagra. Had her eating out of the palm of my hand, when—

Bam!

In walks Kennedy.

I gaze over the model's shoulder. A man whispers something in Kennedy's ear. She looks right at me. Beelines over. I'm so confused, I get tongue-tied. Kennedy handles the introductions. "Hi. I'm Kennedy, the baby momma."

The model gets the point, pats me on the chest, whispers, "I wanted to try that Egyptian Viagra," and walks off.

I frown at Kennedy. "Cockblocker."

She grins. "We need to talk."

"Lead the way."

We walked the entire art nouveau area. Kept walking. Talking. Neither of us wanted to turn back. Ever. I would've kept walking all the way to Switzerland. Kennedy had to pee, though. My baby's pushing on her bladder.

I know—blew my mind too.

The kid's mine!

She wasn't sleeping with Martin, pronounced "*Mar-teen*," after all. She just freaked out when she found out she was pregnant. Wasn't sure I wanted a family. In all fairness, I wasn't sure I wanted a family. I'd never let the thoughts creep in. I knew I was in love with Kennedy, but a part of me always believed she'd never leave her husband.

That's all changed.

Here comes Kennedy now.

"I'm going to be a fucking dad!" I scream with both fists pumping into the night air.

Kennedy's laughing, trying to shush me. I hear people clapping, but all I can see is Kennedy, my baby momma. She lays a kiss on me that would knock a normal sap's socks off. In the middle of it, my phone vibrates in my pocket. I'm positive it's Mikale. He won't go away. *There's an Amber Alert out for a maid of honor missing in Lake Geneva.*

Mikale's assuming I have something to do with it.

"You have to answer him," Kennedy says. "It makes you look super-guilty."

"Me? I was in the middle of being seduced by a Brazilian model when you showed up."

"Charming, I'm sure. Now, answer him. Just deny everything."

"Fine, but he's totally going to know."

"Deny. Deny. Deny," she insists.

I answer. "You're like a bad case of herpes."

"Have you seen or heard from Kennedy?"

"Who?"

"My sister's maid of honor!" He's frantic.

"Oh, that Kennedy. Nope. Haven't heard from her, buddy. Is she missing?"

"Aw, fuck you, David. I knew it. My father's going to shit a spoon."

"Suck it up, ya fag. The wedding's not 'til tomorrow. She'll be back in time." I shrug to Kennedy. *He already knows.*

"What do you mean, back? You're in fucking Dubai. She'll never make it on time."

"I'm in Milan. I left you a message."

"I haven't checked them."

"She'll be back on time. Your sister and mother both know she's here. No one else does, though, so zip it."

"That's why Mother isn't freaking out. What are you going to do if Martin finds out?"

"He abuses her. Who cares if he finds out? She's not going back to him. And the kid's mine. Figure out how to wrap your head around all this because that's what it is."

"Martin and his father are going to pull their investments for sure now."

I'm tempted to ask again about Nova Terra, but I don't.

"So what? It's a few hundred million dollars. I'll have it replaced by week's end."

"I sure hope you two know what you're doing."

"We don't, but we're going to figure it out."

"You're not showing up to the wedding, right?"

"I wouldn't chance ruining Maggie's day. I'm sure it'd be more than a glass being thrown this time."

"Just make sure she's back here before anyone else finds out."

"I will. Gotta go. We're going to make out behind Ferragamo's Boutique."

"You're so disgusting," he says, hanging up.

It's our turn. Buy-bye now.

PART 2

19

CHEEZIN' 24-7

Zurich
Eighteen Months Later

Ultimatums always cost something.

This time, it was the hookers.

Next time, it'll be something different.

This is the way it goes when you tie the knot. Kennedy called it a package deal. Really, it was just an ultimatum. We're hitched. Which is why the hookers are no more. It was her or them. She said there wasn't room for both. I offered to buy a bigger house. She didn't think it was funny. I asked if I could have a day or two to think about it. She didn't think that was funny either.

She married me anyway.

Mar-teen, her ex, got an ultimatum too.

He could give her a divorce in one week and keep everything, or on day eight, she was going to take him to the cleaners for half. He was worth three billion dollars. Still is. His lawyers did the forty-yard dash to the judge, drawing the papers up on the way. Kennedy left with the shirt on her back.

Six weeks later, we tied the knot.

Sasha set everything up. He has an ex-lover who owns a cliffside castle down on the French Riviera. It was a very private ceremony. The only guests were Mikale and his ball-n-chain Eva, Maggie and her new husband, Brett, and Sasha. For our honeymoon, we went to Australia for five weeks. As soon as we came back to Zurich, I sold my bachelor pad, and we bought a chateau up in the mountains…and waited on the kid to get here.

He finally made it.

Kennedy named him Angelo, after her father.

I pushed hard for Tom, after Brady.

Kennedy says I have an unhealthy man crush on the guy. Am I wrong here? He's the GOAT, was married to Gisele the Brazilian supermodel and the rings…huh, he ran out of fingers!

What I'm trying to say is, "Suck it, haters."

Anyhoo, it's midmorning on a breezy day in Switzerland. I find my phone and send Doc a text, telling him to fire up the bird. Doc's my pilot. Yeah, I have one of those now. The bird's mine too. Well, technically it's the company's. I talked Mikale into buying the helicopter. He made me agree to help grow the business, called it a business deal. Really, it was just another ultimatum. I really wanted the chopper, though, and since I wasn't going to be off gallivanting around the globe lookin' for hookers any longer, I said, "What the hell? Let's make it rain at the office."

I've been grinding ever since.

The Boca Raton project is in the rearview. Dubai's under construction. And Mikale's headed to Bangkok, Thailand, to finish up the paperwork on our next spot. I'm headed to Peru. Doc's dropping me off at the airport in Zurich. I'm bummin' a ride to Lima on one of our client's private jets. I've got to see a man about a horse. Not literally (although the guy is a rancher these days). His name's Juan Suarez. He's from Way Out in the Sticks, Venezuela.

Juan didn't have two nickels to rub together.

His ship came in, though.

A few years ago, Juan's out back of his single-wide dump in Venezuela, diggin' around in his garden, and he strikes Black Gold. Texas Tea. The oil shot out of the ground for the next five years. To the tune of four billion dollars. Of that, Juan took fifteen thousand dollars and bought a new used pickup, then deposited the rest of his fortune into his personal checking account at the bank up the block.

A modern-day Beverly Hillbilly.

Word spread fast.

The most recent "elected" incoming dictator got wind of it. But not before someone gave Juan the heads-up. Juan ran out of Dodge fast. Right out the back door with his sombrero in one hand and his *dinero* in the other. He's settled in Peru and now wants to diversify.

Hi. I'm Diversify 2.0.

Mikale's sorry ass was the outdated version….

He was supposed to close Juan a month ago. His daddy got him the meeting. He flew to Peru to meet with Juan and bombed. His daddy had to get us another meeting. Now, I'm being sent in as the relief.

Just so happens Mikale's sorry ass is calling now. He wants to go over what I'm going to say to Mr. Suarez…for the eleventh time. Yeah, no thanks. He had his chance. I'm doing this my way.

I decline the call and go off looking for my family. I find them upstairs playing on the nursery floor. I bend over and plant a kiss on my wife's lips. "Good morning, woman," I say, and tousle my son's hair. "Good morning, Tom."

"Quit calling him that." Kennedy laughs. "You're going to give him a complex."

"A Tom Brady complex? He should be so lucky. Are you positive you two can't come to Peru with me?"

"I wish we could. Next time. I promise," Kennedy says.

Then she jumps up, wraps her legs around my hips, and kisses me like there's no tomorrow. Laughs. Kisses me again. Happens like ten times a day. That's what it's like with us. I set her down and toss my son in the air a couple of times—forty-six kisses and fart-noises all over his face while he giggles. I hand him back to his mother. I get another kiss, cop one more feel, and turn to leave.

"FaceTime me later from the hotel," she says, then flashes me her boobs. "I'll put Angelo down for a nap."

"Who's Angelo?" I shrug and smile.

She covers his ears. "I fucking love you."

I can't picture a day without Kennedy for the rest of my life. Makes some people sick. Plus, I got the boy to boot. I never understood it could all feel like this. I wouldn't trade it for anything in the world.

I'm out the door.

Here I come, *Señor* Juanito….

20

FUCK JUAN'S DINERO!

I'm high as balls.

What? I said I gave up hookers.

Well, and the hard drugs. Kennedy wasn't getting the weed too. She knows I smoke. I'm just not allowed to do it around the baby. I tried to help the kid out. I told her a little secondhand smoke wouldn't kill him. I mean, imagine hangin' out all day in a onesie, suckin' on mommy's titty, and watchin' cartoons. Now try that on a little Blue Dream or Purple Haze.

Talk about livin' your best life.

Relax, everyone, I'm only kidding. Babies should not get high. Imagine their munchies. The li'l fuckers already lie around the house eatin' up all the good shit. They'd never move out.

LMFAO.

I told you, I'm high. Shit looks funny in my head.

I just spent sixteen hours in the air. It's a long-ass flight from Switzerland to Peru. We're now on the final descent into the airport in Lima. I'm planning to leave here tomorrow afternoon, a billion dollars heavier. If you think I sat on a plane for an entire day only to be told "no" by some backwoods lottery winner, then you really don't know me.

Li'l Juanito is coughin' up the cash—today.

Mikale and I have a bet on it.

I close this guy for at least a billion, Mikale owes me a brand new Koenigsegg Agera RS. Next year's model isn't even out for another seven or eight months. The car's going to set him back three million dollars.

Serves him right for opening his big mouth.

I mean, it's common sense. Juan Suarez is a simple man. I told you he was out back playin' in the dirt when he struck oil. And he barely got out of Venezuela alive with his shiny new loot. It taught him a valuable lesson. He knows he can't keep all his eggs in the same basket. The problem is, he's grown to not trust anyone.

Bankers and brokers top his list.

Juan has most of his pesos parked in some money market account, earning him dick. Someone finally convinced him it was time to move some of it around—to diversify. Juan made a couple of calls and, a friend of a friend knows Mikale's father. Like I said, Daddy got his boy the meeting.

His boy's an idiot, though.

Mikale showed up like every other tight-ass banker—polished and proper. A snazzy suit and big words to describe his stupid charts and graphs. It was indexes and futures and blah, blah, blah. Juan wasn't turned on. Mikale left unsatisfied, with blue balls.

I'm going to leave Juan with hard nipples, lookin' for his wallet.

So, Peru…. It's in South America, for those of you arguing Central America. The country sits under Colombia and Ecuador. If you're hanging out in the southeast, Bolivia's across the street. The upper eastside is Brazil. You want to surf, the Pacific Ocean runs up and down the entire coast, that's west. And if you want to make a run for south of the border, and you keep running, you'll eventually make it to Chile.

Lima's considered the second or third largest city in all of South America. It cliffhangs above the Pacific. Juan's ranch is located inland, 'bout 27,000 hectares. Yeah, seemed like an awful lot of room to me too. I decided to look it up on Google Earth. I punched in Juan's address and a message popped up in giant red letters: *WARNING!!! JUAN'S PLACE! KEEP OUT!*

Juan's ranch makes the Dutton Ranch in *Yellowstone* look like Old MacDonald's pop-up farm.

I was supposed to stay at Juan's place. I'm not now. Juan's not happy about this. Too bad. He's already got the four-billion-dollar advantage, he's not getting homecourt too. No, we're going somewhere we can play heads-up. *Mano y mano.*

My secretary called him at the last minute yesterday to say I'd be staying at a hotel downtown, that I had another meeting in Lima. I told her to tell Juan I'd call after I got settled in. My plan worked. Juan called back, insisting to pick me up from the airport and drive me to my hotel.

I told you the guy doesn't trust anyone or anything. Out of the blue, a "banker" from Switzerland shows up to Lima, of all places, and has another meeting on the same weekend?

I said Juan's simple, not stupid. I banked on him wanting to check things out for himself. Curiosity always gets the cat. I'm not stupid either. I did my homework on the guy. I used everything from a hacker to a team of private sleuths.

Juan likes porn, mostly 8th Street Latinas. He searches the site for *white bitches with fat asses* on the reg. (Yeah, I didn't get it either.) That's all the hacker could find. No social media. No business website. No email. Juan doesn't even use a smartphone.

Now, the sleuths…they found the juicy stuff.

Juan's unhappily married. Same woman for twenty-five years. He got rich. She got fat. And old. She's dug her heels in, though, refusing to sign the divorce papers or die. He's tried hard with both. According to a source, there was a botched murder-for-hire not long ago. The wife somehow got proof of the attempt on her life and has tucked it away with her attorney. If she goes missing, the proof lands on some local homicide desk.

Juan's hands are now tied.

He spends his nights in the bottle.

A couple times a week, he stumbles into a brothel for a tune-up. Wife doesn't even give a shit. Doesn't say a word. I *know*, some guys are just lucky. Juan doesn't think so. He's miserable about everything. Hasn't stopped stressing since the day he hit the Pick 6.

His in-laws won't quit showing up, long-lost cousins keep calling, and bankers continue to drop by, which is not helping him. Everyone with their hand out. Juan just wants to be left alone to toss a few too many back and get his rocks off once in a while.

I'm coming at him from left field. First things first, I'm getting him tanked and see where it goes. If I haven't closed him in a few hours, I'll move to phase two. I told Kennedy I might have to buy the guy a hooker. "No problem," she said. "If you touch one, I'll cut it off while you're sleeping." We were in the shower when the conversation took place. She squeezed "it" 'til I promised I would never, ever. Ever. Ever!

There was bruising.

We're finally landing in Lima. I'm being dropped off on the private side of the airport. Juan's waiting when we pull up. He's standing there in off-brand jeans and a filthy cowboy hat, next to his used fifteen-thousand-dollar dusty pickup, alone.

Talk about a no-frills type of guy.

I am too…today.

I'm in faded jeans, holes in both knees, a worn-out black AC/DC T-shirt, shit-kickers, and a George Strait cowboy hat. *Fake it 'til you make it, right?* I walk right up to Juan. He stares me down. I can tell I'm not what he was expecting. He reaches out his hand to shake, formal-like. Nope. I give him the prison yard shake. Pull him in close, pat on the back. "*Qué pasa, cabrón?*"

This catches him off guard. He's not sure what to say. I toss my duffel bag in the bed of his truck and hop inside the cab. "Juan, this place got any good *cerveza?*"

He looks at me strange, then drives off.

We're cruising through the middle of Lima. I turn up the radio. It's that god-awful Mexican-Mariachi shit playing. I bob my head to the beat and play the drums on the dash like I'm Peso Pluma.

126

Some of you may not know this but finding a dive bar in South America is like finding a Starbucks in the United States. The place is plagued with them. I tell Juan to pull over in front of Pedro's Dive Bar. I can't make this shit up! That's the name of the place. Says so on the half-blinking neon sign out front. The rundown building has nine different shades of paint.

All of 'em faded.

"Let's wet our whistle, partner," I say, jumping out of the truck.

Inside, there's a donkey piñata hanging above the bar, one rough-looking waitress waiting on field workers, and a giant Mexican-looking guy behind the bar, with a giant moustache.

Probably Pedro.

We grab a booth in the back and order a couple of room-temperature beers from Consuelo.

Two hours later, Juan and I have polished off two bottles of tequila. We're now the best of slobbering-drunk *amigos*. I'm trying to teach him the Electric Slide...to fucking Elvis. The jukebox doesn't offer much of a selection. It's Elvis or Latin music from Elvis's era. You ever listen to that? No thanks. It's bad enough he has the rhythm of a catfish.

Juan, not Elvis.

Anyway, Juan's money hasn't come up this whole time— 'til now.

He pats me on the back, falling into me. "Why you no ask about *mi dinero*?" he says in Spanglish. (He has no idea I speak his native tongue. I told you, I rarely disclose my multi-linguistic abilities.)

"Fuck your *dinero*, Juan. Let's do another shot." I high-five him.

He follows me to the bar. "Why you tell fuck *mi dinero?*"

Got him. Mikale, order my car!

"You *muy contento, amigo*," I tell him. "You *no necesito me*. You *bueno mucho*."

"No. No. *Mucho* bang-bang *mi cabeza*," he says, pointing to his head. "I *caca* all the day. *Yo te necesito!*" He points to my chest.

"Me, *no tiempo*. My *amigos mucho, mucho dinero*, Juan. Another shot," I say, licking my hand. I pour the salt, slam the tequila, and suck the lemon. Juan's staring at me.

"How much *dinero, tu amigos?*" he asks.

"A billion dollars. *Mas*."

"Me give *dos mil millones*," he says.

"*Cuándo?*"

"*Rapido*."

"*Dame tu teléfono*, Juan," I say in perfect Spanish, turning serious. He hands me his phone. I type in the business account information and return his device. I lick my hand again, pour the salt, shoot the shot, suck the lemon as Juan transfers two billion dollars.

I send Mikale a text with a copy of the transfer: *That's how it's done. Order my Koenigsegg.*

Well, my work here is done. Time to skedaddle.

Hasta luego, Juan.

21

GAME FOR POUNDS

I'm pretty sure I'm being scammed.

By a couple different entities.

We'll start with Sally Struthers. She's been getting me for like fifteen or sixteen years now. It started when I was in college, back in New York. I'd been out all night drinking with the guys. When I got home, I sat in front of the TV, fired up a fatty to go to sleep, and Sally was on an infomercial.

She was standing in front of some mud-hut village somewhere in the middle of Ethiopia. In the background, a bunch of half-dressed, filthy-looking kids were playing in the dirt. There was a little boy standing at Sally Struthers' legs. A fly, so big it had to be a prop, buzzin' around the little guy's face. Sally was selling her pitch: *"For just the price of one cup of coffee...."*

I felt bad for the dirty, little guy. "What the hell?" I said. "Coffee's like fifty-five cents. Send over two cups on me."

They've been banging my credit card ever since.

I get a call from them every couple of years. I hear the same fly in the background. They tell me the kid's doing great. He's always out back chasin' around the goats and chickens. Never wants to get on the phone. He always needs more coffee, though.

Apparently, it's all the little fucker drinks.

He's up to like ten or twelve cups a day now.

Coffee ain't fifty-five cents anymore either. You ask me, he needs to start ordering a water from time to time. Either that or Ethiopian Airlines needs to start kicking in their fair share. I mean, I just gave them eighty-four hundred dollars for a one-way ticket from Lima to Dubai.

And it didn't even get me first class.

They scammed me too.

I'm headed to a kidnapping. I thought I was heading back home to Switzerland. I'm not thrilled about the turn of events either. Last night at Pedro's Dive Bar, coming out of the pisser, I got a text from Ivan.

Yes, the Russian bellhop from Dubai.

He's my eyes and ears there.

Anyway, I was drunk as shit. I had to read the message twice: *ISIS has one of the engineers!!!* There was also a video attached. I watched it. I don't know about ISIS, but there were definitely four ISIS-looking dudes throwin' up Muslim gang signs and wavin' around AK-47s. One of them was demanding that I pay or the guy dies. The engineer was on his knees in the background, blindfolded. I'm not going to say he seemed like he was in good spirits, but he wasn't dead either. He had a couple bumps and bruises, and he was bleeding from the nose, but not much more than that.

It's all part of the game.

We were warned of it in the beginning.

The kidnapping is really just a shakedown. It's usually done by three or four morons looking to score a quick handout. They scream and make noise, but no real violence is ever committed. You either fall for it or you don't. I don't. I know it's a scam.

These particular retards are demanding a million dollars.

They haven't got a shot in hell; I hardly know the engineer. For his sake, he better hope I can wiggle 'em down to something a bit more reasonable. I'll leave his ass there. I promise you. He knew what he was getting into when he signed on to the project. His invoice reflects it. Believe me, all of the contractor's invoices reflect it.

I'm going to try my best, though.

I told Juan Suarez I had to get out of Peru in a hurry; that I had an emergency in the Sandbox. He hustled me to the airport. There was a flight leaving in three hours. I spent those three hours shitfaced, on the phone, planning. I passed out as soon as we got in the air. The flight time was a little over twenty-one hours. I slept the entire way. Trying to drink a fat Mexican under the table and then poppin' Xannies will do that to anybody.

Ah, fuck you, I know Juan's not Mexican.

I'm allowed to say stuff like this. It's one of the only benefits of being half spic.

I'm clearing Dubai Customs now. When I emerge, Ocean—the hooker who kicked the shit out of me—is waiting. Yes, she's on the payroll too. I have a gift for recognizing talent, what do you want me to say? No, not that kind of talent. And, yes, Kennedy knows. She's met Ocean, loves her to death.

Ocean's holding a Louis Vuitton garment bag. She hands me the luggage, then splits. She has to get to the next part of our plan. I go off to find the little boys' room to change. I certainly can't show up in jeans and a T-shirt, looking like the help, and that's all I took with me to Peru.

Back in Lima, while I was waiting on my flight, I called Kennedy and told her what I was planning. She called Ocean and told her, and then sent along my tailor measurements. Ocean went shopping for a custom black suit, Italian loafers, a crisp, white dress shirt, and a pair of flashy cufflinks.

I'm just finishing up getting dressed when Mikale calls.

No time right now to answer.

I didn't even bother telling him I was coming here. Why would I when it comes to shit like this? He's kind of a pussy. I'm no Jean-Claude Van Damme, but Mikale? Muslims start throwin' up gang signs and waving guns around, he'd fold like cheap laundry. And we'd end up paying the inflation the government tells us doesn't exist.

Not on my watch.

I play in an arena full of billionaires where I'm always trying to talk them out of some of their net worth. If you think I can't handle a couple of penniless Bedouins, you got another thing coming. I throw my Peru clothes in the garment bag, hit the hair with a little water, shoot the cuffs, and I'm out. It's time to set a few kidnapping terrorists straight. Mark my words, they're going to get next to nothing.

Believe me, I've got game for pounds.

I'm going to walk in there and give these guys a "take it or leave it" offer, then do a walk-off on 'em. They'll threaten to shoot the guy. Might even put the gun to his head. I'll keep walking. The closer I get to the door, the less I'm going to be willing to pay. I'll tell them this upfront. They won't believe me. They'll let me get to the door. It'll be pennies on the dollar—take it or leave it.

They'll take it.

Understanding this is my gift.

I stroll out of the airport like I've got time and money, truckloads of both. Ivan's illegally parked at Arrivals, the Range Rover running. He steps out and opens the rear door so I can jump in. "How far back are they?" I ask.

"Eight to ten cars."

"Good job. Let's go."

We merge into traffic and head to the downtown area of Dubai. I'm going to have lunch with a smoking hot ex-hooker. And I'm going to make sure the two kidnapping thugs following us watch and report back to whoever's calling the shots. *"Boss, the infidel is having lunch with a smutty woman."* In Arabic, of course.

Ocean's not "hooking" anymore. She's back in law school and working for me full time here in Dubai. She's come in handy over the last year and a half.

Ivan drops me off in front of the valet at an outdoor, Paris-style café. Ocean's waiting, standing there in a dress that'll make you slap your momma. We do the cheek-kiss thing. We have a sidewalk-table reservation. Ocean knows the owner and got us the best seat in the house smack-dab in front of where the kidnappers can see me laughing it up, not a care in the world. Their demands the furthest thing from my mind.

An hour and half later, Ocean and I say our goodbyes mere steps from the kidnappers' front bumper. Ivan pulls up. I get in. We leave. They follow. The hook is set. Now, I'm going to rub it in.

I'm headed to our construction site on the other side of town. I tell Ivan to take the scenic route. He looks nervous about it. Like I'm pushing my luck. Like they might kill the engineer or something. I happen to know they won't. Someone dies over here, or even gets hurt really bad, word'll get back to the big bosses in Saudi Arabia and the whole kidnapping racket will be over for these schleps.

At the end of the day, I'm going to have to give them something, but it's going to be cheap. Super-cheap. And I ain't going to make it easy to come by, either. If I waltz in there with my pants down and pay, I'm going to get fucked, and I'll have to come back for more next week, and every week after. No thanks. We're doing this my way.

I spend almost three hours walking around the site, shooting the shit with our project manager. He has no idea he's even missing an engineer. Obviously, the kidnappers aren't going to broadcast it. And I'm certainly not going to say anything about it.

It's all very hush-hush over here.

Like me, most of these developers are foreigners with really deep pockets filled with other people's money. Unlike me, they're scared to upset the investors footin' the bill— worried they might pull up stakes. Sometimes, these developers even fork out the money themselves, just so their investors don't find out.

Not me.

If I gotta pay. They gotta pay.

I walk back to the Range Rover, texting Kennedy on the way. I'm trying to get a rain check on the FaceTime sex she promised before I left for Lima. Now she keeps telling me she'll think about it.

This marriage shit gets me nothing.

As he closes my door, Ivan tells me the kidnappers are parked right up the block, and they're starting to get restless. They've called him a half-dozen times today and sent along another video. He keeps telling them I'll get back to them as soon as I have time.

"Ivan, can you get me a table at The Naked Fish again?" I ask as he slides behind the wheel. "I'm in the mood for sushi."

He gives me another nervous glance and pulls out into traffic, dialing. He gets me a table, then disconnects. He looks stressed the fuck out.

"Relax, Ivan. I'm not going to get the guy killed. But I'm also not going to let these al Bag-Daddy bums beat us either. You want to go through this again next week?"

"No."

"You may not see it, but I'm running circles around these guys. It's all just a show."

"Why not call the police?"

"Over here? The cops are probably in on it. Plus, if word of kidnapping spreads, the billions of dollars pouring into this place dries up for all of us."

Ivan nods and drops me in front of the skyscraper. I take the elevator up to The Naked Fish. I'm seated immediately. I'm halfway through my sushi when I get a text from Ivan. He's forwarded the latest video from the kidnappers.

The engineer loses a pinky in this one.

The worst of it so far.

Still, he's not dead, but things are starting to get a little hairier. I guess I'd better call. I angle my phone so the other diners behind me can be seen in the background and hit record. "Towelheads, you're starting to get on my last nerve. Put one more of your pork-sausage fingers on the guy, you'll get nothing. If you think I'm playing, try me. Plus, I think the asshole you're holding slept with my wife anyway. You might be doing me a favor." I tell them all this in French.

I know it will take them time to get it translated.

I send the video to Ivan, telling him to forward it to the kidnappers.

This should certainly put a damper on their illusions of overnight riches. Tomorrow, I'll get around to calling them back. It'll be pennies on the dollar, just like I said.

For now, I'm going to my hotel. I'm jet lagged. Plus, Kennedy owes me some skin. A booby shot at the very least.

22

BUSTIN' A MOVE

I've had sex with an Avatar.

Some things you just can't top.

And I'm not talking about any ol' bum-ass Avatar either. I'm talking about a super badass Avatar. It happened last night. And, no, I was definitely not high.

Okay, maybe a little, but not that high.

Last night after dinner, I came back to my hotel beat. I hit the stinky parts in the shower, took a huge pull from the hookah filled with hash, hopped in the sack, and FaceTimed Kennedy. I caught her smack-dab in the middle of her "me time."

Pipe down, you neanderthals. Their "me time" is way different than ours. I mean way, way different, gentlemen. It has nothing to do with sex.

I know. Crazy, right?

Ladies, I'm going to give you the game here. "Me time" for men, means whacky-whacky. Haven't you ever noticed how helpful we become the second you say you have to run to the store? As soon as you say it, *me time* starts flashing across our little brains like *breaking news*.

The second the door closes behind you, we're in the back bedroom, doing the one-finger peek through the window blinds. As soon as your rear tires hit the bottom of the driveway, we turn into the most athletic people on the planet. We're hurdling couches, losing our shoes and socks on the way over. We're sliding, headfirst, across the dining room table, ditching our pants. Then it's a gymnastics floor routine, sticking the landing, ass naked in the chair in front of the computer. We then spend the next fourteen-and-a-half minutes racing through ninety-six different porn sites, searching for this and that.

We finally land on what we're looking for.

Thirty seconds later, we're looking for one of our socks.

Ready, set, go to the finish line: takes us fifteen minutes, tops. It's super-cheap too. Unless, of course, you've signed up for a few of these XXX porn sites, and no matter how many times you call and cancel, they still auto-bill your credit card.

Between Sally Struthers and Biker Bitches in Leather Gear, I'm going broke.

Anyhoo, Kennedy's "me time" had her just hopping out of the shower. The baby was down for a nap. She was wearing a towel…on top of her head, standing in front of the mirror. She was applying a mud mask-thing from head to toe…in Avatar Blue.

Are you starting to see where I'm going with this?

She was laughing, saying I was interrupting her chi. She kept spreading the mud, though. I knew I had to keep her on the phone a bit longer. Sooner or later, she was going to have to stand still long enough to let the mud cake up. When she did, I busted my move. Thirty seconds later, I fell over on my side, spent. We then talked for the next two hours 'til I fell asleep.

I know, I'm so gay. I hear all of you saying it.

You had this chick, you'd be doing the same thing.

In any case, it's approaching lunchtime here in Dubai.

I'm still at my hotel. I'm taking my time. I woke up, ordered room service, then got dressed. I'm wearing a different suit today, a pin-striped navy one this time. Ocean had it sent over this morning. I'm not planning on needing a third. This kidnapping business is finished today. I promised Kennedy I'd be home by this time tomorrow.

When I get downstairs, Ivan's waiting with the rear door of the Range Rover open. The four backpacks I asked him to get are piled on the seat. I slide in, and we pull out into traffic. "Same vehicle as yesterday?" I ask.

"*Da.*"

"Okay, get to the restaurant. The general's military. He'll be early."

Five minutes later, I get a text from Ocean telling me she's in place. I'm going to crash her lunch date. She's meeting General Alsheri. You probably remember him from the night Ocean took me by helicopter out to Abu Dhabi to play blackjack. He was the general drippin' in all the brass, Commander of the UAE Special Forces.

He has no idea he's part of a ruse concocted by *moi*.

I had Ocean call up and invite him to lunch…with just her.

I'm going to "run into" them. Ocean's going to invite me to stay. I'm going to accept. The news is going to make it back to the kidnappers: *"He's having lunch with General Alsheri!"* This will stop the kidnappers dead in their tracks. No one wants this lunatic in brass chasing them around.

Ivan lets me out a few doors down from the restaurant and goes to the other end of the block to watch for the general's motorcade. I'm tucked in the doorway of some high-end boutique, pretending to read the newspaper. I'm sure it's confusing the shitheads following me. It takes exactly sixteen minutes for Ivan to text me the general has pulled onto the block.

I spot him walking up, medals gleamin' on his red jacket, boots spit-shined, his men flanking him, dressed in desert-camo fatigues with pistols on their hips. I leave my hiding spot and arrive in front of Ocean and the general right as they're finishing their hellos.

Ocean notices me first. "Oh, my god, Da-veed! How are you? When did you get in town?"

"Yesterday."

She turns to the general and introduces me. "General, darling, this is my friend Da-veed. He's building a condo-minium development here in town. Da-veed, this is General Alsheri, Commander of the UAE Special Forces."

We shake hands. "Yes, we've met once before, General. A little party out in Abu Dhabi," I say with a wink.

"That's right. You're the banker from Zurich."

"I'd nearly forgotten," Ocean says, lying.

This whole conversation is taking place in front of the restaurant, out in broad daylight. I see it's making the general's men nervous. "Well, it was nice seeing you both again," I say. "Don't let me keep you from your lunch."

The general seems fine to let me go. Ocean says, "Nonsense. Please, won't you join us?"

The look on the general's face tells me he wants me to say no. No such luck. Today, I'm tagging along. "Well, if you insist."

The general turns on a military heel, and I follow them in, knowing the kidnappers are watching everything. At the hostess station we're asked to wait a moment. They were only expecting two. It's kind of making me feel like a third wheel. The general's side-glances aren't helping either. Ocean and I pretend to be oblivious. Truthfully, the general should count himself lucky. Ocean's only having lunch with his old ass because of me. I'm sorry he's unaware of this. He keeps up with the attitude, I'll tell him about himself.

Kidding.

The last thing I want to do is appear to be cockblocking a guy who believes in deadly force. Truth be told, he's famous for it over here. Always on the news, carrying out justice. He's on at least three billboards in town and recognizable by everyone inside the UAE, including the bad guys.

Anyway, five more minutes go by, and a hostess finally leads us to our table. I stay for two glasses of vino. Long enough for the kidnappers to buy my story. I thank the general, kiss Ocean's hand goodbye, and I'm now standing outside, in front of the restaurant.

I pause long enough to slip my sunglasses on and make sure these guys got eyes on me again. I take off, strolling down the avenue, window shopping. I pop in some of the world-famous boutiques, buying things along the way for the wife and kid, letting the anxiety build in my pursuers.

At the end of the block, Ivan's waiting. He jumps out and opens the rear door. When he slides behind the wheel, I tell him to get these guys on the phone. They've been ringing his phone off the hook all morning, which I told him to ignore, and he has.

He pulls into traffic and hands the phone to me. It's ringing. A guy picks up. He doesn't sound very happy.

"Shut the fuck up!" I say, interrupting him. "Now, we're going to do this my way, or I'm going to call a friend and have *him* deal with you, capeesh?" The guy doesn't say a peep. "You've got ten minutes to come up with a place to meet. You bring my guy. I'm going to bring the cash," I say and hang up.

He called back in three minutes.

They're holed up at a house on the outskirts of town.

We pull up to the place thirty minutes later. The guys following pull in and park behind us. The house is made of bricks and mud—mostly mud—built on sand. There are no windows in the cutouts, the roof is thatched, and goats are penned-up right outside the front door. There are two men with AK-47s thrown over their shoulders.

"Stay here. Keep it running," I tell Ivan. His eyes widen like he might shit himself. Like we might not make it out of here. I grab the backpacks and walk to the front door. I'm searched for a weapon, and they look inside each bag.

One of them snarls at me, "*Imshi!*" Towelhead for "*Get a move on.*"

I strut inside, and it's like a movie. The first person I see is the engineer, tied to a chair. He looks like shit. A bloody bandage is wrapped around his hand, flies the size of base-balls buzzin' around. He's gagged but trying to tell me something. If I didn't know any better, I'd think he's cursing me. To the right of him is a wooden table. Behind that are two ISIS-looking dudes. There's a satellite phone in front of one of them. Something about that one tells me he's the guy calling the plays.

No one says a word.

I walk to the end of the table and plop the four backpacks on top. "There's fifteen thousand dollars in each bag. I don't care how you split it, but you're not getting one more red cent, and my guy's leaving with me," I say in English, as tough as I have ever sounded.

The rest of them have crammed into the room. And it's obvious most have no idea what I'm saying. They all start blabbing away at each other. I reach inside one of the bags and produce a ten-thousand-dollar band of bills. I fetch a lighter from my jacket pocket and light the bills on fire.

No one notices.

I toss the wad of burning cash at their feet.

This gets their attention.

One of them hurries to stomp out the flames. "Now you have fifty thousand to split," I say, holding up another band. "Would you like it to be forty?" I position the lighter just beneath the money. Everyone suddenly comprehends. They trip over each other, begging me to stop burning the cash.

"Untie him, then back up against the wall. If I hear from you or any of your friends ever again, I'm sending the general." The engineer is now standing. "Keep the backpacks, I know you need ID to buy them over here," I say as I get the engineer out the door.

Forty-five minutes later, we're dropping the engineer off at the airport. For some reason, he didn't even want to re-trieve his belongings from his hotel. I think he's furious with me. The kidnappers apparently showed him videos of me having lunch with Ocean—twice. He thinks I cost him his pinky. He doesn't understand it saved me a couple hundred thousand dollars, at least. More importantly, it saved me fu-ture problems.

My work here is done.

I'm heading home to Kennedy.

23

OLD SKOOL

Wham, bam, thank you, ma'am.

Yup, that was about the extent of it.

I'm sure it was not what Kennedy had in mind. Me neither. Believe me, I was trying to hang around. Sometimes, things like this just happen. We agreed I owe her one later. She kissed me and jumped out of bed, anxious to try on the clothes I bought her in Dubai.

She's now parading in and out of her walk-in closet, modeling for me. Sir Mix-a-Lot is playing in the background: *I like big butts*….

It's old skool.

Back when hip-hop went off.

Back when it was the shit.

It's Kennedy's favorite music too. She's at the foot of our bed right now, rockin' an off-the-shoulder Coco Chanel dress. The thing set me back close to seventy grand, but man…. She's halfway out of it, in the middle of a striptease.

I'm singing along when my phone vibrates on the nightstand. I don't even look over. I don't care if it's Tom Brady. Well, okay, if it were him, I'd pick up, but it's not. Then the baby monitor crackles to life.

That li'l cockblocker!

I'm praying he rolls back over and gives his old man a break.

No such luck. He's up like it's the crack of dawn. Kennedy thinks it's hilarious. She pulls the top half of her dress back up and runs off to get the li'l jerk, laughing.

"I'm pitching a tent right now. Come back," I yell after her.

"Don't worry, we'll find another three minutes later in the day," she yells back.

Oh, she's got jokes, huh?

I roll over and grab my cell. The missed call was from Mikale. He's in Bangkok. That's where we're headed next. We've been going back and forth for about eight months now. Mikale went there to finalize some things.

I call him back.

He answers, and I strain to hear over the background noise.

"David! My best mate," he yells into the phone. "Hold on." I can tell he's trying to make his way outside of a bar, and he's sloshed. I'm about to be buttered-up.

"Pal, you there?" he asks.

"No, jerk off, I flew away."

"Now is that any way to treat your best chum?"

"Spill it."

"What are you doing right now?"

"Pitching a tent, trying to talk Kennedy back in the sack for round two."

"Gross. Why do you insist on telling me things like this?"

"Best chums. Now what do you want?"

"All right. I need you to come here. Please."

"What? Why? No way. Kiss my ass."

"Please, David. C'mon, mate. I need you. I promise when we get back, I'll pay for a month-long vacation anywhere in the world you want to go."

"I don't want to go anywhere. That would be a vacation."

"Kwan was expecting the both of us," he whines.

"Who cares what Kwan was expecting. Tell him to lick my balls."

"He sent his son to meet me."

"Did he bring the papers?"

"Nope."

"Well, what did he say?"

"He said that his father prefers us both to be here."

"And you're still there?"

"What do you mean? Of course I'm still here. It's a two-billion-dollar deal."

"Grow a pair. Leave. Don't even say goodbye. Kwan'll be calling before you land back here in Switzerland. He wants the deal as bad as we do."

"Just come over. *Please.*"

"The last thing I feel like doing is getting on another plane right now."

"You can take Father's jet. I've already had it ordered to Zurich. You'll make it right in time for the party."

"What party, asshole?"

"This weekend is the Kwan Industries' annual party. A black-tie event. We were both invited. You RSVP'd. I knew you'd never show up, though. I just figured I could make an excuse for you when I got here."

"Best laid plans…. So, now what? I have to show up to save your ass, in a tux nonetheless?"

"Bring Kennedy. Eva is here."

"I can't stand your wife."

"That's why I said to bring Kennedy. Eva loves her. Please, ol' chum?"

"You're a real dick, you know that? I'll call you back," I say and disconnect.

In the kitchen, my boy's in his highchair. Mommy's feeding him. "You and I need to have a little heart to heart about interrupting Mommy and Daddy's playtime," I whisper in his ear. I make the little fart noises on his cheek, as he tries to plaster my face with baby peas.

"That was Mikale. He's drunk in a bar in Bangkok."

"Mikale drunk? And in a bar? Things must be bad."

"No, he's just a pansy. Kwan snubbed him and instead of leaving, he's begging me to come over to save his ass."

"Which you will," Kennedy says.

I kiss the back of her neck. "Know any high-class hookers who might want to tag along? I'll be wearing a tux."

"Not sure about the high-class hookers, but I do know a killer-wife who doesn't care what you'll be wearing."

"Threat noted. Think your mom will watch the kid?"

"You know, he has a name."

"Not the one I picked."

She laughs. "When do we leave?"

"As soon as your mother can get here."

That's all it took. Kennedy's been wanting to get away for a few days.

24

GANG-BANGIN' DWARFS

A crackhead: To be or not to be?

Shakespearian? Nah, but it was the question back then.

I can't believe some of the shit I've talked myself into doing over the years. You wouldn't believe some of it if I told you. Like now. I'm standing in the lobby of the Four Seasons Hotel in Bangkok. Four years ago, I came to right over there, on one of those fancy couches.

I had no clue how I got there.

The last thing I remembered was being in Florida, three and half days prior.

I blamed Mikale. He was the reason I was even in Florida. I had specific plans not to be there. I'd been invited to some billionaire's mansion on the island of Palm Beach. I knew the *soirée* would be stuffy and uppity. Plainly, I didn't want to stomach it. Not my cup of tequila. A party much more suited for Mikale.

Problem was, Mikale was not invited because he'd minced words with this billionaire in the past. The billionaire believed, still believes, Mikale beat him out of several million dollars on a deal long before I came into the picture.

I didn't bother to tell Mikale I was invited.

Somehow, he found out anyway.

He begged, kicked, and screamed until he got his way.

I flew in for the party. My plus-one was a hooker, Esmeralda. I'm married now, so I have to be careful how I say this...let me just go with, Esmeralda was Mama Mia. Cost me over a hundred grand for the evening.

Most of it due to my crackhead shit.

Here's where it all started: I tossed back a couple of pills and hit this billionaire's *fete' champetre* with a super freak on my arm. I worked the room for about an hour, schmoozing it up with people I couldn't stand to be around. It took me that long to work my way to the billionaire. Took me half that amount of time to convince him to invest one hundred million dollars with me...and Mikale.

He called Mikale a shyster and said he was a thief.

Gave me the money anyway.

Just to be polite, I figured I'd hang around for another hour or so. I snuck Esmeralda out the back door of the mansion. Our "new" client kept a two-hundred-foot luxury yacht in his backyard. Esmeralda and I snuck on board. I rolled a joint. Esmeralda confessed she had Molly on her. I sprinkled a little on the joint. There was a hot tub on the third level. We ended up in it.

Neither of us packed our swimsuits.

You can guess the rest.

We eventually left the *soirée* through a side gate, high as balls. Esmeralda said she wasn't ready to call it a night. My kinda hooker. The problem was, there were no more party favors. It turned out I had a hookup right over the bridge in West Palm Beach. As my luck went, he ended up being in Tampa, on the other side of the state.

Road trip!

We hit Alligator Alley out of Miami in the Ferrari I'd rented for the weekend. I mashed the gas, and it still took us almost four hours.

And here comes some of the crackhead shit I was telling you about.

Esmeralda had a guy right there in Miami. She claims to have told me this twice. That's my brain on drugs. What did she care, though? She was high, and her meter was running. She sat back and raked in the cash. We made it to Tampa, and my drug dealer was nowhere to be found. I'd just talked to him thirty minutes prior. He told me to meet him at the Denny's, then never picked up the phone again.

We stuck around and waited for an hour and a half.

I was ready to call it quits, then Esmeralda got a call back. A friend of a friend of hers had a guy in Orlando, "Grumpy." We got back in the car. Two hours later, we met Grumpy. Grumpy was a gangbanger relocated from LA.

A real-life Mexican *vato*: the tattooed head, inked tears running down his cheek, Dickie pants five sizes too big, a Kobe Bryant jersey, and the Mexican push broom moustache. I was not enamored by any of it. The entire situation would've had any sane person throwing in the towel.

Not my dumb ass.

In for a penny, in for a pound.

We followed Grumpy back to his place. He told us that's where the shit was. He lived in an apartment complex on the gangbanger side of town. It was barely past breakfast and there were people already hanging out when we drove up. News of a five-hundred-thousand-dollar Ferrari pulling in spread fast. By the time I put the car in park, seven or eight of Grumpy's homies walked over and circled up.

A little voice told me not to get out.

I never listen to that voice.

Now, remember, I rarely disclose I speak other languages. Esmeralda didn't know I spoke Spanish, and I certainly wasn't going to tell the gangbangers. I got out. The homies closed in. I held up my hands, "*Olah*," I said, super-white. "*Yo no cato de mierda*." I'm not shit of a cat.

They all smirked; like, get a load of this *gringo*.

One of them called me "*ese*" and asked what the fuck I was doing there. I was about to explain that my name was not *ese* when Grumpy finally walked up. They all went back and forth in Spanish. A couple of the homies thought I looked like a cop. Grumpy convinced them I wasn't—that I was their next big score. He turned to me and said we had to go up to his apartment to get the drugs.

At that point, it didn't feel like he was asking.

Esmeralda and I followed him upstairs, with the "homies" bringing up the rear. My plan was to cop the drugs and roll out. Upstairs, there were more villains—all chillin'. Most were high or on their way. We all crammed into the tiny apartment. Grumpy told two of the *vatos* to get up and let Esmeralda and I sit on the couch. They slid apart just enough to let her squeeze between them. They were laughing, patting the cushion. Grumpy told them to quit fucking around and gave them a look.

They got up.

We sat down.

Grumpy whispered something to one of the *cholas*, an Edith, and she disappeared from the room. She came back carrying a sandwich bag full of pills and threw it on the coffee table in front of us. "You gotta take all of 'em, *ese*," Grumpy said, like I didn't have a choice in the matter.

I couldn't have given a shit less.

I just wanted to get high.

I didn't have that much cash on me, though. Luckily, Grumpy's righthand man, Lazy, was a dark web guy. Lazy had a dozen different ways for me to pay for the drugs. We settled on Bitcoin.

At that point, the pills were paid for.

We should've gotten up off that couch and went and found a hotel room somewhere in Mickey Town. Not me, though. I dumped the pills out on the coffee table. Looked around, then yelled, "*La vida loca, putos!*"

The room stopped.

No one batted an eye for like thirty uncomfortable seconds.

Basically, I called all of them bitches.

Grumpy finally stood, walked over to my side of the table and leaned over, staring into my eyes...close enough our noses could touch. He stayed like this 'til I was out of breath, then smiled and said, "You heard what the *gringo* said, '*La vida loca, putos!*'"

Forty-five minutes later, I tried a drug I said I never would, then did crackhead shit for like three more days.

Don't ask me specifics because I have no idea. The last thing I remember was leaning over the coffee table and snorting a line of meth. I turned up here in Bangkok, low on Bitcoin, no wallet, no credit cards, and that five-hundred-thousand-dollar Ferrari was in the wind.

I'm not sure whether Esmeralda was in on it or not. I don't care. She was a hooker. I'm sure she'd hit her fair share of licks on dumbasses like me in the past. I deserved what I got, and that's exactly what Mikale told me for the next two months. Every time Eva busted his balls about it.

At first, he tried to play slick with her.

As usual, he lost.

He knew she'd eventually see the credit card statements. He tried to get out in front of it. Totally backfired. He went with a casual statement, made while brushing his teeth before bed one night. "David's credit cards were stolen," he said.

Eva had been playing possum, waiting on him to dig a hole. "He charged twenty-five-thousand dollars to a place called the Eager Beaver."

Again, it didn't exactly say *Pussy for Sale,* but….

Eva busted his balls for lying. He slept on the couch for an entire month. I avoid her like the Coronavirus. Hasn't stopped her from whispering "Eager Beaver" every time she sees me. Now, I'm expected to spend an evening with her, in the same city she tracked me to the night of the Eager Beaver incident.

I'd rather pressure wash my balls.

But we're back at the Four Seasons, so….

Kennedy and I checked into our suite. Kwan's party starts in five hours. I'm jet lagged. Kennedy is not. She wants to go shopping in downtown Bangkok. I want to go for a romp in the sack. Kennedy wins. That's okay because I have a surprise for her later. I brought some of the Egyptian Viagra Ocean got for me when I was in Dubai.

After this party, she's gonna get it.

We'll see what she has to say about three minutes then.

25

ASIAN CRIBS

Bow chicka wow wow!

That's what Kennedy looks like right now.

No chance these cash cows don't try yakking it up with her at some point tonight. And just so we're clear, I plan on using it to my full advantage. I gotta be here, I'm filling my pockets with some of these Asians' scrilla.

Mr. Kwan sent a limo for Kennedy and me.

We are now in the parade of cars winding up the drive-way. The affair is being held at his personal estate, which happens to be a Japanese palace. It looks like one of those Asian temples in the old Bruce Lee films. Kwan had to dump a hundred million dollars into the place.

Buddha's been good to this guy.

When we arrive at the front doors, there are two Japanese samurais dressed in their very best *kamishimos*. Both are wearing *katanas* at their sides sharp enough to separate a man's head from his body in one swift swing, no doubt. The samurais bow.

I return the ritual, flawless.

Sensei Billy would be proud.

We're led into the palace. A guy who's a spitting image of Mr. Miyagi is standing right inside next to a giant gong. He's also wearing an expensive *kamishimo* and holding the hammer used to gong. He accepts the invitation Mikale had sent over to the Four Seasons, bows, then strikes the gong. "Mr. and Mrs. David Lietch," he turns and announces to the room.

It would be too hard to try and explain what the place looks like. I don't know enough Asian words. Let me just say this, Mr. Kwan is number four on the list of Chinks with the Most Yen. And he's spared no expense on the party. The place reeks of it.

Talk about trying to keep up with the…?

Is it still Joneses over here?

Anyway, everyone's dressed to the nines. I'm wearing my emerald-green tuxedo by Tom Ford. Kennedy's in the Devil Wears Prada. She has a string of rare pearls around her neck, a Cartier on her wrist that starts at six figures, and a pair of legs that should be insured.

I'm not sure if I've told you this—frankly, it's none of your business—but Kennedy played professional soccer for Greece, and from the age of sixteen until she married *Marteen*, she was a full-time model for Givenchy. She's the hottest thing in the room.

She always is.

We just slid into the main "ballroom," and there are probably two hundred and fifty people here, not including the two dozen servers moving around with trays of

157

expensive champagne and priceless caviar. Mikale says there will be close to five hundred people here tonight.

It'll be snug, but I bet we can all squeeze in this room.

The entire long wall to the left is a saltwater aquarium. Inside, Asian arowanas are cruisin' around. Arowana is *Long Yo* in Chinese. Pronounced *giant catfish* to the rest of us. It's the most expensive fish you can buy, hundreds of thousands of dollars for a pick of the litter. Kwan owns the largest collection of Asian arowanas in the world. The fish is a couple feet long, with Rollie Fingers whiskers, and resembles the mythical Chinese dragon.

The fish is believed to bring about good luck and fortune.

Kwan's got a shit ton of both, might be true.

I grab two flutes of champagne from a server passing by, and Kennedy and I sneak off to a corner at the back of the room. She's in the middle of telling me I'm her Superman, while I'm thinking of different ways to peel her out of her dress later. We clink glasses and share a heated look.

Up walks dickface, dragging his wench behind.

The moment's ruined.

"David, I must speak to you urgently," Mikale says as he does the air-kiss thing with Kennedy. "You look amazing," he tells her. His wench Eva is just kinda staring at me, like she's expecting the compliment/air-kiss thing from me.

Don't hold your breath, sweetheart.

I offer her a fist bump.

She leaves me hangin'.

I walk off with Mikale. "Why do you provoke her?" he asks.

"A better question: When you have sex with her, is it like stickin' your dick in the freezer? Brrr…."

"Do you want to keep it up, shithead?" He huffs. "Kwan's going to be here any minute."

"So?"

"So we really need this deal, David."

"Quit being a pussy. I told you, Kwan wants the deal too."

"This time you're wrong."

"You say that every time."

"This time is different. He sent his son to meet me. Do you understand what that means in the Asian culture?"

"That you're just not that important?"

"We shared a ritual tea."

"Yeah, dick breath, he does that with all his new girls. Look around the room. These are the big boys, Mikale. They're all from your dad's type of circle, and for the first time in your life, you're here without Daddy. Now take your finger out of your vagina and start acting like you belong."

"This is your pep talk?"

"Would you rather I talk about your wife?"

"She's really trying to like you now that you've married Kennedy."

"Tell her to blow me, figuratively speaking, of course. I wouldn't go anywhere near that icebox. Now go relax and enjoy the party. I'll handle Kwan. I bet I get him to sign before last call."

"Not possible. Kwan's made it abundantly clear there will be no talk of business tonight. It's like their Chinese New Year or something. No discussions of money after sunset. They believe it messes up their *prana,* their life force or some shit. We're meeting for lunch on Monday."

"Chicken lips, you ever heard of Phuket?" I pronounce it *fuck-it,* instead of *Foo-ket.*

159

He gives me a blank stare.

"The island right off the coast of Thailand here." I wait for him to catch up. "Well, that's where I'm going to be for lunch on Monday. Kennedy and I are leaving for there in the morning. Either we sign tonight or it's *sayonara*, Charlie. We'll catch ya at P.F. Chang's."

"Shh. Someone will hear you," he says, looking over his shoulder. "Kwan will never sign. Not tonight. He has way too much pride."

"It's what comes right before the fall."

We shuffle back over to the ladies. Mikale and Kennedy immediately dive into a conversation. Eva leans in close to me. "Hey, Eager Beaver. I hear you've been keeping your dick to yourself lately."

"Funny, I heard the same thing about Mikale."

She squares up, looks at me sideways. "He told you that?"

"No, but you just did."

She doesn't say anything else, turns and walks away. I step closer to Kennedy and interrupt her conversation with Mikale. "Congratulations, I didn't think you had it in you. Your wife just told me you two weren't bangin', then ran off."

He sees over my shoulder, observes Eva's gone, and scarpers off. "If I'd have known it'd be that easy to ditch those two…. Now, I believe you were in the middle of telling me you wanted me to be Superman later."

"That's not exactly what I was saying, sexpot." She laughs. "Have you figured out how you're going to close Kwan yet?"

"No. He's told Mikale there will be no talk of business tonight. Something with their piranha, or something. I'm expected to be at a luncheon on Monday."

"Ahh, so he's just like you. Terms on your terms."

"Then how do you manage to beat me all the time?"

"I show you things he can't."

"And I'm the sexpot?"

"Want me to help?"

"Do you have to show him anything?"

She leans in. "I don't have to show *you* anything. You're lucky you have a cute ass. Now let's close this guy. I want to jump your bones in Phuket."

"Don't threaten me with a good time."

We mingled. I schmoozed.

Kwan arrived about ninety minutes ago, late. He was away on some kind of urgent last-minute business. *À la Crazy Rich Asians*, he showed up in one of his helicopters. Made his rounds, saying hello to his guests. Stopped in front of Kennedy and me a little over an hour ago and hasn't moved on.

This is his first time meeting Kennedy.

I told you she has this effect on people, especially horny, old men.

She's got Kwan tossing back shots of sake like it's vitamin water. They've discussed everything from the Coronavirus and Trump to Women's Soccer to NATO's stance on climate change.

Kwan is eating out of her palm.

Another round of sake and Mr. Kwan turns to me. "David, why not bring Kennedy to lunch on Monday? We'll get our business out of the way and enjoy the rest of the day," he says.

Kennedy doesn't miss a beat. She sees an opening. "Darling, I told my auntie we'd be in Phuket on Monday," she says to me.

161

"I'm sorry, *cheri*, I haven't had an opportunity to tell you. I just found out myself. You fly over, see your sick aunt. I'll be along later in the evening."

Before anyone can say "chopsticks," Kwan takes the bait. "Your aunt is sick, my dear?"

"Death bed, I'm afraid. She's my great-aunt. Ninety-four years old. She's lived a good life. Been in Phuket for years, wants to be buried there. My mother told her we were headed over here at the last minute and asked that we stop in to see her."

"You must attend to her immediately. David," Kwan says, turning to me, "you must go with her. You two will take one of my personal helicopters over in the morning. Tell Mikale he can come by my office Monday morning. I will have the signed agreement waiting for him."

I shake his hand. "If you think it's best, sir."

He pats me on the shoulder, bows, and kisses Kennedy's hand. "I'm looking forward to dinner with the two of you in the very near future." He bows again, then excuses himself.

Kennedy and I do the golf high-five. "Let's blow this Panda Express," I tell her. "I'll send Mikale a text from the limo. I've got a surprise for you back at the hotel."

"Lead the way, Superman."

Up, up, and away….

26

HAS ANYONE SEEN JOSÉ?

There are eleven Mexicans in Phuket, Thailand.

I've met all of them.

The first thing I did when we arrived was track down weed. The taxi driver knew a guy. We dropped Kennedy off at the hotel, and the driver and I went to meet José—the weed guy on the island.

José was home.

So were the other ten Mexicans.

I ended up hangin' out with all of them for an hour. I spoke Spanish. They got a total kick out of it. No one else on the island knew the language. It was like getting news from home, they said. José ended up hooking me up really nice.

I'm high as we speak.

Kennedy's knocked out, lying in the sand next to me. We're lost somewhere in the middle of the rainforest. It's way more her fault than mine. She wanted to make out. If I'm being honest, I did too. She jumped off the path first. I just followed. Now we're here, next to a lagoon and water-fall.

Her fault, right?

Let me back up. So, when Kwan fell for the okey dokey about Kennedy's dying great-aunt, we skedaddled out of the party. Kennedy began molesting me as soon as our limo driver could get the car door closed. She didn't stop until we arrived at the hotel. And that was only long enough to get inside the room. She was back on me as soon as the door closed. I didn't even have time to pop the little blue pill. (Egyptian Viagra is actually fire-engine red, but you get the point.)

Anyway, lucky for her, I'd downed a half gallon of sake and several flutes of champagne at Kwan's party. She called me Superman…several times. There was even a point where I tied the sleeves of my tux around my neck and jumped off the end of the bed, pretending I could fly.

The next morning, yesterday, we took Kwan's helicopter over to the island of *Foo-ket*. Kennedy checked us into our beach bungalow. I went to meet José. I returned to the hotel, high. We ordered room service for lunch, dinner, a midnight snack, and breakfast this morning—which, not to brag, was served to me in bed by Kennedy wearing a teeny-weeny T-shirt her daddy would never approve of.

After "breakfast," Kennedy wanted to hike trails in the rainforest. I argued the bungalow was costing us five thou-sand dollars a night, and we should stay in and get our money's worth. My argument went nowhere. We packed some snacks and belongings into a backpack. When she went into the bathroom to get beach towels, I rolled up a bed sheet and hid it in the bottom of the bag…just in case the opportunity to "rest" came up later.

I also had a couple of the Egyptian sex pills in my pocket, praying the opportunity would *arise*.

It did, and, like I said, it was her idea.

We'll get back to that in a minute.

So, we headed out just after nine. By lunchtime, we'd been hiking the trails for nearly two hours. For the most part, we'd been staying on the tourist paths that were clearly marked on posted maps with *You Are Here* arrows and rest areas with vendors. We stopped at one of these rest areas for lunch.

After we finished eating, Kennedy asked if I wanted to find a place to fool around. I told her I'd been thinking about it all day. She got up, jumped off the path, and was gone. I had to work to keep up. I had managed to dig around in my pocket for the pills, popped them both.

Two minutes later, I wanted to plop down. Kennedy checked to make sure no one walked up on us…and kept going…and going. Eventually, we ran into this lagoon and waterfall.

It was a race to see who could undress first.

I won.

I know I seem like the kind of guy who's eager to rub it in. I'm not. But I do want to say I rocked Kennedy's world, three minutes at a time, until it was dark. Too dark. By the time we noticed, the sky had turned pitch black. We dressed and tried to hustle back. A couple of wrong turns later, and we landed right back here.

We were trapped, some real *Gilligan's Island*-type shit.

We decided it would be fun to just make a night of it. We threw our shoes in the corner, spread the sheet back out, and I started a campfire with supplies from her emergency kit. I looked around and found a log and dragged it over. Kennedy sat on it, and I sat on the ground and leaned against it. We split a box of granola bars and a bottle of water. Eventually, Kennedy curled up next to me in the sand and fell asleep.

I dug through my emergency kit and fired up a fatty.

We're flying home late tomorrow night, provided we find our way out of here in the morning. I'm leaving again when we get back to Switzerland, almost immediately. Kennedy is still unaware of this. It's a surprise. I must keep it that way. I have something up my sleeve—a "nooner" scheduled in the South of France for the end of the week.

A sudden rustling in the bushes startles me.

It's not the weed either.

I cover Kennedy's mouth with my hand. When she opens her eyes, I'm shushing her. "Something's out there."

She sits up and listens.

We hear it again and hustle to put our shoes on.

It's probably some kind of animal coming down to the water to get a drink. I'm not trying to find out. I grab a log from the fire and start waving it around like I'm fucking Zorro. Out walks two teenage boys with two girls behind them. I'm six five, waving fire.

All of them pale like they've shit their pants.

Makes us even.

I throw the log down. "We're lost," I tell them, holding up my hands.

Their English is good enough to understand. The first boy tells us he can show us the way out of the forest. Before I respond, Kennedy tells him to go do what they came to do, and just to grab us on their way back out. I look over at her. *What gives?*

She winks. "They probably snuck out here to fool around."

"Ooooh! In that case…."

I hand the boy a hundred-dollar bill and tell him to not forget us. They all promise to come back, and they walk off. I wait for them to disappear into the trees. When they do, I'm out of my shoes and clothes before Kennedy's back from peeing behind the bushes. I'm laid out on the sheet next to the fire when she emerges.

"Well, that didn't take long," she says.

"We can fool around too. If we hurry, maybe we can do it twice."

She laughs.

Doesn't stop her from undressing.

27

GETTIN' RAMBO WITH IT

Weed gives me wings, like Red Bull.

Weed does not give me brains, like common sense.

Between us, this is the way shit goes when I rip huge bong hits right before I have to do something important.

We're back home in Switzerland. Right now, I'm high. Earlier before, I was stupid-high…for four hours. The kind of high where you promise to never smoke again if it just goes away. It's some new shit from Amsterdam. There's a warning label on the packaging: *This shit is serious!!!*

I read the ingredients.

"Extreme paranoia" was there.

Didn't give me pause, though. I threw a decent-sized nug of the stuff in the five-foot water bong I call *El Burro*. The Donkey. I pulled until the smoke was all the way up to the rim, then covered the top of *El Burro* with my hand so none of it could escape. I took a deep breath, filling my lungs to the max. I held it as long as I could before choking to death for the next fifteen minutes.

Kennedy heard and brought me a glass of water.

I finally got it under control.

Kennedy went off to do shit around the house. I told her I was going to piss around in the garage for a few hours. She kissed me and told me to have fun. I went to the basement. I had almost twelve million dollars in cash stashed down there in a hidden safe.

No one knows about the money—not Mikale, not Kennedy, not my priest, not the government. No one. I've stockpiled it over the years. You never know when it might come in handy. Like now.

I needed to sneak eight of the twelve million up to the garage right under Kennedy's nose. Last night, not high, I split the eight million into two duffel bags. All I had to do was march the two bags up the basement stairs while Kennedy was somewhere on one of the upper levels.

Should've been two trips max.

Enter *El Burro*....

When I finished choking and finally made it to the basement, I realized I'd landed in space, delusional. And, let me tell you, the disorder is a real motherfucker up there. I convinced myself Kennedy was watching, waiting for me to move the bags of cash. Like she was going to mug me.

The only obvious thing to do, I decided, was to move the eight million dollars upstairs, little by little...under my T-shirt. Took me like forty trips. Up-down. Up-down. Up-down. Up-down—forty fucking times! After like the fourth trip, I had myself convinced Kennedy was a lethal operative, and I was Rambo.

All true.

I was slipping behind doors, jumping behind furniture, sliding around corners—a total machine. At one point, I was coming up the basement stairs and almost ran into Kennedy coming down from one of the upper levels. I could hear her talking to the baby. Thought it might be a cover-up. By this time, I was shirtless with a belt cinched tight around my forehead.

Rambo for real.

I hurried across the kitchen and hid in the pantry. I cracked the door to listen. Silence. Kennedy and the baby must've moved off to another part of the house. I tightened the belt, assumed my Rambo stance, and made a break for it across the kitchen, out through the dining room, and did a double-knee slide to the garage door.

I made it.

I'm fucking Rambo, bitches!

Rambo looked down. He was shirtless…and the cash was still in the basement.

Shit went on like this for four hours.

I'm not sure what they're putting in weed these days, but it'll get you there fast. You just have to figure out where "there" is.

So, the cash made it past Kennedy. Now, I have to get it to the French Mob. Tomorrow, at noon sharp, I'm meeting one of these mafioso clowns who fancies himself a French Marlon Brando. The guy's a total douche if you ask me. He's the "nooner" I was telling you about back in *Foo-ket*. And, check this out, he doesn't even know I'm coming. In fact, doesn't even know who I am.

That's not going to stop me from waltzing right into his place of business and making it clear to him that it's in his best interest to take the money…or else! If I must, I'm prepared to hold his life over his head.

The balls on me, right?

This is just the way it has to be with these types.

They respect violence, not boardroom chatter. He's got something I want. I've got what he needs. It's a matter of presentation from there. Tomorrow morning, I'm taking a private flight down to the South of France to have a "sit-down" with him.

In the meantime, tonight, Kennedy and I are having dinner with Sasha. He's bringing his new boy toy, Addison. (Addison just graduated from college.) I'm told they're moving in together. I guess things are heating up between them.

It's a big gay secret.

No one knows Addison's queer, including Addison's parents.

Ain't that a bitch. Imagine being a fly on that wall when he tells them: *"Mom, Dad, I love men. And I'm in love. We're moving in together. Dad, you're gonna love him. He's your age."*

Kennedy says I can't say stuff like that tonight at dinner.

It's not going to be easy.

Kennedy calls out from the other room.

"I'm in the kitchen!" I holler.

"Sasha had to cancel tonight," she says, coming around the corner.

"What's wrong? Addison have homework?"

She rolls her eyes. "Sasha says this is the one, babe. Love is blind to age. Just look at us," she says, wrapping her arms around my neck.

"But you have a vagina."

"What does that have to do with anything? And why are you wearing a belt on your head?"

"I lost a bet."

"With who?"

"Rambo."

"I don't even want to know. How 'bout we stay in, watch Netflix and chill?"

"More chill or more Netflix? And who gets to pick the movie?"

"Rock, Paper, Scissors. Same as always," she says.

"If you win, are you going to pick a chick flick?"

"Yep, but the last one with the Rock had action. You left in the middle anyway. I found you in here, scrolling through Tom Brady's Instagram."

"So?" I shrug.

"I'm calling Gisele and telling her you're stalking her husband."

"He traded her in for a younger version."

"No, she dumped him for the karate guy."

"Dude's a fag."

"He'll beat up your man-crush."

"I'm done talking to you about this. I will leave you and the kid for Tom Brady. Pick the movie."

She does the karate sound effect and punches me in the stomach. "He'd still beat him up. I'm going to put on something sexy," she says. Kisses me, pinches my butt, saunters off.

Hard to argue with that.

28

KEEPIN' IT GANGSTA

First impressions are critical here.

I look like I could be carrying eight million dollars.

Which I happen to be.

I'm in my white, linen Hermes suit, a pink Tom Ford pullover, brown Gucci loafers, brown Gucci belt, brown Gucci sunglasses. I'm carrying the two duffel bags of cash through the airport in Saint Tropez.

Actually, it's pronounced *San Tro-pay*.

No idea why.

It's the French—they do all kinds of weirdo shit.

Saint Tropez is in the South of France, along the French Riviera. The backdrop is the Mediterranean Sea. The town has an estimated population of 4,352 residents. That's it. It has everything, though. Just ask the Beckhams, Leonardo DiCaprio, Jay-Z and Queen B, Rihanna, Lady Gaga, Kate Moss…should I keep going? Karl Lagerfeld, Joan Collins, Elton John, even Armani's sister has a summer pad here.

The place is the shit.

There are three hundred vineyards, over forty beaches, a crazy nightlife scene, restaurants and galleries…and the French Mob. I'm here to buy Kennedy a two-year anniversary present: our summer home. The mobster I'm buying the place from has no idea he's selling.

He will.

Like it or not.

Everyone refers to this mafioso don as "The Count." Not like the Count of Monte Cristo. More like count to three and he's sending Pierre with a bat or banger. One, two, three…. *Bada Bing! Bada Boom!* Believe it or not, he's a crowd favorite here in Saint Tropez.

The locals love The Count.

His problem is no one from Corsica likes him.

Corsica is an island right off the coast. It's the mecca for bad Frenchies. One of them is the new boss of a rival family. When he took over, he looked in the "cash reserves" and went to pokin' around. Bumped into The Count with his hands in the cash register.

The new boss knows The Count's been skimmin' off the top of the casino profits. To the tune of eight million dollars. The profits are supposed to be divided between the two main families on the island. The deal has been in place for twenty-five years.

An old friend of Mikale's from way back when they were sucking on platinum-plated pacifiers told me about The Count's ordeal over drinks one night in Zurich. Brett Murdock with a "k"—no relation to Rupert Murdoch with an "h"—said The Count has a very small window in which to produce the cash, or Pierre's comin'. Special K—he hates when I call him that—said The Count doesn't have the ability to pay. He told me the mobster had assets here in town that no one knows about.

It piqued my interest.

I sent a team of my investigators to find out what those assets were.

Turns out The Count owns a piece of real estate here in his dead mother's name. It's a home and vineyard. He could put the property on the market and easily get twelve or thirteen million dollars...if he had that kind of time, which he does not. I've brought along the eight million dollars he's risking his life for.

He can take it or leave it.

He leaves it, he rolls the dice.

I'm going to make him see that.

I take a taxi to the downtown area. The Count owns a French bistro right on Main Street: *The Count's Place*. The driver lets me out at the front door. It's straight-up noon. The Count's guy is standing out front of the place, just like my investigators told me he would be. The guy gives me a hard look. I stare right back and walk up, carrying the duffel bags. He steps in front of the door. "What's in the bags?"

"None-ya."

He curls his lip and shrugs. "None-ya?"

"Yeah, none-ya. Like none-ya fuckin' business. Tell your boss I wanna see him. Zippity-zap like."

He takes a threatening step toward me. There are people around, though. Lucky for him. He's now close enough I can lean in.

"Listen, you tart. You wanna keep your boss on this side of the curtain, you'll tell him I'm out here."

"And just exactly who are you?"

"A guy who's brought eight million dollars with him."

"That what's in the bags?"

"Hard to believe you're not a doctor."

He bites his cheek, tells me to wait outside, and goes inside the restaurant. I follow him. He turns and glares at me. Can't do anything about it, though. There are patrons. I spot The Count at his booth. There's an attractive woman sitting across from him. Two more of his guys are at the table in front of them. The guy from the front door gives them a look. They stand up, shoulder to shoulder, blocking my path.

I'm not getting past without violence.

I bite my tongue.

The guy leans over and whispers in the boss's ear. The boss looks over at me. I wink. He glances down at the bags. Bingo. He waves his hand to the blockheads in front of me. They let me through. I walk right up to the table and drop the bags at his feet. "Take a walk, honey," I tell the woman. She doesn't move, looks at me, looks at The Count. "I'm your solution to Corsica," I tell him. "You wanna discuss it in front of the lady here, that's your business."

The Count tells her to go powder something.

I sit in the woman's seat and make myself comfortable.

The Count's got both elbows on the table, staring at me. He takes a long pull on his cigar and exhales, like no one's ever died from secondhand smoke. His eyes never leave mine. He starts to say something. I hold up my hand, cutting him off. "Listen, Frenchy, save me the *do you know who I am? I'll kill everyone in your family* bullshit. You mob guys don't rattle me. Never have. Now, you've got a problem. I'm your solution. It's simple. I've brought the cash."

The waiter walks up. "Um, your food is prepared, Mr. Count," he says, timid.

"Perfect timing," I cut in. "Bring the food."

The Count takes a deep breath, gives the nod. The waiter turns and walks away. "Where'd you get the cash?" he asks.

"Right to business, I like that. Where I got the cash is not your concern. What your concern should be is, what do I want for the cash?"

"What if I just take it?"

"What if I don't let you?"

"What do you want, Mister…?"

"Lietch."

"What do you want, Mr. Lietch?" he asks, all wiseguy.

"Your home and vineyard."

"*Vas baiser ta me're!*" he snarls.

It's fancy French, telling me to go fuck my mudda.

I take it on the chin, totally laid back. Like I'm a real gangster. "I know you're into these guys, capeesh?" As I'm telling him this, I'm shaking my wrist, like the Italians. "Take the fucking money, or you know what it is."

"Are you threatening me, Mr. Lietch?"

"Merely pointing out the obvious."

"My home and vineyard are worth a lot more than your eight million dollars."

And just like that, we're in a negotiation. "So is your life," I tell him as the waiter arrives with the food.

The woman ordered French onion soup. Happens to be one of my favorites. I lean over the bowl and slurp two spoonful's before casting a glance back up at The Count. When I do, he's staring at the top of my head. He wants to put a bullet in it. Clearly, I'm beginning to get under his skin.

Everything about me has him backed in the corner. I go over his options again, real slow like he's impaired. "Pierre, Frenchy, whatever the fuck you call yourself, take the cash, pay back the money you skimmed, and—"

Wham! The Count slams his hand on the table, interrupting me.

I lean over the bowl, slurp another spoonful of the French onion, and settle back into my seat. "Then get on with your life."

Before he can pound again, glass is shattering, and guns are firing.

Shards from the windows scatter across the floor. A water glass right in front of me explodes. "Fuuuck!"

Before I can dive under the table, I'm hit.

It's in the leg, so I'm not gonna die, and it was probably a good thing I didn't go low. Hurts like a motherfucker, though. I scurry under the table with the money. The Count's slouched over in the booth, bleeding out from the hole in his head. Dead.

We were just getting down to the nitty-gritty, too.

Hate to say I told you so.

Talk about a day late, dollar short.

Now I'm hiding beneath the table, a giant pile of cash next to me, a bullet in my leg, and a bumped off mafioso don above me. It'll be front-page news. I can picture the headline already: "The Count's Been Whacked! His Swiss Banker Hiding Under the Table…with Millions!"

Mikale's going to shit a brick.

The cops are going to have questions. I peek my head out from under the table. The place is a total ruckus. Seconds later, a cop is coming through what's left of the front door. I drag myself up into the booth, accidentally pulling The Count off the seat. He hits the floor like a concrete block.

The officer walks over, looking at me like I'm crazy. "What? I just moved his feet so I could sit." I hold up my leg. "I've been shot. Hurts like a motherfucker."

He examines my leg, shakes his head. "What's in the bags?"

"That's your first question? There's a dead guy at my feet."

"He's not going anywhere. Who are you? And what's in the bags?"

"I'm David Lietch from Switzerland. There's eight million dollars in the bags."

"Cash?"

"No, a really big check."

He doesn't smile. "Who does the cash belong to?"

"Me."

"You a banker?"

"No…yes…no, I don't know. Do I need a lawyer?"

"Did you kill The Count?"

"No."

"Know who did?"

"Nope."

"What's the money for?"

"I was trying to buy The Count's vineyard here in town for my wife. It's our two-year anniversary."

"Why cash?"

You can't be serious. "C'mon, the guy's in the mob…. When in Rome."

"You're not in Rome, Mr. Lietch," he says, his expression unreadable. "Is your government aware of the cash?"

"Not really. It's my getaway fund. Well, in my case, it's my 'buy a castle for my wife' fund. But you know what I mean. Everyone has one."

"Get away from who?"

"You're missing the point. Is this an interrogation?"

"Just a conversation."

"Then, am I free to go?"

"No."

"Can you call me an ambulance?" I hold up my leg again.

"No. The bullet only grazed your leg. It's not even bleeding."

"It is bleeding. Maybe not like an ax to the head, but it hurts."

"You'll be fine. How do you know The Count?"

"I sent a team of private detectives over here to find out everything about him."

"For?"

"An angle to buy his property."

"If this were a trial, you'd be digging yourself a hole."

"Honest to a fault. It's a blessing and a curse."

"Got some ID?"

I hand him my passport.

"Stay here and don't touch anything," he says and walks off.

Where am I gonna go, asshole? I've got a bullet in my leg.

Ten minutes later, the place is crawling with cops...all three of them. "Defund the police" must've hit here too. Although, I'm pretty sure Saint Tropez is not at the top of the list for mob hits. Three cops probably make up the entire force anyway.

The officer returns, holding my passport. "I'm going to need to hold onto this, Mr. Lietch. The Americans have some questions for you. Give me a couple of minutes here, and I'll find someone to drive you over to the station. You can wait there until they show up."

Huh?

PART 3

29

THINGS HAVE GOTTEN SPOOKY

The Good Ol' US of A
A Year and Some Change Later

Twelve months, four days, thirteen hours…and just about nine minutes.

The Count's been dead that long.

Where has the time gone, right? It's flown by.

Yeah, fuck you, flown by. It's moved so agonizingly slow, I've wanted to claw my eyeballs out. Time. It's just been creeping along…for twelve months, four days, thirteen hours, nine and half minutes, and counting.

A lot has changed.

For starters, I'm busted. And I don't mean busted as in guilty—actually, I'm busted like that, too, but I'm pretty sure my lawyer's going to get me out of it. I mean, I'm busted as in broke. We'll get to that bit about the lawyer and the alleged charges in a second.

Let me tell you about being broke first: it sucks.

Happened on the double too.

The French DST—Directorate of Territorial Security—took the eight million dollars from under the table back in Saint Tropez. And they didn't stop there. The following week, these monkeys in ill-fitting suits called Switzerland, and the FIS—Federal Intelligence Service—knocked on the front door of our chalet with a warrant and ransacked the place until they found the hidden safe in the basement. That's when they seized the rest of it, close to three million in cash. And they took the keys to the house on the way out. They then called the NCA—National Crime Agency—in London, and they seized my downtown flat. On their way out, they called these USA pricks back to let them know they followed through and took it all.

Meanwhile, while all this was going on, someone at the Home Office of the Feds froze every financial asset they could put their grimy, little paws on—stock accounts, bank accounts, and every credit card. And the final kick in the teeth, they took possession of my beach home in Boca Raton, Florida, until the judge realized Kennedy and my son had no place to live.

The fucking United States of America has turned my life upside down.

I've got some explaining to do, I know. Believe me, it's all I've been told by every three-letter agency on the face of the earth for twelve months, four days, thirteen hours, and…ah fuck, you get the point.

Let me start from where I almost lost my life from a bullet wound.

Fuck you, it hurt.

So, I get shot. The Count gets whacked. And the Americans would like a word.

An hour later, I'm being marched through the single-front door of the Saint Tropez Police Department, past two desks facing each other to their only two cells—both empty, and not a gun in sight—at the back of the room.

Some real Podunk, out-in-the-sticks type shit.

Anyway, the cop who brought me over told me to pick a cell and get comfortable. It was going to take the Americans a couple of days to get there. I had no idea what the fuck was going on. I asked for a phone call. The officer laughed and said I wasn't in America. I chose a cell. He then undid the cuffs and locked me in. I figured they'd at least give me an attorney if I asked.

Wrong. The cop said, "No phone. No attorney. No visitors. Period."

Orders came from up top.

"What about a bandage? I've been shot."

"It's not even bleeding. Rinse it off in the sink."

Hmm.

At that point, I began to get a little nervous. Like what the fuck could I have done? I was racking my brain and staring at the wall clock. It had been exactly two hours and forty-one minutes since I plopped my ass on the end of that cot.

Now, I want to remind you, I was down in the French Riviera, basically a two-hour flight from the rest of civilization.

186

I'd only been in custody for like three hours when in walks four guys, single file through the front door. They were all sporting dark sunglasses, ball caps pulled low, dressed like they just left the GAP. *Tourists looking for directions?*

What else could it be, right?

Wrong.

Try the Central Intelligence Agency. You know, the spooks runnin' around in foreign countries, killin' people up close in broad daylight. Always some slick shit too. Shit no one ever sees them do.

So the CIA GAP models circled the desks to have a hushed conversation with the officer who locked me up. He fixed a stare over at me, then nodded. *Yeah, that's him.* There were more whispers. More nods. The cop picked up his desk phone, mumbled out a conversation with whoever-the-hell, looked over at me again, hung up, and gave the four spooks another nod.

I was pretty sure something wasn't right.

Like shit was about to get fucked up.

They walked over to my cell, still didn't remove the sunglasses, and told me I was leaving with them. I asked who *they* were. No answer. I asked to see some ID. They said it was outside in the vehicle. The cop unlocked my cell, and they walked my ass right out the front door, threw me in the back of a delivery van emblazoned with *St. Tropez Dry Cleaners* across the side, and peeled out.

In broad daylight.

And no one saw shit, right?

We turned the corner, and they put a black bag over my head. I kept asking questions. They kept ignoring me. No one said shit to me for an hour and a half until we stopped again. The side door opened, and I was assisted out of the van.

The black bag didn't come off until they got me inside.

I ended up in a small, bedroom-like room—smelly, dusty, no windows, a metal folding chair in the center, and a Muslim prayer rug rolled up in the corner. They left and locked the door behind them. I was in total darkness.

Felt like some Netflix shit without the chillin'.

Still no phone calls. No attorney. No bologna and cheese either. It sure seemed like a whole lot a fanfare for li'l ol' me, even if I had killed The Count. He was a mobster, not a president. I knocked, kicked, screamed, threw a fit.

That went on for an hour or so.

No one gave a shit.

In the middle of the night, I pissed in the corner. I wasn't the first to do it either. The spooks didn't bother to come back until the next morning. I was sleeping on the prayer rug when in walks the same four dudes, plus a woman. Finally! Someone I could talk some sense into.

Yeah…right.

She came through the door, snarling, itchin' to snap on me. "You've got some explaining to do, Mr. Lietch," she growled. Turned out, she was the one responsible for having me picked up in the first place, then blindfolded, and holed up. A real battle-ax.

Obviously, I had no idea what she was getting at. She started peppering me with questions. I answered each one honestly—"I have no fucking idea what you're talking about."

She didn't seem to believe a word I was saying. She tried grinding my answers into something more, looking to trip me up somehow. I was still, "I have no fucking idea what you're talking about, lady." It went on and on like this.

She then showed me some 8x10s.

"What about this one? You know him too?" she asked.

"No. I don't know any of these people."

More 8x10s. More trick questions. Same answers. For eight straight hours.

On their way out, one of them tossed a brown paper bag at my feet—bologna and cheese, and a bottle of off-brand water. Still no phone call. Still no attorney. This, though, they were nice enough to kick a bucket inside the room.

Still no lights.

I ate in the dark, and pretty sure I missed the bucket.

I never got to find out.

The bologna and cheese was laced with something. I woke up on the floor in some run-down motel room in who-knew-where? One of the spooks was kicked back on the other bed, flipping through channels. Two more of his buddies were standing right outside the door—I spotted them through a crack in the drapes. There was a change of clothes on the end of the bed and a bag of McDonald's on the table.

"You have a long flight in front of you. Take a shower and eat," the spook said.

I got lippy, said I needed to speak to my wife. "Now!"

He said not to worry. I'd sent her a message. I yelled that that was illegal. He didn't seem to care. Told me to get in the shower. I gave up, took a shower, and ate. In the middle of my McSomething, in walked this butch bitch. She had more questions. This time, there was no trickery. She got right down to business; tossed six or eight 8x10s on the bed.

"Tell me about these," she said.

Fuck. Fuck. Fuuuck!

The first photo was of Jargons. Remember the fat-ass in all white, the lawyer to the king of Belgium dickhead? The next several photos were of the tattooed American Kyle, who rolled up in Yemen with Jargons—the fucking prick who wouldn't shake my hand, just took my bags of cash and went on his merry way. The last photos were of the bad joke, one that was hard to forget: "*Three men walk into a deserted hotel in Yemen carrying a hundred million dollars in cash....*"

I thought I was a real card.

Fuck. Fuck. Fuck.

The fucking arms deal had been a reverse sting operation, conducted by the United States.

The charge carries up to life without parole. My day in court is tomorrow. They've got everything they need to send me up the road too. The spooks delivered me up on a silver platter. They'd laced my food for a second time at the run-down motel. When I woke up, I was handcuffed to the bed frame. FBI agents, in their little fucking gay jackets, were standing around the room looking at all the 8x10s and file folders.

No spooks in sight.

"Where are they?" I asked the Feds.

They said they had no idea who I was talking about. Said they showed up to the motel on some 1-800-CRIME-FIGHTER-type shit. They walked in and found photographs of me in Dubai, standing in front of the hotel while Ivan and Bundu's pilot loaded the black duffel bags of cash into the Range Rover. The Range Rover ended up tracing back to the Khaleed brothers, who eventually traced back to the opium business. There were more photos, thirty minutes later, of the same duffel bags being loaded onto the seventy-five-million-dollar Gulfstream, which they traced back to Bundu and all his family craziness. To seal the deal, there were pictures of the transaction in Yemen.

The fucking spooks had been following me ever since Mikale and I agreed to lend Jargons the hundred million for his arms deal. Jargons was a rat the whole time, working for these Americans. The lawyer to the king of Belgium got pinched for some kind of big financial scam a month and a half prior by Interpol. He was looking at some serious time and couldn't take it. Said he had some information on weapons of mass destruction and knew an American—this Kyle—who was trying to round up a hundred million dollars for the deal. Jargons figured it would be enough to earn him a *Get Out of Jail Free* card.

"Not on your life," the officials said.

The authorities decided they wanted more, or Jargons was going to the big house.

"What if I can get you a billionaire to finance the arms deal?" he'd asked.

Aah, a billionaire. Now he was singing their tune.

Jargons set up Kyle Something or Other, then gave up "the billionaire"—Mikale and his father. But by proxy, my dumb ass got ensnared. I showed up to Yemen with the cash. Case closed, right? All they had to do was nab me. The problem was these fucking American Feds squirted all over each other when Jargons told them I could lead them to even bigger fish beyond Mr. Lars Van der Broeck & Son.

He made up some tale that's still unclear to me about me being involved in some major nefarious enterprise with billionaires.

Wrong.

The Americans fell for the "fish story."

They let me walk away from Yemen to see where I'd lead them next. They started in on their cloak-n-dagger shit right up front, wiring the hundred million back to Mikale and me, like it was coming from Jargons per the agreement, with Mikale's father's ten-million-dollar profit on top. We, in turn, wired the agreed upon five million to Daddy.

The Americans then followed the three of us around. Every move we made, they were right there. Not a problem. One, we didn't know they were there, and two, we were clean. The American supervisors began to think the same thing—we were leading them nowhere.

They pulled the plug on the investigation.

Three days later, there's an Interpol warrant out for my arrest, sitting on a judge's desk, waiting to be signed. I was down in Saint Tropez having lunch with The Count. He gets himself whacked, my ID gets ran, a call goes out, a response comes back: "*Sending in delta-niner-four for an extraction.*"

Wham! Wham! Wham!

No phone calls. No attorney. No visitors.

The spooks picked me up. I told my side of the story 'til they laced me. I woke up and the Feds were there, FBI and ATF. They had IDs to prove it and my civil rights up their ass. They gave me my fifteen-minute phone call. I called

Kennedy. I was then flown to the Gun Club County Jail in West Palm Beach, Florida.

My bail hearing was set for two days later.

Went like this:

"Your Honor, Mr. Lietch handed over one hundred million dollars in cash to finance weapons that kill women and children. He's connected to drug lords in the Middle East, war lords in Morocco, and Chinese billionaires in Thailand, and now an arms deal in Yemen.

"Judge, in this last month alone, Mr. Lietch has flown to Peru, Dubai, Thailand, back to Switzerland, then on to Saint Tropez, where he had lunch with a refuted mob boss who was murdered over his soup and breadsticks. And, Your Honor, there was eight million dollars in cash found under the table, which Mr. Lietch has admitted belonged to him. It is the Government's belief that Mr. Lietch is part of a much bigger organization. He has the financial ability, and contacts like his business partner to help his skip town. Your Honor, we strongly believe he will. The Government asks you to deny bail."

That was the pitch for the United States of America. A motherfucking best seller.

Now it was time for my glossy, high-priced New York attorneys to step in.

They looked at each other, looked at me, then asked the judge for a ten-minute recess.

The judge granted it.

My high-priced attorneys turned to me and asked if anything the prosecutor just said was true.

"Most of it," I confirmed.

Bail was denied.

Five days later, the Feds started knocking on doors and freezing assets. They didn't even allow me to continue paying the high-priced attorneys, causing them to ditch me like a bad investment. The judge appointed me a free federal public defender—a civil servant with a caseload out the wazoo.

I'm going in front of the judge again in the morning.

My attorney says tomorrow can go either way.

Ya think?

You get what you pay for, I guess.

I know, I still have a bunch more to tell you, but I'm back in my cell, and the deputy's screaming, "Lights out!"

I'm going to lay here and stare at the bottom of the bunkbed above me until the Guatemalan wannabe-rapper up on the third bunk shuts the fuck up so I can go to sleep.

Twelve months, four days, thirteen hours….

30

RISE AND SHINER

People say I have tendencies.

I've heard it my entire life.

It usually goes something like this: "David tends to let his mouth get him into trouble. One day it's gonna get him fucked up."

Like today.

Doesn't pay to be witty in jail.

I've got a black eye, a cut above my eyebrow, and my upper lip is the size of a watermelon. The judge would have to be Stevie Wonder not to notice. I can't wait to hear what he has to say about it. If he asks me, I'm snitching. He's going to read it in the report anyway. These pussies filed assault charges, and they started it.

Ain't that some shit?

I was sleeping, when a three-hundred-and-fifty-pound redneck swung down from the middle bunk and landed on mine…in his da-dunt-da-dunts.

Things escalated from there.

Up until the middle of last night, I lived with two other dudes in a 6x9 jail cell. There's a steel table and chair pushed up against one wall, three lockers are bolted to the opposite wall, the back wall is stacked with triple bunk beds, and at the front of the cell, there's a one-piece toilet/sink combo with a steel door that locks from the outside.

A chateau, it is not.

Definitely not enough room for three people to scrap.

Like I said, my cellies started it.

Well, one of them anyway. The other jumped in. I mean, literally, he jumped from the third bunk. He's this crazy-looking, gang-bangin' Guatemalan with tats galore, including an "MS13" across his Adam's apple. He goes by Bimbaito.

Pronounced *Bimba-e-toe*.

Means little fat lip.

Bimbaito wants to be a rapper. A black American rapper…who's Guat-e-malan! He's been learning to rap in English for the last year. He's up to like seventeen words already. He practices all day. Shit's painful to listen to. Atrocious, actually. Take my word for it. I've told him on several occasions that he should give up and keep selling drugs for his gang.

In fact, I told him this again last night.

He was up there on the top bunk, rappin' away, same seventeen words, scrambled a bit but basically on a loop. I was down on the bottom bunk, trying to tear my ears off until I couldn't take it any longer. "Oye, nigga-ito, you sound like el shit-o!" I yelled up to him. "Give up. Sell drugs."

He leered over the side of his bunk, gave me the finger, and went back to butchering two languages simultaneously...out of tune.

The other cellie, the one in the middle bunk, was snoring his ass off. His name is Justin. He pronounces it with a lisp. Not a gay lisp, but a hillbilly lisp. Like "Juuh-stin."

Juuh-stin is one of these fat, inbred, redneck crackers from Okeechobee or some other Bumfuck part of Central Florida. He's here because he and his mother were caught cooking meth in the single-wide trailer where they cohabitate. Juuh-stin tells Bimbaito and me the same story every day. "I swearz, Momma and me whattin' makin' meff to sell. We only duz it."

Aw, good ol' Ma.

He feels the same about her.

He's got the proof tattooed on his left shoulder: the trailer park heart with *Momma* inked through the banner. The Confederate Flag is on the other shoulder, and the tramp stamp reads *White Pride*. Every night after chow, the nurse comes by with Juuh-stin's meds. They knock him out almost immediately. By seven thirty, he's snoring his ass off. It's so loud, I've considered holding a pillow over his face.

Yes, until he dies.

Never Gonna Be a Rapper and Trailer Park Boy were cellies before I came along.

So, it's like 12:55 in the morning when Little Fat Lip finally decides he's practiced enough for one day. He leans over the side of his bunk and asks if I'm still awake. I ignore him and pretend to be asleep.

Five minutes later, I doze off.

At 2:32, I'm jarred awake.

Justin rolls out of his bunk, loses his balance, and lands on the end of my bunk. "Sorry, bruh," he says, standing there with his huge gut hanging over his tighty-whities. He walks to the toilet, farts on the way, pisses and doesn't wash his hands, then crawls back in his bunk.

I fall back asleep.

Exactly twelve minutes later, the fat redneck leans over the side of his bunk. "Psst.... Bruh, you awake?"

I lift my head and stare at him. He holds up his headphones, country music twangin' away loud as hell. "Is this too loud? Like, is it keeping you awake, bruh?"

I ask if he understands irony.

From his expression, I gather he does not.

I then tell him his momma should've flushed him when she had the chance and roll back over.

He either didn't hear me or didn't catch my drift, because he rolls over and goes back to his country music. Me? I proceed to toss and turn. Can't go back to sleep. And I keep mentally strangling him, while he's up there humming, occasionally mumbling a verse.

And it's starting to get to me.

I smack the bottom of his bunk with the back of my hand. The headphones come off. He shifts and looks over the side of the bunk again, like, *What's up, bruh?*

"You're humming. Cease!"

His face is priceless. I roll back over.

Five or six minutes go by. I hear him up there mumbling, getting himself all worked up. He's telling himself that he ain't no bitch. I've seen this skit of his a few times. He always talks himself out of trouble. The guy wouldn't bust a grape. However, I'm not stupid. This is jail, anything's possible.

198

I roll back over, quietly move my feet to the side of the bunk, and slip out of my T-shirt, just in case. As I'm reaching for my booklight, Juuh-stin jumps out of his bunk. He's pushing three fifty. And don't forget, he's in his skivvies.

He stands over the top of my bunk and asks if I think he's a bitch.

"No," I tell him. "I think you're a *retrasado*."

He stares at me, confused.

"It's Spanish for 'retard.'" I sit up. "I need to piss. Can you back the fuck up?"

He takes a couple steps backward—enough so I can get out of the bed.

Right as I stand, he steps in with a haymaker. One that came with a three-day notice. I duck, pivot behind him, and use the momentum to catch his arm.

I'm choking him out with his own arm.

This is when Bimbaito decides he wants to be fucking Super Beaner, jumping from the third bunk. He lands on top of us. Mostly, on his buddy's head.

I quickly ran the numbers. Weighed things out if you will. I was fighting roughly five hundred pounds between the two of them, in a very small space. Three hundred and fifty of those pounds was seconds from going to sleep. I tightened the chokehold around Trailer Park Boy's neck.

Night-night, li'l bruh.

Now, it was Tu Paco's turn.

The wannabe rapper was around my neck. A metallic taste flooded my tongue. He got a few good licks in. I pulled him off me and was in the middle of trying to cram him into one of the lockers when the lights switched on.

"What the hell's all this noise about?"

I turned and spotted one of the deputies glaring through the sliver of window in the steel door.

Without hesitation, I released Bimbaito. He fell to the floor, trying to catch his breath.

I held up my hands. "Hey, I was just trying to get a little sleep."

The deputy screamed for me to get against the bunks and put my hands up.

A pack of guards entered the cell ninety seconds later, breaking out the pepper spray as if they had an endless supply. They called for more backup. No idea why. Juuh-stin was out cold at my feet, Bimbaito was on all fours still catching his breath, and I was blind as fuck, not to mention the pain I was in…. Then, they hog-tied me and carried me out like a six-pack of beer.

I'm now sitting in an isolation tank that reeks of piss and puke. My eyes and skin still burn from the pepper spray, and I'm freezing my nuts off. I'm waiting on the US Marshals to pick me up and drive me across town to federal court.

Over the last year, we've developed a rapport, the Marshals and me.

31

YOU HIDIN' ANYTHING UP THERE?

Trump's got the same record as Pussy.

Undefeated.

In fact, he's beaten Pussy. Hell, there are rumors of him even grabbing a few. Who knows? And I don't think anyone cares, especially not here in West Palm Beach, Florida. The streets are lined with his supporters.

Looks like a parade.

It's USA flags, *We Love Trump* signs, mugshot shirts and hats that say *3 Peat*. Everything red, white, and blue. A lot of white if I'm being honest. I don't see many reds and blues. I'm handcuffed and shackled, wearing an orange jumpsuit, sitting in the back of a US Marshals' van, tryin' to get a closer peek through a metal-grated window, so....

We're in bumper-to-bumper traffic, making our way to the federal courthouse on Clematis Street in downtown West Palm Beach. My life hangs in the balance—kinda. Yes, I'm facing life without the parole, but it's very unlikely the judge would give that to me. He'd have to be a real dick. Like a total dick.

This judge isn't that guy.

Don't get me wrong, he doesn't like me. I've been a thorn in his side over the past year, but so has the federal prosecutor, and the judge has let her know it. He's "beefed" with her almost as much as he's "beefed" with me.

The judge is a dick, but he's a fair dick.

My freebie attorney doesn't believe that's going to be the case, keeps ranting about my mouth getting me into trouble. I keep telling him to spare me the dramatics. He's one of them anyway.

Did you know that all these mofos get their paychecks from the same place? And I'm talkin' from the top down. The CIA spooks, the FBI, ATF, Homeland Security, the judge, the prosecutor, and even my federal public defender.

Sure seems like a lot of people on the same team.

A black or brown don't have a chance.

I decided early on I wasn't going to make it easy on them. After all, they started it. I know, seems like a recurring theme with me, but they did. I was minding my own business. They swooped in, lookin' to pick a fight. And that's what they've gotten the whole way...tooth and nail.

I keep "beef" with all of 'em.

Right down to the US Marshals.

Again, paid by the same people as everyone else.

These Marshal pricks show up in their matching uniforms: khaki cargo pants, too-tight black polo shirts, and their pointy little star badges. All biceps, short on brains. I call each one of them "Biff."

Today, I have extra-beef with the transport Marshals.

Started first thing this morning, at around six thirty at the county jail. I heard them come in at the other end of the tier. They were dragging their chains, licking each other's doughnut, drinking their Gaybucks, and making as much noise as they possibly could.

I was crabby.

They stopped at the front desk to chat it up with the county deputies. I couldn't hear exactly what they were talking about, but they were laughing and cutting up. All shits and giggles.

For sure my middle-of-the-night cell-extraction was a topic of conversation.

The Biffs finally got around to me.

They walked down the tier and got a load of my busted-up face. Thought shit was funny. I wasn't in the mood and told them as much. I'd been locked in a smelly-ass, isolation tank. My eyes and skin felt like fire ants were setting up camp, and I was shivering my nuts off...for hours. These asinine pricks show up, and they got jokes.

On top of all that, I'd just learned that Bimbaito and the fat hillbilly Juuh-stin filed assault charges against me.

I snapped.

Told the Biffs to lick my balls.

They got huffy and puffy. I said more things. Included their wives, mothers, and daughters in my castigation. They got even huffier and puffier. One of them was like five-four, arms the size of coconuts. I really hurt his feelings. His coworkers had to restrain him. I laughed.

"Take it easy, li'l D-ball," I said, patting his head through the bars.

I don't think he liked it. I know his buddies didn't. Took some time to get things settled down. Two Biffs returned a few minutes later. They moved me out of the isolation tank and into one of the holding cells in Receiving and Discharging. They were not very nice.

There were five other inmates inside, also being processed out to the custody of the US Marshals for federal court. I picked an open seat on the concrete bench to wait. No one said anything to me. Rumors of a fight had already found their way through the halls of the jail.

I looked like I'd been in a fight.

Gave the impression I might not mind doing it again.

I leaned my head against the wall and closed my eyes.

Twenty minutes later, the Biffs returned. "It's time to get you ladies dressed out," one of them said, opening the cell. "Gimme three at a time."

I was closest to the door and stood up. Two other "ladies" followed me out. The Biffs led us around the corner to the subzero, dress-out room in R&D.

"All right, ladies," Biff 1 said for the second time. "Up against the wall, shoulder to shoulder, facing me. Watches, wedding bands…. Any of you bitches wearing ear or nipple rings?" He looked us up and down. "Everything goes in the bin with your name on it. You'll get all your property back when you return from court later today."

I kissed my wedding band and put it in my bin.

"All right, sissies, lose 'em. Everything goes into the laundry cart. Pants, shirt, socks, your panties, even your shoes," Biff 2 barked.

The three of us got stark naked and stood shoulder to shoulder, facin' Biff 1. I already told you, the room was an icebox, so all of us were tied down there.

At this point, I could still look my mother in the eyes.

"Arms to the sky," Biff 1 ordered. "You ladies just missed being a man." He examined us from head to toe. "Open your mouths, let me see under your tongues. All right, turn around, hands on the wall, let me see the bottoms of your feet. Wiggle your toes."

The three of us followed his demands.

"Okay, ladies, drop it like it's hot!"

We squatted and coughed.

"Now stand back up and grab your ankles. Let me get a good look up there. Make sure you ladies aren't trying to smuggle in any drugs."

He used a megatron flashlight.

The backs of my eyeballs were glowing.

We stood back up and were asked what size jumpers we needed. Because of my height, I asked for a 6XL. Biff 2 threw a 3XL at me, said it was all they had, and laughed. The stack of 6XLs were right there in front of him. He gave the other two guys the sizes they asked for. Meanwhile, I was standing there, staring down the 6XLs.

Ultimately, I ended up in super-tight handcuffs and ankle shackles and an orange jumpsuit three sizes too small. I can no longer feel my hands or feet. They've gone numb. Not to mention, I have a huge camel toe.

That's numb too.

I'm sure you would agree, the "transport" Marshals are total dicks.

Well, the courthouse ones aren't much different. They've still got the beefy arms, but they've gone soft in the middle, from sitting around on their fat asses all day. The same smart mouths, though. Just watch what I tell you.

We've finally made it to the federal courthouse.

We're standing in front of the elevators in the underground parking garage, waiting to be cleared to enter the building. When we get clearance, I'm escorted upstairs and handed off to the courthouse Marshals. I'm then shuffled into another holding cell. I don't have to be in front of the judge for another four hours, so they remove the handcuffs and shackles.

I'm going to lay on the cement bench and await my fate.

32

SOMETIMES YOU GET LICK'T

Lick't.

Pronounced *licked*.

It's what the US Marshals at the courthouse call me: David Lick't, instead of David Liecht—pronounced *Leeched*. It's been a thing now, for goin' on six months, at least. It all started over my lunch. They never brought it to me. I was hungry and aggravated. Words were exchanged. I said something to the effect of their daughters being cheap prostitutes. They took it personally. From that day forward, it's been an uphill battle.

The least of which is them calling me Lick't.

Like, Lick't my balls. Lick't my ass. Lick't my ass and balls.

Fuckin' Biffs, nothing gets old to them.

One of them is yelling down the tier right now. "Lick't my scrotum! Attorney visit! Get! Ready! Now!" The other Biffs laugh in the background. "Do you hear me, David Lick't my ball sack?"

I never answer them. Ever. I make them walk their fat asses down the tier to tell me. Sometimes, I pretend to be sleeping when they walk up. Other times, like today, I'm standing in the middle of the cell, holding up both middle fingers.

One of them trudges down the tier. He stops in front of my cell. His shift must've just started. He gets his first look at my face…and my camel toe. "Yeah, Biff," I say, still flipping him off, "I heard your dumbass. Attorney visit. Now lick't these balls." I pelvic thrust my camel toe at him.

"You'd better hope your mouthpiece is on his A game today. Otherwise, you're headed up the road where someone's going to put that mouth of yours to work."

"Ooh, scary. Just do your job, shithead. Take me to see my attorney."

He handcuffs and shackles me again. Makes sure everything is super-snug. He then steers me by my elbow, squeezing as hard as he can get away with in front of the cameras, all the way to the attorney-client rooms in the back.

My "mouthpiece" is sitting at the metal table, working with his head down when Biff unlocks the steel door. It's customary to remove at least the handcuffs. Most of the Biffs do it. Not this one. He shoves me in the room. "Hope he can save your ass," he says and winks.

"Can't wait to show you my balls later. Make sure your flashlight has new batteries," I yell through the steel door.

I turn to my freebie attorney. "Do you hear how these Marshals speak to me?"

He continues to scribble notes on a yellow legal pad. I shuffle over to the table. "I'm glad to see you're working so hard on my case. 'Bout time."

"This is on my last client. I'll be right with you," he says, like it's a walk-up service.

A minute or so later, still without looking up, he says, "You want to tell me about your two cellmates?"

"Sure, if you're interested. One's super fat and snores. The other one wants to be a rapper, and he sucks at it."

He glances up and lays his pen on the table. All business. I can tell he doesn't find me funny. Not one bit. He uses his index finger to push his glasses farther up his nose, sees my busted-up face and swollen lip for the first time.

I shrug. "I slipped on a bar of soap in the shower."

He holds up a sheet of paper. "Pedro Gomez has filed assault charges."

"He's the rapper."

"Yeah, thanks for the clarification. I guess that makes the fat one Justin Simms," he says, deadpan. "He's filed also." He holds up another piece of paper.

"Can I file? They started it."

"The judge is going to ask about this."

"Great. Looking forward to it. What are the chances of him dropping the other charges today?"

"Never going to happen. The best it can ever be is three or four years and a lengthy probation term. And you have a next-to-nothing shot at that. He's likely going to sentence you somewhere pretty close to what the Government is asking for. Seventy-two to ninety-six months."

"Bitch!"

"Let's not call her that again in open court."

"She started it."

"Seems to be a pattern with you."

"I was just telling my friends about that. Is Kennedy here?"

"Yes. Sitting right up front. She's showing lots of skin too. We've talked about this."

"I don't know what to tell you. I've told her. I don't dress the woman. It's a cat thing between her and this prosecutor bitch. I'm staying out of it. You should do the same."

He leans in like he's going to say something smart.

"Save it," I say, raising my hand. "Just get me out of here. There's a big tip in it for you if you do." I wink.

This strikes a nerve.

"Mr. Liecht, you don't have anything left to tip," he hisses, slamming his palms on the metal table. "Do you understand what you are facing today?"

"Seventy-two to ninety-six months…and I get all my money back."

"Wrong. The judge can sentence you to life if he wants to. Wouldn't shock me if he did. And I've told you a thousand times, you're never, ever, ever getting your money back."

"I had money before I went to Yemen!"

"Where you handed over a hundred million dollars…in cash. For guns. Forget the money. It's never coming back. Consider yourself lucky those weapons didn't actually kill anyone. The judge would bury you under the prison. All right, I'll see you in there," my freebie attorney says, standing and tucking his notes away.

"That's it? Just like that? There's nothing to write down, like on your last client? Nothing more to go over?"

"Now that you mention it, yes. Refrain from using the word 'fuck,' or any other explicative in the courtroom today."

"I apologized!"

"You're the first client I've ever had where the judge actually hates you as much as the prosecutor does."

"I'm misunderstood."

He strides toward the door and tells Biff that I'm ready to go upstairs. My attorney is going to be walking through the front doors of the courtroom like a human being. I'm going to be shuffled through tunnels, like an animal, with two Biffs escorting me.

Ten minutes later, I'm walked through the back door of the courtroom. Kennedy is right up front, whispering to my attorney. She does a double-take when she sees my busted-up face.

I shrug.

She mouths an *I love you.*

It breaks my heart. My eyes say as much. I take my seat at the defense table. As I lean back to tell her I love her, the bailiff enters at the front of the courtroom.

"All rise," he booms. "The United States of America versus David Liecht. The Honorable Judge Walker McDaniel's presiding."

The judge comes through the door behind his throne. "Please be seated," he says. "Are we ready to proceed with sentencing today?"

My attorney stands. "Uh…Your Honor. I have two separate motions before this court on behalf of my client—"

"Denied," he interrupts my attorney, while staring me down.

I hold up two fingers. "Both?"

He slams the gavel so hard, it must've left a dent. "Both!"

He's obviously still upset about my last appearance. I'm not sure why. It cost me the fifteen thousand dollars, not him. Freedom of Speech or not, no "fucks" allowed in the courtroom. He held me in contempt of court and charged me a thousand dollars every time I used the word.

My attorney clears his throat. "Your Honor, my client is terribly sorry for his courtroom decorum last time he appeared in front of you."

The judge continues to glare at me. "Is that so, Mr. Liecht?"

"Terribly, Judge. I've been beating myself over it." I hold up my cuffed wrists, point to my face, and stick out my busted lip.

The prosecutor can't take it. "Judge, we have copies of two separate assault charges filed against Mr. Lie—"

"I'm fully aware," he stops her in her tracks. "Mr. Liecht, I'd like to hear the highlights of your morning from you. In your own words."

"Ah, Your Honor, I have to advise my client not to do that," my attorney says.

The judge narrows his gaze, kinda like he's daring me to recap the story. I've talked myself out of way worse situations than this. I raise my cuffed hands. "May I use the podium, Judge?"

"No. Talk from there."

I decide not to fight it.

"Judge, this is exactly what happened. I was in my bunk, trying to sleep. The fat fu—sorry, Judge, the fat redneck swung on me first. I was in the middle of choking him out,

212

trying to diffuse the situation, when the MS13 gangbanger jumped down from the third bunk. The fat guy finally went to sleep. Then the cops walked in. That's it."

The judge looks through some papers on his desk. "And what about you trying to stuff Mr. Gomez in the locker?"

"My attorney says I can't talk about that."

This blows the bitch's mind. She's on her feet again in a flash. "Your Honor, Mr. Liecht is way out of line."

The judge holds up his hand, silencing her. She sits back down. He gives me a stern look. "Mr. Liecht, I do not believe in violence. However, I've reviewed all three of your backgrounds. Between a three-hundred-pound methamphetamine trafficker, a MS13 gang member who has stabbed his last two cellmates, and you, you are the least likely to start a fight."

Stabbed his last two cellies? WTF? I should've paid closer attention to his rap lyrics.

"That brings us to the matter of sentencing today," he says, leaving the prosecutor no room to argue.

Although, she's on her feet again. "Your Honor, we'd like to postpone Mr. Liecht's sentencing for a later date. We are still gathering intel."

"No."

"Your Honor—"

"No. Present your case for Mr. Liecht's sentencing, or I will move forward without hearing the Government's argument."

"Judge, I'd like to take a recess to converse with my colleagues."

"Proceed with your argument, Ms. Colm, or forfeit the option."

She heads toward the podium.

I lean toward my attorney. "Sure seems like he's in a hurry to sentence me."

"Yeah, I think you're fuck't," he whispers.

Bureaucratic humor.

"Your Honor," the prosecutor says, "Mr. Liecht has admitted to handing over a hundred million dollars to Mr. Kyle Matson for the purpose of financing weapons of—"

"Objection!" My attorney butts in. "Your Honor, let the record show my client did not hand the money over to Mr. Matson. He handed the money over to someone he believed to be an officer of the court. Mr. Jargons was a lawyer to the king of Belgium. My client reaffirms he believed he was acting completely within the lines of legality."

"Sustained. I believe the record reflects this. Ms. Colm, you're walking a tight rope here. Continue."

"My apologies to the court. The defendant, Mr. Liecht, handed the cash over to Mr. Jargons. Mr. Liecht was doing that to avoid the tax authorities of Switzerland."

"Objection! Calls for speculation," my attorney says.

"Overruled. Let's hear it, Ms. Colm."

"We believe Mr. Liecht had, maybe still does, a large amount of cash hidden in Dubai. We believe he's been slowly sneaking the money out of Switzerland to avoid the tax authorities."

"Objection!" I say, half standing up. "This woman is a loon, Judge!"

He slams the gavel so hard this time, I'm positive it leaves a dent. "Mr. Liecht, I'm warning you. One more outburst…." He shakes his head like he's in complete disbelief.

"Maybe Mr. Liecht would like to tell us the whole story then," the prosecutor says.

"Forget it, Colm." It's my attorney again.

"Continue, Ms. Colm," the judge says, "but I should warn you, it is not the duty of the United States to prosecute Mr. Liecht for crimes you believe he committed against other countries. Mr. Liecht is no longer a resident here and hasn't been for more than eight years. What *is* the United States charging him with?"

This shakes her off her tracks again. "Okay, um, so Mr. Liecht takes a private jet, owned by some very suspicious individuals, from Dubai to Sanaa, Yemen, with duffel bags full of American currency on board. He then carries the cash by taxis south to Aden, Yemen, where he hands it over for the purpose of funding an illegal arms deal—"

"Objection! My client had no idea he was involved in anything illegal."

"Overruled. Counsel, do not think for one second that this court believes your client is squeaky clean in all this. Please, finish your argument, Ms. Colm."

"Thank you, Judge. After Mr. Liecht delivered the cash, he sat back and waited for the hundred million dollars to be wired to his business account, with an additional ten million dollars on top. The ten million has been labeled as the "introduction fee" previously marked as Exhibit B in the original indictment. This was the profit Mr. Liecht and his partner Mikale Van den Broeck agreed to split with Mr. Lars Van den Broeck, Mikale's father, before the transaction."

"Objection! Ms. Colm is playing fast and loose here, Your Honor. The worst and only thing the Government can claim is Mr. Liecht may or may not have skirted the tax authorities of Switzerland, where he is a citizen."

"Before we get to the objection, Ms. Colm, I have a question. Mr. Lars Van den Broeck and his son, Mikale Van den Broeck, seem to be wrapped up in all this, yet I don't see them in the courtroom. For the record, this is not lost on me. The objection is sustained."

An uncomfortable look settles over the prosecutor's face.

Mikale is off the grid. Daddy's whereabouts is anybody's guess.

"Ms. Colm, I have given the Government plenty of time to find a thread of evidence to the contrary of what Mr. Liecht's attorney is arguing. These are, in fact, affairs of another country. I'm inclined to drop the charges altogether. It is very clear to me that Mr. Liecht was duped into this arms deal in Yemen. The Government has had ample time to prove otherwise. You have come up empty. Your confidential informant, this Mr. Jargons, set out to entrap Mr. Liecht in order to save his own skin.

"Now, I do agree Mr. Liecht should have some explaining to do to his own country. But for now, they have chosen to forego charging him with a crime. I don't believe it will happen in the future either. However, I do believe Mr. Liecht should bear some responsibility. He may choose to appeal, and the conviction may be overturned, but I am going to charge him with a minor role in the offense. Does the Government wish to add anything before I proceed with sentencing?"

Ms. Colm stands back up. "The Government would ask the court to sentence Mr. Liecht within the guideline range of seventy-two to ninety-six months."

"I was thinking less."

"Your Honor, this is highly irregular—"

"So is entrapment. Need I drop all charges, Ms. Colm?"

"No, Your Honor."

The judge turns to me. "Mr. Liecht, please stand. Normally, this is where I'd ask the defendant if they would like to say something on their behalf, but frankly, I don't want to hear anything else from you. We've all heard enough over the last year."

My attorney kicks me under the table. "I'd advise you to be quiet here. The only reason he'd behave like this is because he knows you won't appeal whatever he's about to give you. For your own good, shut up," he whispers out of the side of his mouth.

He might be right.

I keep quiet and stand.

"The United States of America will be keeping the majority of your assets, Mr. Liecht. I will allow you to keep the home in Boca Raton that your wife and child have been staying in. I will release the Aston Martin vehicle, and I'll allow you to keep the Wachovia Bank account with just over one hundred and fifty thousand American dollars in it. You shall receive a prison term of time served, and a term of sixty months of federal supervised release, which is probation.

"You are to refrain from working anything more than nine-to-five while you are a guest of the United States. You are not to leave the country without prior written permission from the Probation Department. Welcome back, Mr. Liecht." He bangs the gavel.

My freebie mouthpiece was right. The judge knows I won't appeal his sentence. I knew I wasn't going to get my money back. At the end of the day, I did hand over a hundred million dollars for an illegal weapons deal, whether knowingly or not. It could've gone a lot worse.

I'm no longer a jailbird.

33

ONE SIZE FITS ALL

Fucking Biffs!

The motherfuckers got me again.

I'd been sitting around all day, antsy, waiting on my name to be called. The fucking judge sentenced me to time served, then took all day getting around to signing the release order.

The Biffs got a real kick out of it.

And they didn't stop there.

Half an hour ago, the release order was finally signed. I was then escorted to Receiving and Discharge by two of the county deputies. When we came through the doors, there were two US Marshals standing there. I waved like a smart-ass. They flipped me off.

I was told to sit and wait for my name to be called. Took about ten minutes. The R&D deputy called me to the front desk to sign my release forms. She then handed me a black garbage bag with my personal belongings inside from the day I was arrested over a year ago. She told me to go change in the inmate bathroom.

I was so happy to be going home, I accepted the bag like it was a gift and toddled off to change. The deputy snickered behind me, but I didn't give it much thought. I went into one of the stalls in the bathroom and ripped open the garbage bag.

I about gagged to death.

It smelled like rotten bait fish and jalapeños that had gone bad. That was where my olfactory sense immediately went. Which was pretty funny, because that's exactly what the US Marshals put inside the bag—mackerels from the jail commissary and jalapeños. I could hear the halfwits in the hallway, listening to me gag, laughing their balls off.

And they weren't quite finished.

Obviously, there was no way I could wear the clothes. I returned to the front desk and asked the deputy if I could just purchase the jail scrubs I was wearing.

"Absolutely not," she said, then handed me a paper sack. "The Marshals send their regards."

Hmm.

I peeked inside the paper bag and frowned—a pair of paper pants and shirt. Navy blue and one-size-fits-all. It's what the county hands out to homeless individuals when they're being released back into the wild.

The "one-size-fits-all" is not accurate.

In fact, it's a bold-faced lie.

I'm sitting here waiting for the R&D deputy to finish up my release paperwork. She keeps looking over and laughing. The paper suit has torn everywhere. The shirt, what's left of it, is showing one of my nipples, and don't even get me started on the nut-huggin' waders, missing the ass....

I look like a twerker in a Cardi B video.

Fuckin' Biffs!

To be honest, I don't even care. Kennedy's bringing me a change of clothes anyway. I just want to get the hell out of here. There's so much shit to tell you about. Shit I couldn't tell you from inside. Things I couldn't say over the phone. Like, "So-and-So is dead."

Like *dead to me* dead.

I have a list.

Starting with whoever served me up on a platter to the US government. I suspect he's fat, wears white, and knows a little legal *jargon*. Next, I'm going to need to speak with whoever has my fuckin' money. It's not been confirmed yet, but I'm 99 percent sure it didn't vanish into thin air. We're going to know very shortly.

I have to get on a burner phone.

I need to check my secret Bat account.

Mikale and I both have them. Not very many people know about the accounts. If he's hidin' out where I think he's hidin', then he's had to dip into his by now. He ain't callin' back and forth to Daddy.

We set up these accounts three and a half years ago through one of our clients who owns a nine-billion-dollar security company in Israel. Not like rent-a-cop security either. I'm talking about some secret spy-type shit. Everyone calls the place The Firm. Mikale and I flew into Tel Aviv and sat down with them. We each spent a little over a million dollars on one of their packages. We have secret Bat phone numbers, secret Bat accounts, 24-7 access to jets, fake passports, IDs, credit cards, and even to plastic surgeons who can change our appearance overnight, if need be.

There's a go-to plan for almost everything.

Including, if one of us has been arrested.

When the Feds showed up to the motel on a "crime tip" and found me "passed out," I was finally given my one phone call…to Kennedy. She in turn called Mikale and delivered the message: "*Meet me in Gotham.*" Mikale knew it was code for: "*Shit's hit the fan.*" He called The Firm's hotline. They tracked down a team of velvety New York City criminal defense attorneys and sent one of their esquires, Igal.

Igal was in Tel Aviv when he got the call.

He went wheels-up within an hour. He made it to the Gun Club County Jail in West Palm Beach for an attorney-client legal visit before the New Yorkers could get to town. When Igal showed up, I'd already been processed into the county jail. I was sitting on my bunk, wondering what the fuck was going on, when one of the deputies popped my cell door to tell me I had a "legal visit."

I'd never been so happy to see an attorney in my whole life.

I walked in the room, and it was this guy, Igal.

I started slamming him with questions. He didn't have any answers, nor the slightest idea what was going on with me. He wasn't even sure exactly what I was being held on. He wasn't there for any of that. I was agitated by this news. He reminded me The Firm was a security company, not litigators.

Fuck me.

Igal removed the lining of his briefcase and slipped me a phone half the size of my pinky finger. Said the little spy phone had a three-hour battery life. He recommended I use it right there, but if I chose to take the phone with me, it was on me. I wanted to be able to speak with Kennedy after I spoke with the criminal defense attorneys.

I decided to chance it and "cheeked" the phone.

Igal wished me luck and ended our legal visit.

The county deputy escorted me back to my cell. I walked slowly, squeezing my cheeks the entire way. It felt like everyone was staring, like they were leery of me. I later found out why. I'd been labeled an international terrorist with lots of cash. I was given my very own jail cell.

Some super high-profile shit.

Everyone looked at me like I was crazy as fuck.

Like these murderers, rapists, and drug lords would've never dreamed of calling me "Lick't."

The deputy locked me in my cell. When I heard the steel door at the end of the tier lock behind him, I called Kennedy. Now, at that point, I still had no real clue as to what was going on. I mean, I knew there were some incriminating photographs, but they didn't tell the whole story.

Kennedy was all business, trying to hold it together.

She was booked on a flight the next morning, heading to South Florida. I hated to hang up with her, but I needed to speak with Mikale to make sure he was okay. I called his secret Bat phone number. It pinged thirteen different countries before a computer picked up somewhere and asked for my eight-digit pin.

A minute and a half later, I was connected to my business partner.

He'd been waiting on the call.

I asked Mikale to take care of my family with my secret Bat account and not to comingle any of our funds. And we agreed for the sake of Valtara Enterprises and our clients, he needed to immediately separate himself from me until things could be worked out.

Two minutes after that phone call, Mikale went *underground* underground.

We haven't spoken since, in over a year.

I'm not quite sure what to do moving forward. I don't want to set off flairs. And let's face it, no one wants to be associated with an International Terrorist Wannabe. Hell, it's even taken a toll on Kennedy. When she came to visit this past weekend, she didn't look so good. She hasn't been feeling well lately. The doctor said it's likely stress-related, that she needs rest.

"David Liecht," the R&D deputy finally yells, "You're free to go."

I've got knots in my stomach.

I've had them all day.

Kennedy and I haven't shared a private moment since I left for Saint Tropez over a year ago. All our visits have been through glass, and every word has been recorded and gone through with a fine-tooth comb by Colm. We've had to exchange messages on the palms of our hands during visits.

All that's about to change.

34

CASH...OFF THE BOOKS

Kennedy was a hot mess.

I was in a paper suit.

When they finally buzzed me out of the back of the county jail, Kennedy came running out of the SUV rental. She ran into my arms, bawling. Made me cry too. It turned into high school sex in the uncomfortable back seat. The kind of sex where you never want to let go of each other.

Made us both cry...again.

She just dropped me off at the county impound lot on the other side of town. The judge was nice enough to let me keep *my* Aston Martin. I'm here to pick it up. Kennedy tried making arrangements for us to swing by and get it tomorrow. The person she spoke to told her they had specific instructions from the US Marshals to pull the car outside the gates today, and to leave the keys in the ignition. The county impound lot is smack-dab in the middle of the hood.

The car's a pearl-black Aston Martin Vanquish.

Vintage James Bond.

In a pinch, I can get a quarter mil for it.

The car's ruined.

I'm staring at it through the fence, waiting on the lot attendant to bring me the key.

It's been parked outside, under a huge ficus tree, apparently for the entire year. It's covered in four inches of caked-on bird shit, just baking in the South Florida sun.

The lot attendant walks up, tossing my key up and down in his hand. "Do you know what that purple stuff is in bird shit?" he asks, unlocking the fence while staring at my busted face.

I glare, wondering what the judge might do if I karate chop this guy in his larynx. He claps, and seventy-five hundred, nasty-ass pigeons take flight. The vast bunch of them take a shit on the way.

He hands me the key. "The purple shit, well, it's just more bird shit." He chuckles, turns, and walks away. "The Marshals send their best," he says over his shoulder.

I practice my *whoosah* and unlock the doors. As I'm pulling away, I glance in the rearview mirror. Someone's taken the time to draw a huge dick across my back window.

Fucking Biffs! Again!

They're lucky I have other things to focus on right now. Like getting my life back, and I'm not talkin' about getting back to So-So either. I'm talking about right the fuck back to where I was: the Swiss chateau, the helicopter, the exotic cars, and 50 percent of the multi-billion-dollar company I helped to build.

Fuck you, So-So.

I'm now at a red light, waiting to turn into the Walmart parking lot. On my left is a car full of college kids, giving me the thumbs-up and smiling. All of them have their phones out the window, recording. I cannot tell which they like better, the bird shit, or the dick mural on the back window.

I wave like, *yeah-yeah*, and make the turn.

I park and go inside. I need to buy a burner phone. I don't believe for one second this prosecutor and her Big Brother are going to let me get on with my life. And they're slick, too. In my discovery there were hundreds of pictures of me, taken less than a foot away. They were literally underneath my feet the whole time. The cocksuckers even managed to get a mole inside Kwan's party, all the way in Bangkok. Not to mention they recorded every phone conversation I had in that time period.

Even the dirty ones with Kennedy.

I don't trust them as far as I can throw 'em.

And I'm working under the assumption they've bugged everything in my life—my car, the house, the phones…everything.

If I've been fucked out of all my money, I won't be able to just waltz through the front door and ask for it. Laws are going to be broken to get it back. I'm going to have to steal it—from behind the scenes, in a very gray area.

I head to the counter and pay cash for three prepaid phones and a value pack of SIM cards. Back outside, I connect one of the burners and leave the other two in the car. I walk back inside, to the far back corner of the store.

Now that I'm out officially, I should call Mikale. He needs to know I'm a free bird, which means he can unclench his arsehole. I kinda miss the creep. My first call is to his secret Bat phone. I wait to punch in the eight-digit pin. It rings and rings. I try again with the same result.

Next, I try his cell phone. He's not picking up. I leave a message. "I'm around."

I call the office after that. It's a new girl at the front desk. She tells me Mikale's been out of the office on extended leave. I don't bother leaving a message. He'll figure it out. No sense in wasting more time trying to reach him. Eventually, he'll make his way back to civilization and find out the charges have been dropped.

I wonder briefly if I should call his Daddy. The problem is I don't know where he fits in all of this. Someone was cunning enough to cripple me. There aren't many with this kind of foresight. I'm having to start over from the very bottom. To do so, I need a million and half dollars cash at least.

Money Uncle Sam and his buddies can't sniff out.

These types of funds aren't typically advertised on the front page or talked about in the conventional circles I once belonged to. Especially not now since I'm the jerk-off who was "caught"— it's bad for business—playing with guns in the Middle East.

With Mikale still MIA and my unwillingness to call Daddy, I'm going to have to visit a different circle.

A circle with vigs and a Russian named Yakhov.

Yakhov is purported to be some rich oligarch from St. Petersburg, Russia, who got lucky in the vodka business. He supposedly "retired" here to South Florida. An upstanding citizen. Yeah, that makes two of us. I admit, he does look good on paper, but I'm smart enough to know that retired oligarchs don't lend cash out the back door…at break-your-kneecap interest rates.

Not to mention, I learned of Yakhov from a retired hooker.

Ocean.

Of course she's still around. Never left. She and Kennedy have become BFFs over the last year. Ocean's flown in from Dubai at least half a dozen times. She's visited me at the county jail every time. She's in on the plan. In fact, she plays a major role. I've spent hours and hours writing her letters. We've exchange them through Kennedy and the attorney.

Right now, it's the middle of the night in Dubai. Kennedy has Ocean on standby. She's my next call.

Halfway through the second ring, she picks up. "We ba-ack!" I say.

"I'm so happy for the both of you."

"No time to celebrate. You ready to get these motherfuckers?"

"Been waitin' on you, Boss."

"Call your Bolshevik. I need the money. Like, yesterday. There's nothing left."

"Kennedy told you as much. You men never want to listen. Yakhov's in New York. Apparently on Russian business. Really, he's just been shacked up at the Waldorf with a couple of hookers. I called and spoke to him this afternoon. He's flying home. You have an appointment at his home tomorrow morning at ten o'clock."

"Ahh…the power of 'shh-at.' I've missed it. Text me his info. I'll call you tomorrow after I leave him. And, Ocean, thank you for all your help this past year."

"Anything for you and my girl. Now get home to Kennedy. She needs you," she says and disconnects.

I remove the SIM card from the burner and chew it until it's destroyed. Tomorrow, I'll go see this Russian, see if he'll give me a couple of suitcases full of his "upstanding" cash.

Off the books.

35

I'M A MEME

It's winter in South Florida.

Actually, it's winter everywhere.

Everywhere else is not South Florida, though. It's nine o'clock in the morning and seventy-one degrees with an expected high today of "Fuck you. Bet you wish you were here!" The problem, because it is South Florida, is every wank-off with enough cents to have saved for a retirement fund keeps a winter home here. And, every day at the crack of dawn, they get up and start driving around, lookin' for shit...all day.

Because of it, I'm stuck in bumper-to-bumper traffic.

And just FYI—I'm driving my two-hundred-fifty-thousand-dollar pile of bird shit.

The giant dick still in the back window.

Last night, I left the Walmart and rushed home. Kennedy was lighting scented candles around our master bath. Deep house was playing softly in the background. You know how all of that ended. This morning, we did it two more times before I had to get on the road.

It was that or the car wash.

And because of my decision, I'm now the virtual laughingstock of I-95.

The next car creeps up. The people inside record and take pictures. I wave and smile. Like, *yeah-yeah, fuck you*. It's a red convertible Porsche now. A platinum-blonde at the wheel. Big sunglasses. Big lips. Big tits. Lots of makeup. Wearing a NY Yankees hat. She turns her head and gives me a look, like she's so disgusted to be driving next to me, like she's never seen a giant dick before.

Yeah, fat chance.

I just hold up my hand. Smile. *Yeah-yeah, fuck you.*

Only nineteen more miles to go.

I finally exit the highway in Fort Lauderdale. Yakhov lives right off Las Olas Boulevard. He and everyone around him are mega-millionaires. Yakhov's house is probably worth twelve or thirteen million dollars. The waterfront mansion was purchased five years ago out of foreclosure. The deed is registered to a Russian company in the Canary Islands. No forwarding address on file. No phone number listed.

If it sounds shady, that's because it is.

Yakhov is exactly who I thought he was.

TAZ confirmed this around four this morning. When Kennedy fell asleep, I snuck out by the pool and made some calls from the burner. My first call was to TAZ. He lives somewhere in the Netherlands, so he says. One can never be sure with his type. I know him from a past life. He's one of these dark web hackers. We've traded favors over the years.

I told him I needed deep state on Yakhov. The stuff no one's supposed to be able to find.

TAZ called me back two hours later.

Yakhov comes from a long line of Russian thugs. His grandfather, his dad, and two of his uncles…all KGB. His dad works for Putin right now. The "I got rich from vodka" story is partly true. But only partly. Grandpa KGB mysteriously acquired it in the '90s. He left it to his only grandson, Yakhov.

It was a gold mine.

All Yakhov had to do was sit back and get fat. He couldn't keep his ass out of the sling, though. Human trafficking, the sex trade, kidnapping, arson, murder, murder for hire…you name it. He did it.

TAZ said he had to dig deep to find the stuff.

It's all been made to go away.

TAZ thinks they grew tired of cleaning up after Yakhov. Believes he was *told* to retire, and to get out of Russia. Yakhov picked South Florida. He was given instructions to lay down and do nothing. He's not listening. Instead, he lends cash out the back door. And, if you don't bring the cash back, he sends Igor.

Igor drives a black Cadillac and carries a bat.

I'm going to ask Yakhov for two million dollars in cash.

Ocean doubts he'll do it without collateral.

I've brought along the deed to the home in Boca Raton, but I'm hoping to not have to use it. The home sits on the water and is worth around four million…if I had the time or desire to put it on the market. The problem is, I don't.

My GPS takes me right to Yakhov's front door.

I've rung the bell three times already. I'm getting ready to lay on it again when the door finally opens. It's Brock Lesner's big brother, Braun. He looks me up and down. "Vhat?" he asks with a scrunched-up face.

"Your boss," I say, holding up my briefcase.

Braun looks over my shoulder at the Vanquish, shakes his head, then meets my eyes. "James Bond, *da*?"

"007."

"Ocean's friend, *da*?"

"You're two for two."

Braun's still trying to work out what I said as he closes the door behind me. I follow him through the mansion and out back to the pool area. He stops on a dime. "Wait here," he says.

Yakhov—it's got to be him—is sitting in a hot tub at the far end of the pool, chewing on a cigar. There's a topless bimbo in each arm and one standing up in the middle, dancing.

Braun walks over and says something to him.

Yakhov barely pulls his attention from the dancing bimbo to answer Braun out the side of his mouth.

Braun walks back over and stands right behind me. Like in my space behind me. Doesn't say a word. I figure it's some kind of Russian tough-guy bullshit. All part of the show. Probably works on most people. I decide to let him get it off. I'm here to borrow two million dollars. If I'm successful, I'll be seeing Braun down the road.

We stand like this for every bit of six or seven minutes. Silent.

Yakhov finally decides he's had enough dancing and stands up in the hot tub. He's five-four at best and, in his sixty-plus years on this earth, hasn't missed a meal. He rolls out of the hot tub, naked, one leg at a time.

Should have come with a *WARNING* label.

Halfway between us, there's a table underneath an umbrella. Yakhov walks to it. Doesn't bother to grab a towel or robe on the way. He takes a seat at the far end. Braun nudges me to get a move on and follows on my heels. I stop at the opposite end of the table and reach down to pull the chair out. Braun stops me with his arm across my chest, like a crossing guard. I glance at Yakhov. He wags his finger at me. Doesn't invite me to sit.

"Take off your clothes, Mr. Liecht," Yakhov says.

"Huh?"

Braun moves in even closer. "Yesterday you were in the American gulag, facing a life sentence. Today, you're here to ask me for money. It's precautionary. Now get naked. I will not ask again."

Yakhov doesn't trust Big Brother either. I get it. I really need the two million dollars, and I've gotten naked for much less. I strip down to my birthday suit.

"Now get in the pool," Yakhov tells me. Like I might be wearing some kind of listening bug in my hair or under my nuts.

I walk over and dive in. By the time I'm coming up, Braun has grabbed all my clothes, walked to the edge of the pool, and is now dropping everything in the water—shoes, clothes, burner phone. He turns and walks back to the table and grabs my briefcase. He opens it, hands the papers inside to Yakhov, then tosses my forty-five-thousand-dollar briefcase in the deep end. Inside is a matching pair of

Montblanc Pens that Mikale gave me for my fortieth birthday. They set him back thirty grand.

Fuck the pens.

Same goes for the clothes and briefcase.

I swim to the edge, pull myself up out of the pool, stroll over, and sit in the chair across from Yakhov. Naked. I wait for him to speak. He doesn't. Instead, he snaps his fingers. Braun walks over to the bimbos, picks up something from the backside of the hot tub, walks back over, and sits a mirror with drugs on top in front of Yakhov.

Braun walks off.

Yakhov does a line.

He looks back up. Shakes his head. Rubs some of the drugs on his gums. "I'm supposed to be in New York City right now, with three more of them," he says, pointing over his shoulder to the bimbos. Like it's all my fault.

I shrug.

"I'm told you're broke," he says, pushing the mirror across the table to me. "Do line. We have conversation."

"I'd rather not."

He looks offended. "Suit yourself. I'm told you speak the language of the Motherland."

"*Da.*"

"How?"

"With my mouth."

He either doesn't get sarcasm or doesn't care for it. It's hard to tell. His head's the size of a watermelon and about as expressive as one. He taps his fingers on the table like he's waiting on an answer.

"Growing up, I had a Russian nanny. Ingrid. Ingrid was a schoolteacher before leaving Russia. My father insisted she teach me to read, write, and speak Russian."

"Why do you need the money?"

"Why do you care?"

"I understand why someone did that to your face. What are you looking to get?"

"Two million, at the very least."

"Collateral?" he asks, holding up the deed to my house.

I shake my head. "No."

"Then the answer's no."

"Typically, this is the part where you offer a counter proposal."

"No collateral, no money. That's the counter."

Doesn't seem like he's going to budge.

"The home is worth every bit of four million. If you're keeping the deed, I need three million. In cash."

"Let's say it's worth three. I'll give you a million five. A point and a half a week, and I'll be keeping this in a safe place," he says, still holding the deed.

There's no wiggle room on the dollar amount, I can tell. "Fine. The mil and a half will have to do. A point a week, though. Cap of sixty grand a month."

He thinks about it. "Because of your friend. Now do a line," he says, pushing the mirror to me again.

"Not today, Yakhov. I'm meeting my parole officer at twelve thirty for the first time. I'll have to give them a piss test."

"We got a guy there. He knows you're coming. He'll be looking after you. Call it a favor," he says with a creepy wink. "Go ahead, do a line."

"Still, I'd rather not."

The bimbos are calling him over to the hot tub. "Don't forget the drugs, *zolotse*," one of them says. Means *golden one*. Yakhov jerks his eyes to me, then to the drugs. Shrugs. Grabs the drugs and walks his fat, "golden one," hairy ass back to the hot tub. "Boris," he yells over to the Braun dude, "get our friend here a million and a half. Arrange to pick up fifteen a week."

I stay seated as the Boris/Braun dude walks over to me. "You stay here," he says. "Make sure he doesn't do anything stupid. I'll be back in an hour or so with the cash." Braun turns and walks inside the house.

Apparently, the cash is not kept on site.

36

BIMBOS AND HOMERUNS

Ugh! I just ate.

Some things you can't un-see.

I've been trying all day.

It's my fault. I went looking for Yakhov to find out what the holdup was. I was tired of sitting around the pool, waiting on this Boris character to show back up with the cash. I walked inside the mansion. No one was on the bottom floor. I went up to the next story. At the end of a long hallway, soft music drifted from behind one of the doors. I knocked lightly. No answer. I knocked again. Harder. Still no answer. I turned the knob.

My life was changed.

Maybe forever.

Yakhov was strapped into a sex swing. Still butt naked. Still old and fat. He was facedown, facing the wall. The red leather tassels clipped to his nipples didn't help the situation. He had no idea I was at the door. Neither did the bimbos.

They were all facing the opposite direction. And I was about to abort when Yakhov screamed, "Spank me!"

I was curious.

So I stayed put.

The bimbos stood behind him. At first, I didn't notice one of them was holding a wooden paddle at her side. She wound up and swung. It was a decent swing, but she hit like a girl. It wasn't what Yakhov was looking for. He screamed even louder this time. "Harder, you filthy cunt!"

All the fun evaporated from the room.

She swung again. Harder. Still, not what Yakhov was looking for. He went ballistic. "You filthy whore! If you don't hit me harder, I'm going to slit your fucking throat and dump you in the ocean. Then I'm going to kill your parents."

The bimbo wound her arm back like she was ready to spank him into the next dimension.

I strode into the room. When she noticed me, I held my finger to my lips. Then I walked over and grabbed the paddle from her. She had tears in her eyes. The other one didn't look much better. Yakhov was still popping off at the mouth.

I moved in behind him, spread my feet shoulder-width apart, crouched into a Shohei Ohtani stance, and wound up like it was the bottom of the 9th with two outs and I was the winning run.

WHACK!!!

I hit a homerun.

I broke the bat doing so. Literally, I was holding just the handle. Yakhov was howling. Almost to the point of hyperventilating. I considered choking him the rest of the way out but figured it might cost me the money. I couldn't afford that. I mouthed a *keep quiet!* to the bimbos and left the room.

At the end of the hallway, I turned around and headed back, yelling for Yakhov on the way. "Yakhov? Where are ya, Yakhov? I need to get going." I opened the door, feigning surprise. "Uh, is this a bad time?"

The paddle-sized welt across his ass was glowing. Practically pulsating.

I almost laughed out loud.

I walked around to the front of him and knelt. He was in the middle of some kind of tantric sex thing. He was so high. His head was just hanging there. I slap-tapped his face a couple times. "Yakhov! Hey, buddy...you in there?"

The guy was toast.

He'll likely never even remember I was there.

I left the room, shut the door behind me, and went back outside by the pool to wait for Boris. He didn't bother to return until just after one thirty. He didn't seem sorry about it either.

I counted the stacks of hundreds as fast as I could. Made sure it was all there, then got back in the car and raced the forty-five minutes all the way back up to West Palm Beach to meet my probation officer for the first time.

I'm over two hours late.

Before leaving, I asked Boris about what Yakhov told me about having a "guy" at the Probation Department. Boris said, "Oh yeah. You're all set." He didn't seem sure.

We're about to find out.

I'm in the elevator now, going up to the third floor.

Ding.

I follow the hallway around until I find the door that says, *The United States of America Federal Supervised Release.* It opens into a cramped waiting room with cheap-ass government furniture and decor. Smells like crime. There are at least a dozen and a half plastic chairs. All of them occupied. There's a receptionist area on the far side of the room, shielded behind bulletproof glass. I walk up and greet the woman sitting behind the desk.

"Good afternoon," I say, through the little circle of holes in the glass.

She doesn't bother to look up.

She's in the middle of painting her nails…orange.

I tap on the glass with my knuckle. "Hi. I'm David Liecht. I have an appointment to see my probation officer."

She takes her sweet time pressing the button for the intercom. "Orientation was at twelve thirty. You're late."

"Yeah, I'm aware. Do I reschedule?"

"Yeah…just reschedule. You let us know what's good for you," she says, words dripping in sarcasm.

I start to explain I can come back tomorrow, and she holds up her hand like she's heard enough. She points behind me. "Sit and wait to be called."

I'm gonna kill this Yakhov and Boris.

I opt to stand against the wall and wait for a seat to open. It takes twenty minutes. At this rate, I'll be stuck here all day. At a quarter to five, I'm still here. It's down to two of us. Me and some kid in his mid-twenties, tattoos and looks like he's probably got drugs on him.

Naturally, he gets called next.

Now it's thirty-five after at a government nine-to-five. I walk up to the bulletproof glass. The smart-ass receptionist is no longer there. The power-saver on her computer is on. I tap the glass with my wedding band. "Hellooo…" Nothing. Seems like everyone's left for the day. I decide I'm not going to stick around either. They're certainly not going to throw me back in the slammer for being tardy, right? Plus, this PO is supposed to be some kind of "friend" of the guy who just lent me almost two million dollars. He can't expect me to pay if I'm locked up, right?

I'll just call and reschedule.

I reach for the door to leave the lobby, and the intercom clicks on. "Mr. Liecht! You will sit down and wait." It's a woman's voice. And nothing about it sounds Russian…or friendly.

This fucking Yak-off and his nut-licker Boris.

I return to my seat. At ten after six, a door on the far wall opens. It's her. The voice. Has to be. She's white, looks mean, and she's dressed like she doesn't give a shit. I'm guessing she's been at the job her entire life and has seen and heard it all. A real ballbuster. She doesn't say a word, just stares at me.

I stand up. "Hello. I'm David Liecht."

"Yeah, no shit."

This should be fun. I walk over.

"In the future, Mr. Liecht, you will call and tell me if you're going to be late for our appointment," she says. "Do we understand?"

"I'm pretty clear."

"The next time, I might not be so nice."

"Peachy," I say with a French accent. She's not sure what to think and holds the door open for me.

Inside, there's a metal detector I have to pass through. "Put your phone, keys, anything metal in the tray, and walk through."

"Just the keys," I say, holding them up. "I'll be stopping on the way home today to buy a new phone. Your friends never bothered to return mine."

"I can see that you're going to have a hard time, Mr. Liecht," she says, matter-of-factly. "Judging by your face, you've always had this problem."

I walk through the metal detector. Nothing beeps. We head down a couple of long hallways, and I follow her into her corner office. Obviously, she's a supervisor. Her window faces the Intercoastal Waterway. The nameplate at the front of her desk reads *Linda Livingston,*

Federal Parole Officer, Supervisor.

Just my luck.

I'm sure this is the prosecutor's doing.

Linda Livingston drivels on for twenty minutes about what I'm allowed to do. Basically, it includes just breathing. She then asks if I have any questions. I do, but I keep them to myself. She seems happy about this. "I'll need a UA on the way out," she says.

"A who?"

"A urine analysis, Mr. Liecht. I do not tolerate drugs of any kind," she says, standing up.

I follow her back out of her office, down a different hallway, and stop in front of a door that says *Restroom.* There's a countertop and cabinet right outside the door. She has me initial some papers and hands me a cup. "Fill it up." she says and stands with the door open as I face away, pissing in the cup. She then drops the cup and papers into a sealable bag and leaves it on the counter. "I need to have a look at your car and take a couple of pictures. Then you can be on your way," she says walking back down the hallway.

Shit.

The cash is in a gym bag in the trunk.

I really didn't plan on the PO having to examine my car. Linda grabs a camera from the receptionist area and follows me outside. We walk to the visitor's parking lot. She stops at the sight of the only car still there. Looks at me. Looks at the car. Looks at me. I nod. "I'll take the photos next time, Mr. Liecht," she says.

"I'll make sure to have it washed."

"Open it. And pop the trunk."

Shit. Again.

She just grilled me upstairs, like she was snoopin' around, looking for a reason to bust my nuts. There's not a chance she doesn't ask, "What's in the bag?" I open both doors and let her take a peek inside. "All right, Linda," I say. "I'll call you with my new cell phone number."

"It's Ms. Livingston, Mr. Liecht."

"Sorry, Ms. Livingston." I start to climb inside the vehicle, like I forgot about opening the trunk.

"The trunk, Mr. Liecht," she says.

"Oh, yeah. I almost forgot."

Fuck!

As I slip out of the car and walk to the trunk, a vehicle pulls in next to us. When the guy gets out, I know right away he's the Russian PO. He walks over, shields himself from me, and has a hushed conversation with Linda. She then turns and walks inside the building without another word.

The guy turns to me. "That could've gone really bad for you," he says, eyeing the trunk.

"What took you so long?" I ask.

He holds up a cup exactly like the one I pissed in two minutes ago. It's filled to the brim. Looks toxic. "It's not always easy to find a crackhead this time of day. I had to go all the way across town to get your urine," he says, expecting me to say something.

I just stare at him. I get it. He's going to say it's my piss in the cup. If I get out of line or miss a payment somewhere down the line….

"You mess up, the judge gets this," he warns, shaking the cup.

"Yeah, no shit. Can I go now?"

"For now. Don't spend the cash all in one place," he says over his shoulder, walking back to his car. "By the way, my name is Mr. Vladco. I'll be in contact soon."

"Can hardly wait."

Fucking Russian Americans.

I've got to find a cell phone store right now. I need to call Kennedy. She's probably worried sick.

37

HOUSE OF CARDS

Sometimes I figure shit out.

Sometimes I'm late to the party.

Like right now. I'm being pulled over. I've got a million and a half dollars in a gym bag in the trunk, a bag of brand-new burner phones on the seat next to me, and when they run my name, they're going to find out that I've been out of the slammer for like nine and a half minutes.

I'm every cop's wet dream.

Can't wait to hear what the judge has to say about this.

The officer is walking up now. He looks like the serious type. I lower my window.

"License and registration," he says.

I hand over the registration and an expired insurance card. He just looks at me, like he's waiting for an explanation. "I'm sorry, Officer, I don't have my license with me," I tell him.

"Why?" He's like a robot.

"I just got out of jail last night. I haven't had time to get things back in order." I point to the bag from the cell phone store. "I'm just now leaving from purchasing a new cell phone."

That's two of his bullets.

He studies me for a second. "Who beat you up?"

"I slipped in the shower."

He motions to the dick. "The artwork on your back window is offensive. This car is an accident waiting to happen." I nod, but before I can get a word in edgewise, he continues. "There's a twenty-four-hour car wash at the next light. You're going to follow me there. Or I can write you a citation for being a public nuisance and impound the vehicle."

He pauses, seemingly waiting for my response.

Like I have a choice.

"I'm on your six," I say, and he marches off.

The car wash is right where the officer said it would be. I pull into the lot, and he keeps going. I'm sure he'll double back in a bit, just to make sure I stuck around. He's lucky I have to get it done anyway. I head inside and ask for "the works." The girl at the counter looks out the window to my car and cringes. She tells me it's going to be three hundred dollars plus tip, and that it'll take at least three to four hours, making it after ten before I can get out of here.

I explain that I'll pay three hundred dollars more if they finish in an hour.

Two hours pass.

My Vanquish still looks like shit. They've just run it through the car wash for the fourth time. The detailers are standing around, like they don't get it. The bird shit is just smearing. I'm sitting at a table twenty paces away. A couple of them glance over at me. I just smile and keep on working.

The gym bag of cash is on one of the chairs. The bag of burner phones next to it. I've opened and connected three of them so far. They're sitting on the table. I'm on my "every day" phone, surfing, waiting for callbacks.

My first call was to Kennedy. She'd been freaking out. I could hear the relief when she realized it was me. She thought something had happened. The pain in her voice was overwhelming. The last time I disappeared, I'd been kidnapped by the American spooks.

It didn't help the situation that this PO Livingston called her twice this afternoon, looking for me. In all her drivel, she failed to mention that she told Kennedy she was going to violate my supervised release and send me back to jail. It took me a minute to get Kennedy settled back down. I told her I'd be home as soon as the car was finished.

So far, we've sent ten or twelve *I love you* texts back and forth.

After hanging up with her, I called Ocean.

She's going to be here tomorrow to be "the front man" in my plan. Ocianna "Ocean" Zigmond is now Olivia Fitz. Her new passport says she's from Prague. TAZ spent almost four months building her file.

Olivia is from old, old money.

Like, she's got a bunch of it.

Day after tomorrow, I'm picking Olivia up from the airport in Fort Lauderdale.

My next two calls were out to California. The first one was to an old fraternity buddy. We called him "Meat" back in the day. Meat liked to drink. A lot. A few drinks in, he was the guy you could dare to do anything. Didn't matter what. A lot of heart. Very little sense.

Meat is back home in LA working for his father's company. He sells small-time corporations up and down the state. Like, *Pizza Shop for Sale! Owner Retiring* type deals. I caught him at the bar. Same shit. Still goes by Meat. Meat Senior, on the other hand, is one of these super-serious, hotshot dealmakers. He's in his seventies and, according to Meat, still killin' it. Meat's dad handles the big-ticket items. Like dormant, public shell corporations and tech companies.

I told Meat I had a close friend—this Olivia Fitz—who's in the market for one of each. Told him she needed them cheap too. He said he would put in a good word to his dad, get the best price he could. It's still going to cost me somewhere around a third of the cash.

Olivia and I are flying out to Cali next week to meet with Meat's father.

The second call was to an attorney out in Beverly Hills. A shiesty Jew, Richard Bernstein. Ol' Dickie and I crossed paths eleven or twelve years ago. I faced him in court. He cheated to win. Afterward, on the courthouse steps, he called me "Sport." Like, "Hey, sorry, Sport. It's just part of the game," then handed me his business card. We've been in contact over the years.

TAZ has been keeping tabs on Dickie for a while now.

I know a lot of Dickie's secrets. Same goes for Dickie's clients' secrets. At the end of the day, I need board members who can be controlled. Manipulated, if need be. Dickie has a client list full of people just like this I'm going to use. In fact, I know exactly who I want already.

When Mr. Bernstein picked up, he didn't seem thrilled to discover it was me on the other end of the line. He'd heard through the grapevine that I was involved in some shady shit with the Feds. I explained I was out of prison, and that all that was behind me. I told him I was building a consulting business here in the States. "On another matter," I said, "I have a very wealthy business client, a Ms. Olivia Fitz, who's in need of a good attorney in the Los Angeles area. I thought of you."

Next week, Ms. Fitz and Mr. Bernstein are meeting at his Beverly Hills office.

I'll be outside…in the back of the limo, callin' the tune.

I told you, I spent hours writing Ocean letters, going over her Olivia role. She's got it down pat.

Now, where in the hell is my car? It's after eleven thirty already. I walk around to the back of the car wash. They've pulled my Vanquish into a detail bay, underneath fluorescent lights so bright every bug in town is here. The car still looks like shit. Like it has a bad case of herpes. Two guys are working their asses off, scrubbing. Used rags are scattered on the ground. I walk over. One of the guys look up. Seems pissed.

"How much longer?" I ask.

The guy starts going off in Spanish to his coworker. None of it's very nice. The gist of it is, they've been scrubbing bird shit for hours, for this "*puto gringo*."

Rude.

I let it go. "My keys. I'll have to come back another day to let you finish," I say, in perfect Spanish.

They both get that *oh shit!* look.

"*No hay problema, amigos*," I say and hand each of them a hundred and fifty dollars.

They scatter to move their buckets and rags from around the car. One of them holds open the passenger door so I can throw the gym bag and the bag of burners on the seat. The other one races around to the driver's side to open my door. "*Muchas gracias, Señor*," he says, shutting it behind me.

I hit I-95 South, heading home.

Shit's starting to look up.

I've got the cash I need to get started, which means by this time next week, I'll be in control of a public corporation. The giant dick in the back window is gone, along with most of the bird shit. And I'm about a half hour away from having Kennedy wrapped in my arms.

All that's left to do is to is squeeze someone for my money.

There's very little traffic. I make it to the Glades Road exit pretty quickly. I head east, toward the Atlantic Ocean. As I near the front of my subdivision, I'm forced to the side of the road by an ambulance. There's a squad car following closely behind. They turn into my subdivision. I wait for them to clear the guard gate before turning in after them. I need to stop and speak to the guard on duty. My sensor for the gate has probably expired.

I reach up and grab my golf course membership ID from my visor and hand it to the guard. He studies the car. Examines the photo. Looks at me, sees my bruised face. Steps back inside the hut and swipes the card. The gate begins to swing open. "Mr. Liecht," he says, handing my ID back, "I'm sorry, there's an ambulance at your home right now."

Without another word, I hit the gas and race around corners to make it to my house. Flashing lights are bouncing off the neighbor's homes. Porch lights are starting to come on. I throw the car into park and nearly trip over my own two feet as I exit the vehicle. The front door is wide open with an officer posted right outside. "I live here!" I tell him, approaching. "My wife is inside."

It's obvious I'm not going to stop for questioning, and the officer steps aside.

I race through the house and find everyone in the kitchen. They're all working over the top of Kennedy. Someone's yelling out her vitals. Someone else is yelling something I don't understand. A pool of blood covers the floor. Kennedy's cell phone is nearby.

Everything stops making sense.

Someone's yelling at me now. It takes me a second to answer. "Yes, yes, I'm her husband, David Liecht."

"Does she have a history of seizures, Mr. Liecht?" a paramedic asks.

"No."

"Is she allergic to anything?"

"Not that I'm aware of."

"Would your wife…take anything?"

"Like to kill herself? No! Never."

"Mr. Liecht, your wife is in a coma. We're going to transport her to Boca General Hospital," she says, as two paramedics hoist Kennedy onto a stretcher.

"I'm coming with you."

38

DREAMS OF PORCH SWINGS GONE

It's ten o'clock the following morning.

Kennedy's still in a coma.

She has swelling on her brain. No one's been able to tell me why. They've had her in and out all night, running tests, trying to rule things out. It's killing me. I've never been so scared in my life.

I'm sitting in the chair next to her hospital bed. She looks so helpless lying there. The golf ball-sized lump on her forehead and the six stitches running across the bottom of her chin don't do anything to help. At first, everyone believed the injuries were the reason for the swelling on her brain—*she fell and bumped her head*. It took Kennedy's mother calling from out of the blue to determine the injuries are biproducts of the swelling and not vice versa.

I'd decided there was no reason to call and panic her mother. She was in Brussels and couldn't do anything anyway. I'd just call her when I had news on Kennedy. So imagine my surprise when at three o'clock this morning, I was pacing the floor of the ICU waiting room and in walks a nurse to tell me I have a call at the front desk from my mother-in-law.

Turns out she'd been on FaceTime with Kennedy.

They were talking about me being home. Everything was happy go lucky. Then Kennedy stopped making sense. Her mother said she started speaking gibberish. Said her daughter went ghost-white, then passed out and fell.

Because I'd just come home from jail yesterday, her mother didn't have my new phone number. She doesn't speak English very well. She ran to her neighbor's house, and together they called the Boca Raton Police Department. Boca PD sent a squad car and the ambulance to the house. When my mother-in-law called back to find out where they'd taken her daughter, things were lost in translation. It took her some time to track me down.

When I gave her the news about Kennedy being in a coma, it crushed her.

Her and my son are boarding a flight right now, heading here.

A nurse just walked in the room to chart Kennedy's vitals. "Do we know anything yet?" I ask, standing up. "No one's been in to give updates."

"I'm sorry," she says. "I'm just here to monitor the vitals. The doctors should be doing their morning rounds here soon. I'm sure they'll be in to see you."

Right on cue, in walks a doctor wearing a lab coat. The elderly, black lady with him is wearing a dress. She has an ID clipped to her collar, says she's the chaplain.

What the fuck?

All the blood drains from my face, and my knees go weak.

I fall back into the chair, dizzy.

With blurred vision, I watch their fuzzy frames walk over and stop in front of me. None of their words are making sense. All I can hear is my heartbeat pounding through my head. It takes a second for the ringing to clear. When it does, the doctor's asking if I'm okay.

I look up and let my eyes focus the rest of the way.

"Just tell me, Doc," I choke out in a whisper, lowering my head again.

He steps closer and rests his hand on my shoulder, causing any shred of hope I had left to evaporate. I fall forward out of the chair, limp. The doctor kneels beside me. "I'm sorry, Mr. Liecht," he says. "Your wife has terminal brain cancer."

My heart breaks into a million moments spent with Kennedy. "How much time does she have?" Tears cloud my vision and rain down my face.

"It's hard to say right now. We need to get the swelling to go down. I've spoken to a specialist. She believes medications will do for now. We're going to be administering them. Over the next twenty-four hours, the specialist believes your wife will regain consciousness. The fact she's breathing on her own is a very good sign.

"I want you to understand, though, even if she does come out of the coma, the cancer will still be there. I don't want to give you false hope. You also need to be prepared that your wife may have suffered brain damage. She may not be herself when she wakes up."

I feel like I've been kicked in the gut.

"Will I be able to take her home, Doc?"

"We believe so, but the coming months are going to be tough on both of you. Your wife is going to need round-the-clock care."

"Is there any chance at all she can beat this?"

"In cases like this, it's very rare for a person to live more than four to six months. Sometimes not even that long. To save her life, it'd take a miracle. Again, I'm truly sorry. Would you like some time with Ms. Thompson, our chaplain here at the hospital?"

The chaplain kneels next to me, like she's going to say something that will make me feel better. I know all the lines already. I don't want to hear any of them. "I just want to be alone with my wife," I tell them, but it barely comes out.

She nods and tells me to have her paged if I need her. They both turn and leave.

I grab Kennedy's limp hand and cry into it 'til there are no more tears left.

My silver lining was just yanked from underneath me.

PART 4

39

THIS LEMONADE TASTES LIKE SHIT

Boca Raton
Five Months Later

Life chucks lemons at you.

Sometimes, those lemons are filled with shit.

Since the day I got out of jail, lemons keep smacking me in the face. Splattering. Everywhere. One after another. Shit! Shit! Shit!

Like now…

I'm in a shady part of town, behind a house, ducked down next to an air-conditioning unit. It's after midnight. I've been running through the neighborhood. I just stuck-up a drug dealer for his heroin. A couple of his buddies on the corner saw me.

They came running.

I didn't stick around.

The scenario I came up with in my head didn't go as planned. Now I've got a group of non-white guys on my tail. I just have to make it a couple more blocks over. My Vanquish is parked in the shadows at the end of a one-way street.

None of this would even be happening if Paper, my main dealer, would just give me a little more credit. He's all bent out of shape, though. I owe him like seventy-five grand. And he wants it. Pronto. He's made that abundantly clear.

Twice.

Back-to-back reminders.

The first time his guys got the jump on me, I woke up in the trunk of a gold BMW. Paper was smacking me awake with his gun. My heroin bill was past due. He gave me a week to come up with the cash. Said he wasn't takin' anymore shit either. Which, as a side note, is a good thing, since I don't have any "shit" left to give him. He's already got all the jewelry, the electronics, and the furniture—inside and out.

Hell, the motherfucker's even taken the good pots and pans.

Yeah, like some real crackhead shit.

Anyway, his goons removed me from the trunk and threw me to the ground. For good measure, Paper kicked me in the ribs, screaming that he didn't want to see my stupid ass again until I had his "cheddar."

And, yes, he said "cheddar."

Two days later—which was the second time, my stupid ass showed up at Paper's front door—I was still cheese-less. I told him I was working this big, overseas deal, that my ship

GC BROWN

was about to come in, and that I just needed a little more of the heroin to get me through.

I even slapped him on the back, like, *I gotcha! No worries, mate.*

Paper just let me keep on talking.

He seemed receptive to what I was saying. I followed him through the house and out to the garage, where I knew he kept the shit. He let me walk in the garage first, all polite-like. Two black guys were inside. One was duct-taped to a folding metal chair, slumped forward. He was missing a couple of fingers.

They hadn't gone far; I could see them next to his feet.

Paper introduced me to the other guy, Link—holding a pair of pliers—adding that he was who was going to kill me. Shit. What?!

I'd missed something.

Before I could process the situation, Link was ramming his gun in my eye socket like he was looking for my G spot. I started singin' and dancin'. Saying anything I could to keep Paper from killing me. I even tried telling him some of my shitty lemon stories. He said something like "all lemons not making pink lemonade," or something to that effect.

I wasn't about to ask him what he meant.

Link was still eye-fucking me with his gun.

Out of the corner of my other eye, I watched Paper walk over to a cabinet and open it. He pulled out a sheet of plastic and spread it over the floor. Link rammed his gun deeper in my eye socket, 'til I had no choice but to walk over and kneel on it.

I was shitting my pants.

262

I could feel the pressure of Link's finger closing in around the trigger. I thought I was dead. Kennedy and my son flashed before my eyes. I screamed out, "I'm a bank robber! I can get your money!" There was a tiny release of pressure from my eye socket.

Paper walked around to the front of me. "You've got five seconds," he said. "Talk."

I told him again that I rob banks. Like with a ski mask. He didn't believe me. Frankly, it was the first time I'd said it out loud, and hearing it, I didn't believe it myself.

Unfortunately, it's true.

I walk right through the front doors of a bank, wearin' a ski mask, wavin' a note around.

I leave with a bag of cash.

I wish it weren't true, but it is. I'm out of options. I'm being blackmailed to save Kennedy's life...for the second time by the same doctor. This time, I need three hundred and fifty thousand dollars. I have most of it in cash. I've got just over three more weeks to get the rest. I'm exactly sixty-four thousand dollars short.

Plus, now Paper.

That's another seventy-five large.

He's expecting to see me this Saturday morning with it. I tried telling him I wasn't planning on robbing the next bank for a few more weeks. He wasn't in the mood to hear any of it, and I wanted to make it out of that garage alive. I agreed.

Honestly, I would've agreed to anything.

I'm "pennies" away from *possibly* saving Kennedy's life.

The money goes to her London research doctor. He's the guy doing the blackmailing. The funny thing is, this whole charade started out with me blackmailing him. He flipped the script.

Let me start at the beginning…back to the day when the doctor and chaplain showed up to Kennedy's bedside to tell me the love of my life only had a few months to live.

"To save her life, it'd take a miracle," the doctor had said. That day and the next, I came apart. I was spinning out of control, then it dawned on me he said "miracle." I pulled myself from the dark, kissed Kennedy on the forehead, and left.

I went home and started looking for that miracle.

For the next fourteen days, my head never hit the pillow. The phone never left my ear. Around the clock, I spoke to cancer doctors, research scientists, pathologists, professors, and cancer survivors from all over the world. I even spoke to a few conspiracy theorists who believed the government was behind all cancer. Everyone said they were sorry, but no one could help. Everyone said Kennedy was doomed.

Life was starting to feel like a house of cards.

I tried to keep going, but I began falling asleep on my feet, behind the wheel, and at my desk. I was losing my pace. Yakhov sent his lackey Boris around to pick up the weekly juice payment. I had the cash ready. I added a few extra hundred and told Boris I needed a little pick-me-up.

"No coke, though," I'd said.

He got me speed.

I doubled the recommended dose and went back to working the phones.

A few days later, I was on a call with a retired genetic pathologist in Sydney, Australia. His wife had passed away seven years earlier from the same type of brain cancer

Kennedy has. They were married for forty years. The irony of the ordeal was that the doctor had dedicated his entire professional life to eradicating the very cancer that took everything from him.

Talk about a kick in the teeth.

The conversation lasted more than four hours.

Both of us cried at points.

But at the end of the call, he, too, apologized. There was nothing that could be done to save Kennedy. We hung up, and I went back to researching.

Sometime after midnight, the doctor called back. Said he hadn't been able to stop thinking about our situation. He confessed to knowing about a top-secret cancer research outfit in London with an experimental case study underway.

He explained it as a medical breakthrough. The case study involves genomic sequencing, which identifies the exact type of cancer cell variants that are mutating. Once the cells are identified, precision medicine is used to treat them. You can compare these cells to healthy cells and create a weapon aimed at the gene and protein changes to eradicate them.

"The study is showing promising results," he'd said.

However, he explained that he was bound to secrecy and to please not ask why. All the retired geneticist could give me was a name—Michael Tenpenny.

I immediately researched the guy.

Tenpenny was one of these mega ego philanthropist billionaires who was always throwin' money at the cameras, talkin' about his latest contribution to the world of cancer research. All very loud and public. Top secret? Not so much.

I called TAZ.

TAZ called me back three hours later to brag he'd already broken through Tenpenny's Mickey Mouse firewall and was currently snooping through his personal shit. I told him to dig deep and find me something. Later that night, he sent me dossiers on Tenpenny and two of his billionaire cronies—also involved in cancer research.

TAZ included financials on these guys that most people don't even know about. Through hidden offshore companies and nominees, the three of them were funneling private money to a research laboratory in London. It didn't take a rocket scientist to figure out this was where the breakthrough experimental study was being conducted.

I needed to get to London and fast to talk our way into this "top secret" study.

The speed wasn't going to cut it.

I called Boris.

He gave me the number to a new guy. I met this guy, Paper, across the street from the Fort Lauderdale International Airport the next morning before my flight. He handed me my first little baggie of China White. "Go easy on the stuff, you'll feel like a superhero," he said. "Too much, you'll just be another junkie."

Man, he was spot-on.

I've tried stopping, but shitty lemons keep smacking me in the dome.

That morning, I slept for most of the flight over to London. On the final descent into Heathrow Airport, I did a tiny line of the heroin in the airplane loo. By the time I deboarded, I felt like I could leap tall buildings in a single bound.

I was a man on a mission.

While I was in the air, TAZ continued to digitally invade Tenpenny and his posse's lives, looking around for a way in. Maybe something juicy. I didn't know what or how, I just knew I was getting Kennedy into this study.

Talking billionaires into or out of shit is what I do.

By the time I landed, TAZ had an easier way.

We thought.

TAZ did a deep dive into their head research doctor—Dr. Norman Stallings. He found something in the doctor's personal emails that didn't smell right, the screen name *Lilly-Dilly16*.

"Lilly-Dilly" is the research doctor, pretending to be a sixteen-year-old boy…who likes other boys who don't look sixteen on their tallest day.

There were thousands of images of naked boys on his computer.

The next day, I waited for Dr. Lilly-Dilly outside the research laboratory and followed him home. I sat across the street, watching his house for close to an hour. Finally, I walked up to the front door. The doctor answered. His wife and kids were in the background. I handed him an envelope with images from his computer. Inside was a note, with a time and place to meet for breakfast the following morning.

I turned around and walked off.

He showed up the next morning right on schedule.

I told him I'd destroy his whole life if he didn't help Kennedy. I even leaned across the table and grabbed him by his shirt collar to make my point clear. He took me very seriously.

Two weeks later, he stole the first of four rounds of the experimental drugs from the freezers of the heavily guarded laboratory. Kennedy and I flew in the night before and waited at the hotel around the corner for him to show up and administer the drugs.

The next day, we flew back home and prayed.

Three weeks later, Kennedy's brain swelled again, and she ended up back in the Intensive Care Unit. This time she left with paralysis and some brain damage. The following month, we had to be back in London for the second round of experimental drugs. After returning to South Florida for the second time, we began to see a sliver of light at the end of the tunnel. Kennedy was starting to show signs of improvement—or at least she wasn't getting any worse.

The following week, the child molesting doctor flipped the script…started blackmailing me.

On top of being a child predator, the guy is also a degenerate gambler. He likes to bet heavy on soccer and polo, and really sucks at it.

At the time, he was into the wrong people for more than a million and half pounds. They'd already kidnapped him once. I couldn't chance it happening again. Kennedy still had two rounds of the treatment to go.

I put together two million dollars in cash and sent it over with Ocean.

We traveled to London for Kennedy's next-to-last round of shots.

The following morning, we were all set to return to South Florida when Dr. Scumbag called to say he was going to need another two mil before he would administer Kennedy's final round of treatment the following month. I left Kennedy and my mother-in-law at the hotel and went to his house.

I beat on the front door until he answered. Then I kicked his ass all over his living room…in front of his wife. He kept crying they were going to publicly ruin him if he didn't pay. I beat him some more, then stormed out of his house. I went back to the hotel and postponed our trip home. The following morning, I returned to his house.

His wife answered the door. I barged right in. The shit-bag was in bed, still sleeping it off. I marched into the bed-room. His face was black and blue and swollen.

I grabbed him by his broken nose and yanked him out of a sound sleep.

His phone was on the nightstand. I beat him with it, then made him use it to get an appointment with the people he said he owed the money to. Ninety minutes later, I was sit-ting in the back of a run-down pub on the seedy side of London, waiting on another character in this disastrous pro-duction to show. He finally walked in, puffed out chest, tuff guy swag, and sat down. Right away, Dr. Scumbag started fast-talking in French. I sat back and played dumb.

Neither of them knew I spoke French.

Lilly-Dilly told the guy that I believed the gambling debt was for two million American dollars, and that I'd pay. Basi-cally, I'd already coughed up a bunch in the past. The guy shaking down Dr. Scumbag said that if I didn't pay, he was going to ruin him in front of the whole world. And he wasn't taking anything less than 50/50 split, after the debt was deducted.

The perv complained it wasn't fair since he really only owed around two hundred and seventy-five thousand pounds, which is around three-hundred and fifty thousand American dollars.

That's where I chimed in, in French.

Long story short, I smacked the doctor across the face for lying to me, then told the other guy I'd pay what he owed, and not a pound more.

The next day, we flew back home to Florida. I'll spare you the boring details, but I had nowhere left to turn for the money.

I robbed my first bank.

And didn't get caught.

I decided to do it again.

Between the two bank heists, I stole just over two hundred and eighty-six thousand dollars. The cash is hidden in the attic above the garage in a double lead-lined bag. I'm sixty-four thousand from the finish line. Well, plus Paper. After that, I can sit back and take five. Then it's onto the list of people I'm going to destroy.

At the moment, though, I just need to avoid the authorities.

I've managed to ditch the group of non-whites chasing me. I'm back in my car, parked at the end of the block. At the opposite end, a cruiser is parked in front of a coin-operated laundromat. Two cops are standing outside, talking to a streetwalker and what appears to be a pimp. They all just look like they're kickin' it. I'll have to stop dead-even with them at the stop sign.

It's the middle of the night, in the hood. I'm "white" and driving an expensive foreign sportscar. Do you see where I'm heading with this? For sure there's going to be racial profiling. There are only so many reasons why I'd be around here. None of them favorable. To further complicate matters, to go along with the two hundred dollars' worth of shitty heroin in my pocket, there's a gun under the seat with a scratched-off serial number.

Ever the cop's wet dream.

As I approach the stop sign, both officers turn to face me. Fuck, even the streetwalker and pimp look over and stare. Like, *What the fuck are you doin' around here?* I keep my attention straight ahead and act nonchalant, like I'm supposed to be here. Then, like a sixteen-year-old newb, I keep my hands on ten and two while I look left, right, left, and go.

I make my way over to US1.

I'm headed home.

40

SHIT OUTTA LUCK

It's nine the next morning.

I haven't gone to sleep.

I just finished feeding Kennedy her breakfast. Her speech therapist is with her now. They're downstairs in our home theater. We turned it into Kennedy's room when the stairs became too much for her. I'm upstairs, standing in front of my bathroom mirror, the last of the stolen heroin on the sink.

It's Dog Food.

Paper sells China White.

There's a huge difference between the two grades. Dog Food is found in neighborhoods with liquor stores and coin-operated laundromats. China White is found uptown. If this were Paper's shit, there'd be enough here to last me a few days. This Dog Food won't get me past tomorrow after-noon.

I've split it into three hits, one for now, one ten to twelve hours from now, and the last for this time tomorrow, right before I rob the bank…a day early. Yes, a day early. I decided this last night on the drive home from robbing the drug dealer.

I did the pros and cons thing.

Cons trumped all.

I'm still goin' in.

Twenty-four hours from now, I'm going to be out of heroin and headed for dope sick by tomorrow night, the night before I was originally supposed to rob the bank. If I wait, I'll have to rob another drug dealer at gunpoint. How many times can I possibly get away with that?

Plus, Paper and his killer Link are the only other people on the planet who know the "when" and "where" this is supposed to go down. Paper's not stupid. He'll for sure have someone in the parking lot on Friday. Doing the job a day early alleviates the chance of any funny business with him or any of his guys.

On top of these two reasons:

What if I only get away with enough to cover fucking Lilly-Dilly?

Paper would be SOL.

I stare into my bathroom mirror. Don't worry, I see myself. I just can't do anything about it. Not today. When Kennedy's in the clear, I'll begin my exit strategy. Right now, I must get the rest of this money. Apart from hurting someone, there's nothing I won't do to get it.

I tighten one of my neckties around my bicep, tie it off, and squeeze my fist 'til I find a vein. I plunge the needle in, and the drug melts through my entire body. The aches and pains disappear, and I'm ready to start my day. I tuck the needle and necktie between the stack of towels in the back of the linen closet and walk into my bedroom to get dressed.

Jeans and a hoodie today.

I'm going to be casing the bank again.

As I'm walking downstairs, my phone beeps with a new text message. It's from the security guard at the front gate. I slipped him a hundred bucks yesterday to give me a heads-up if Yakhov's meatheads came back. Well, they're back, sitting across the street in a silver Dodge Durango.

Yakhov has sent them around to collect.

As if I don't already have enough shit on my plate.

The two meatheads were here yesterday, trying to catch me coming or going. Yakhov has recently suffered another one of his meltdowns. It's become a recurring theme with him. He's developed a number of serious issues. All having to do with me. He doesn't want to hear about my shitty lemons either.

He really is on my last nerve.

I call him "Yak-off" these days.

Makes him irate, and I don't care.

I paid him the first of several weekly payments on time. That was like four months ago. Since then, not so much. To add insult to injury, when this blackmailing pedophile called me to say he needed more money before he would give Kennedy her next treatment, I went to see Yak-off.

On top of the one and a half million I already owed him, he let me sweet-talk him out of another four hundred grand. Dummy. With "accrued" interest and late penalties, I owe him around two and a half million dollars. He calls. When he does, I tell him, "Now's not the time." He doesn't listen. Calls again.

Last week, he rang yet again.

I was still nice. Nonconfrontational.

I simply told him things didn't look good for him or his money. He started to get lippy. I told him to go fuck his mother in his native tongue and ended the phone call. He psycho-called me for the next two hours. I finally answered and told him I thought he was a little thick in the skull.

I spoke slowly…as if he were Joe Biden.

Then I hung up on him again.

Now, here we are.

Ocean has offered to make some calls to Russia to get him off my back, but so far, I've declined. I don't want anyone else in my business. Especially more Russians. I know Yak-off won't kill me. He wants his money. Badly. And thanks to TAZ breaking into the County Records database, the deed to my house—that Yak-off's holding for collateral—is now worthless. Same goes for the title to my Vanquish.

To make sure he doesn't jump the gun and do something stupid, TAZ triggered the county to mail the "updated records" showing no liens on either piece of collateral directly to Yak-off. Now he can't just kill me and sell off the assets.

All this sent Yak-off into a tailspin.

He sent a couple of guys around to break my legs.

I sent 'em right back.

I'm downstairs now, standing outside Kennedy's room. The speech therapist is talking on the other side of the door. They're going over Kennedy's flash cards. I'm not supposed to interrupt. I've been told this a handful of times. I'm a "distraction," they say.

I can't help it.

It makes her so happy.

I pop my head in the room. Kennedy is propped up in her hospital bed. The therapist is sitting in the chair with her back facing the door. Kennedy looks over. I do the *shh* thing with my finger. She smile-laughs and starts shaking her wrist—like stuttering—trying to point at me. She wants her therapist to hurry and turn around. She's trying to get me in trouble and loves it.

It makes my day.

I walk into the room. Kennedy goes silent, starts wringing her hands…anticipating. The therapist stands and turns toward me. She's holding the flash cards. Kennedy starts smile-laughing again, trying not to.

She can't hold back.

She knows I'm busted.

Even the therapist gets a kick out of it.

She nods toward Kennedy and tells me we have two minutes, then it's back to work. I walk over and smooth Kennedy's hair back. It takes her a couple of fits and starts, but she catches my hand and squeezes it to her chest. I press my lips into her forehead, then bury my face in her neck. "I fucking love you, wife," I whisper in her ear as she squeezes tighter.

Tears flood my eyes.

I just want my Kennedy back.

I leave my head buried in her neck until the tears dry.

Once our two minutes are up, I walk out of her room and into the garage. I keep an aluminum baseball bat in the trunk of my car…just in case. I move it to the front seat. I'm going to have to deal with Yak-off's meatheads. Obviously, I can't let them follow me to the bank.

As I'm backing out of the garage, my mother-in-law pulls into the driveway. She's been staying with us. She and my son went grocery shopping. I roll down my window and tell her that her daughter got me into trouble again with the therapist. She also gets a kick out of it. She holds Tom up to the window. He gives me a sloppy kiss and squeezes my head with his little hands, and I cry again.

"I love you guys. I'll see you this evening," I say, before my mother-in-law can ask me what's wrong.

I back out of the driveway.

The meatheads are there. I spot them in the silver Durango across the street from my subdivision. As I drive by, I play it cool, making sure they see me. In the rearview, I watch them pull out. They're five or six cars back. A couple of miles up the road, I pull into a grocery store plaza slowly, making sure not to lose them.

I have a plan.

They're not gonna like it.

I drive all the way to the far end of the plaza and circle around to the back, to the loading zone. They take the bait. They're on my bumper now. Halfway down the backside of the stores, there's a row of trash dumpsters. I slam my brakes and thrust the gearshift into park. Before the meathead driving can exit the SUV, I'm out of my car, carryin' the bat.

I run up and homerun-smash the driver's side window.

The end of the bat meets the guy's jaw.

He catches a nap.

His buddy scurries out of the vehicle and comes around the front. By the time I spin around, he's charging me at full speed. The bottom of my shoe meets his face, causing a sickening crack. Nighty-night. I'm not sure if he's going to make it or not. Sorry, not sorry. I reach inside the SUV, grab the keys from the ignition, toss them on the plaza roof, and walk back to my car.

Yak-off is not going to be happy about this.

Something's going to have to give here and soon.

I'm heading north on I-95 to the airport in West Palm Beach. I'm doing a practice run today. It'll be my only one. With the first two banks, I did this step over and over 'til I had it down. Now that I've decided to do this a day early, there's no time.

It was one of the cons.

I merge onto the airport overpass and circle around to Arrivals. I pull into the short-term parking garage and take the automated ticket. I find parking on the fifth floor and walk the skybridge over to the airport. Inside, I take the escalator down to baggage, walk right back outside, and jump in a taxi.

Four miles away, I'm dropped off at the airport long-term parking. This is where I keep the rental car, an olive-green Honda Accord. I rented the vehicle this past Saturday from one of the airport agencies around the corner. I've changed the plates and spent three hours installing do-it-yourself window tint.

I'm heading to Parkland, Florida.

Parkland Savings and Loans Bank is number six on TAZ's list.

There are a total of fifteen banks left on the list. It started off with over a hundred. I told TAZ I needed to know all the banks in high-income, low-crime areas within a sixty-mile radius of Boca Raton. He informed me there were one hundred and twelve. I then asked if he could do a search for registered medical marijuana dispensaries in the same area. There were thirty-one in the same sixty-mile radius.

TAZ merged the two lists and came up with the top fifteen banks, based off cash deposits.

I pull into the plaza at eleven o'clock sharp. It's the start of the lunch rush. It takes me a couple of laps, but I find parking about seven rows back, diagonal from the front doors of the bank. There's steady foot-traffic, and the drive-thru is starting to fill up. I'll sit here watching until 12:45. Then I'll slip my hoodie on, walk inside, grab a brochure, and walk right back out, like everything's hunky-dory.

Tomorrow, I'm hoping to be leaving with a bag of cash. Like everything's hunky-dory.

41

THE NOTE

THIS IS A STICK-UP! CASH GOES IN THE BAG! NOW!

Ten words that won't get me ten years or more in prison.

There are other words, too, but these are the ones I've chosen for my note.

I stroll into the bank, right up to the teller, slide the note across the counter, and wait to be handed the money. *Zip. Zoop. Zing.* No one panics. No one reaches for their phone. The rent-a-cops don't spray me with pepper spray.

And, before anyone knows what happened, I'm *adios*.

Best of all and worst-case, I get caught, and I'll catch three years tops in a federal prison camp, where everyone's got a phone, there are no fences, unsupervised visits every weekend, and fuck, there's even liquor and drugs galore. No rules. I mean who wouldn't want this as a worst-case scenario? The exact same bank job with a gun, I'm up the road with "Bubba" and "Don't Drop the Soap" for who knows how fuckin' long. My luck, I'd draw the same judge and that sweetheart of a prosecutor who tried to bury me after the whole Yemen ordeal.

No, thanks, I'll stick with the note.

I'm two for two with it.

I got the idea from a documentary I watched while in London, waiting on Dr. Scumbag to show up to our hotel room. The two bank robbers are, apparently, still foot loose and fancy free today. They've managed to pocket millions over the years...using a note.

A fucking note.

Who knew?

The bandits discovered some very beneficial things about robbing banks. One, bank tellers are trained to hand over the cash, no matter what. *Gun, note, or singing telegram—the cash goes in the bag.* Defying this means the bank's insurance policy is null and void, and there goes millions. The second beneficial thing these guys learned was that if they were to be captured, they'd get a little more than a slap on the wrist.

These two reasons were enough for the dynamic duo to "pull the trigger," slide the note across the counter, and come up big.

They're still coming up big today.

At the time, this was all just useless knowledge. Fast-forward to now, and I'm livin' it. I've run out of options. I'd even gone so far as to ring Mikale's Daddy for help. I even left a message, telling him Kennedy was dying. Still haven't heard back. Not even Bundu will call me back. However, some time ago, he did send me a text. Wished he could help but confessed to blowing most of his family money and was banking on the NT deal. Said there were legal issues with it, though, and it might not end well.

The Nova Terra deal.

That again. *Is that why Mikale is still underground?*

It dawns on me, not for the first time, that he might be dead. Once Kennedy is in the clear, I'm going to get off drugs, get squared with everyone I owe, then start choking people out for some answers.

But that day is not today.

So, here we are.

D-Day, T-minus roughly five and a half hours.

I'm back home now, sitting next to Kennedy's bed, scrolling through pictures on my phone. She's sound asleep. She looks so peaceful lying there. Like none of this is even going on. Like she just knows she's going to pull through. Her local doctors say her chances are better than 50/50 now.

Leaps and bounds beyond where we started.

From day one, everyone, including her cancer doctor here, told me Kennedy would be dead by now, or just shy of. it Her doctors believe it's Divine, as in a miracle. They do her blood work every two weeks and are amazed at the results. If they only knew, right? Fat chance of that, though. What would I look like telling someone I blackmailed a sleazy, cancer research doctor in London out of some breakthrough experimental drug no one's supposed to know about? It would turn into a global scandal the next day. Lilly-Dilly would get canned, and Kennedy needs him for one more round of treatment.

After that, it's open season on his child molesting ass.

Yesterday after casing the bank, I returned the rental car to long-term parking at the airport, then came home.

Kennedy was napping after a long day of therapy. I played in the pool with little Tom for an hour, while my mother-in-law made dinner. At the table, she said I looked like shit. I couldn't argue. I haven't seen a barber's chair in four months. I have dark circles under my eyes that resemble sandbags, and I've lost thirty pounds I didn't need to lose.

I didn't eat again last night.

I was dope sick.

It'd been nine hours since I'd taken the hit in front of my bathroom mirror. I had the shakes, my stomach was in knots, and a freightliner was screaming through my head. I kept pushing myself to hold off. I needed to stretch the time out.

I made it three hours longer.

By that time, I was on my bathroom floor, curled up next to the toilet. I'd worn myself out, dry heaving. Finally, I couldn't take it any longer. I pulled myself across the tile, reached inside the linen closet for my necktie and the heroin, and got high right there on the floor.

As soon as I could pull myself together, I came back downstairs to sit with Kennedy.

I've been here in the recliner all night long, just staring at her and scrolling through my photos.

I'm waiting to wake her up so I can feed her breakfast.

Kennedy doesn't speak these days. Not to us anyway. She's embarrassed by her new speech impediment. Oddly enough, her speech therapist thinks it's a good thing. She knows Kennedy's dying to talk to us. Thinks it's giving her an extra boost toward recovery. I'm good with it. I'm good with anything that helps.

I'm doing any little thing I can do, including being here every morning when Kennedy opens her eyes. When it's time for her bath at night, it's me who gives it to her. Last night, I ended up in the tub with her. Twenty minutes beforehand, I tried lifting her out. She resisted and then started bawling. I got in the tub with her. Didn't even bother taking my clothes off. I held her tight and cried with her. We didn't get out 'til our fingers were wrinkled, our teeth were chattering, and our tears had dried.

It's time to wake her.

I rub her arm until she stirs. When she opens her eyes, it takes her a second to recognize it's me. When she does, the corners of her mouth curl into her new smile. A couple of tries and she finds my hand and squeezes. I kiss the top of her head and tell her how much I love her. Over and over. I try to feed her breakfast, but she doesn't want it today.

She just wants me to talk while she listens.

Some days, I make up stories. Other days, I tell her about the moment I fell in love with her. Today, since I'm scrolling through the pictures on my phone, I turn my chair around and lay back into her, to let her look over my shoulder. I start with the pictures from the day our son was born. It's her in the hospital bed, the baby laid across her chest. Then it's the baby between us in our bed, the baby crawling around, the baby in his highchair, in his playroom.... The baby, the baby, the baby.

Nothing's changed, except I call him "Tom the Baby" throughout the entire montage.

Kennedy smile-laughs every time.

Now it's on to the photos from our wedding, photos from Foo-ket, photos from our life together while she was still married to her ex. I'm scrolling and scrolling. Clickin' and clickin'. I tap on a video I don't recognize. When it plays, I realize it's one from the kidnappers in Dubai. It's the video where the engineer lost a finger because I was out having lunch with Ocean, a "woman of the streets." Kennedy goes frantic behind me. She has me rewind it two times.

I do.

She recognizes the engineer.

"Do you know him?" I ask.

She shakes her head, trying to say yes. I help her sit up in the bed. I don't push her to say anything, though. I can tell she's trying to get it out, trying to put her words together. She takes a deep breath. "Th..th…th…tha…that's Mu…muh…muuhah…teen's bu…butha."

"Brother?" I ask.

She shakes her head, like a yes. "Heeee…muh…muh…muh…da." She's trying to make a gun with her with her fingers. "Pri…prr…hih…hihson."

"He went to prison for murder?" I ask.

She shakes her head with a tilt to it again for yes.

There are obvious questions I want to ask, but it's upsetting her. And her mother is in the room now to get her ready for the day. I hug my wife and rest my head against her neck. "Baby girl, settle down. There's nothing to worry about. The video is from a long, long time ago. I'll be back this afternoon." Kennedy squeezes my hand tighter. "I love you with every milliliter of blood I have in me, wife." I kiss her on the lips and hold on until I get that shock, then turn and exit the room.

Upstairs, I rush to get high in front of my bathroom mirror.

I wish I could say I was okay with it. I'm not, though. I've been bangin' high-grade China White for months. I'm full-on addicted. I'm not going to be able to just stop or walk away from this with a snap of the finger. The physical withdrawal symptoms are going to require God. It's going to all but kill me.

Right now, I'm not prepared to deal with it.

I inject the heroin into my bloodstream and wait for it to work out the kinks.

That's the last of it. There's nothing left to sniff, smoke, or shoot.

Today, I'm going as the old me—spit-shined, slicked back, and looking like I belong. I'm wearing a camel-hair pullover shirt with a pin-striped custom suit that, two years ago, set me back eight grand. Today, I'm adding black tennis shoes and all the Visine I could find in the house.

Once inside the garage, I grab my stick-up note, the lead-lined backpack, my gloves, and the nylon ski mask from a storage box on top of one of the shelves. As I'm backing out of the driveway, my mother-in-law and son are standing at the front door, waving goodbye.

Just another day, heading to the office.

So it would seem.

42

GOIN' HAM!

Talk about comin' and goin' at the same time.

It's Yak-off and his meatheads.

They're comin', and I'm goin'.

Only this time, they're in a different car, sitting at the guard gate of my subdivision. It appears they're trying desperately to gain access. I come barreling out of the exit and exchange a quick glare with the driver. Same guy from yesterday. The bandage around his head gives it away. The one in the passenger seat is different, though. The guy in the back, not so different. It's Yak-off.

He doesn't look happy.

I take the corner like a pro, cut through a business complex, come out the back of a subdivision, and ditch them before they get turned around at the gate. I wind my way over to I-95 and tuck into northbound traffic. Next stop: Palm Beach International Airport. The same routine as yesterday ending with me at the rental car in long-term parking.

I'm on the way to Parkland again.

There's a wooded picnic area on the backside of town a couple of miles from Stoneman Douglas High School. I pull in and park. In the trunk are two good-sized car door magnets that advertise Boynton Beach Skin with a phone number and a doctor's name on them.

Pretty sure I stole them from the doctor himself.

He was wearing the scrubs.

His magnets are now on the doors of the rental car.

I drive through Parkland and ease into the plaza with Parkland Savings and Loans Bank. It's the beginning of the lunch rush. I find a parking spot at the back of the lot, where I have a clear view of the front doors. The plaza traffic is picking up. People are stopping by the bank, in and out of the grocery store, there's a nail salon, barbershop, and a couple of cafés. I'm watching everything. The heroin has me dialed in.

If things stay like this, I'm going in at 12:45 and asking for a withdrawal.

At 12:39, I move to the front row.

The bank's doors are right in front of me. It's time. I lower my head, slip the ski mask on, and roll it back up to my forehead like it's fashionable. I slip on my black gloves and grab the lead-lined backpack from the back seat. Keeping my face hidden from possible cameras, I exit the vehicle.

At the front door, I roll the ski mask down and go in.

There are no customers and only one teller behind the counter. I walk right up. The teller has her head down, looking at her computer screen. She doesn't notice me until I'm standing right in front of her. When she looks up and sees me wearing a ski mask, it sends a visible jolt through her. I hold up my hands. "Stay cool. This is a robbery. Just do what the note says," I say, sliding it across the countertop.

THIS IS A STICK-UP! CASH GOES IN THE BAG! NOW!

I toss the backpack on the counter. The teller casts a nervous glance at the door leading to the back room, where her coworkers are probably on their lunch break. "Let's go! I ain't got all day here, honey. No slick shit like dye packs either."

She empties her drawer into the backpack.

"C'mon, c'mon! Now the rest of the registers."

She empties six more drawers. There's cash in every one of them. "Now the drive-thru. Make it quick. No funny business."

She clears out the registers.

It's been one hundred and fifteen seconds.

Time to bounce.

I slam my hand on the counter. "Let's go! Gimme the money!"

She hustles over with tears in her eyes. I feel bad for her.

"If you only knew. I'm sorry," I tell her as I turn to leave.

Back outside, I'm gone before anyone notices. I stay on back roads, away from the city limits. There's a quiet park, eight and a half miles away. I pull in and drive all the way back to the baseball diamonds. I park and take my first real look inside the backpack. There's more than a hundred grand.

I did it!

No time to celebrate right now.

I quickly strip the do-it-yourself window tint, change the license plate back to the original, and remove the door magnets. Everything goes in the garbage bag I brought from home. I toss it in the trash on the way out of the park. I stay out west, using all back country roads to make my way to the airport. Finally, I arrive at the car rental agency.

I leave the car in Drop-off, carrying an oversized red gym bag. Inside is my jacket, the ski mask, the gloves, and the backpack of money. Before I catch the shuttle, I pull on a baseball cap and dark sunglasses. I jump off at Departures with everyone else and walk through the airport, like I've got time, over to Arrivals and head back outside to short-term parking to pick up my Vanquish.

As I get closer to home, I'm on constant lookout for Yak-off and his jerk offs. That'd be just my luck…I get away with the cash, then immediately run into those clowns. At some point, I'm going to have to pay this guy. He's not going to let up, but neither will I, and eventually someone will get hurt—again. Now that I'm out of the woods with Kennedy, at least from the blackmail side of things, I can sit back and take a deep breath.

First things first, the heroin habit is getting the boot.

Then, I'm going to dial back in on my life.

I make it to the house unscathed. Inside the garage, I take the money from the trunk, pop my head in the back door to make sure my mother-in-law isn't coming down the hallway, and head over to my workbench. I take sixty-four thousand from the lead-lined bag, climb up into the ceiling, and add it to the rest of the cash in the other lead-lined bag.

The heroin's beginning to wear off.

Back at the workbench, I take the rest of the cash, around forty thousand, and throw it into a small gym bag I found under the counter. I toss that on the floorboard of the Vanquish and head inside.

I open the door to Kennedy's room, only to discover she's not there. I walk through the house and into the kitchen. Everyone's out back in the pool. Kennedy's mom is helping her through her walking exercises while my son naps in the shade. I'm not going to interrupt them. I'm not staying anyway.

I've got to go see Paper.

"Local Bank Heist…Again!"

It's headline news, everywhere. And "local bank" happens to be the same bank I planned on robbing tomorrow. Paper is not going to just brush this off as coincidence. He ain't dumb. Paper's going to think I'm trying to fuck him over on his money. He'll call Link.

Just what I need, that psychopath chasin' me around.

It's bad enough I'm only showing up with forty thousand of the seventy-five thousand I owe him.

I run upstairs to my bathroom and grab my drug paraphernalia from the linen closet. On the way out, I call Paper. He doesn't pick up. Probably thinks it's a setup. I send him a text.

Need to see you. $$$

He'll understand. I don't have time to spare. I'm heading to his house down south.

As I exit my subdivision, I'm on the constant lookout again for Yak-off. By the time I make it to I-95, my stomach is already cramping, like someone is repeatedly stabbing me with a steak knife. The withdrawals are kicking into high gear. I have a guy right here in Delray Beach who sells some mid-grade heroin. He calls himself Bugatti. No way I can risk making it all the way to Paper's house. I dial Bugatti.

"You'd better have cash," is all he says.

"You know I do. I'm ten minutes out."

"Hurry the fuck up. I'm going to the mall."

This is what my life has come to.

Bugatti is waiting for me at the same gas station we meet at every time. He drives a Maxima. Not a Bugatti. I walk up to his car. He starts to get out. I punch him through his open window, connecting with his chin. He's dazed but awake. I grab him around the neck. "It starts today. You motherfuckers are going to start respecting me like you've got some sense. Now give me a thousand dollars' worth, and forget I ever called you." I let go of his neck and throw the money on his chest. Bugatti stares at me for a second, then hands me a baggie.

Back in my Vanquish, I shove the heroin in the gym bag with the money and head toward Paper's house. There's a park a few blocks away. I've gotten high there before. It's safe. Besides, it's not like someone's going to suspect somebody is sitting inside a two-hundred-and fifty-thousand-dollar Aston Martin in broad daylight bangin' China White.

I leave Paper a voicemail this time. "I'm local with cheese in hand."

I pull into a spot all the way at the back of the park, near the ball fields so I have a clear view of every direction. I reach under the passenger seat and feel around for the sock I keep the needle and rubber band in. Instead, my fingers land on something hard and cold. "Shit!" It's the gun I used to rob the drug dealer. I have to get rid of it.

I find the sock and grab the heroin from the money bag and mix a little of the powder with five or six drops of water in the lid of the water bottle. I draw the liquid into the syringe and find a vein to sink the needle in.

Instant delirium.

The feeling is indescribable.

It's the deepest breath I've taken in six months. I haven't stopped from the moment the doctor told me Kennedy was going to die. Knowing I've worked against all odds to save my wife's life…the feeling is overwhelming. Now, I just have to get Kennedy to the finish line.

I lean against the headrest and close my eyes. All I can see is her. Kennedy. I can't lose her. I wouldn't know how to breathe. I've spent my entire life pushing love aside. I never did the serious thing. I relished being able to come and go as I pleased. Then Kennedy popped back in my life, married.

When she went back to her husband, I felt alone for the first time. Yeah, I played it tough for everyone, but the truth is, it broke me. The absence of Kennedy consumed me. I never called, though, and I never took her calls. I buried myself in work. When she strolled into the fashion show in Milan, my dreams came true. From that moment forward, we've been riding that wave of love that makes people sick to their guts.

I'm going to get our life back.

I just need to tie up a few loose ends. Like trying to figure out how this engineer, Kennedy's ex-husband's brother—with a rap sheet to include first-degree murder—ties into all this. What's the play here?

Why was he pretending to be an engineer? Did he fake his own kidnapping? If so, why? But he lost a finger. Would he go that far? Was I the actual target in that shitshow of a charade? Did "running into" Ocean with the general save my life?

If so, who all is involved?

Ivan? Was he selling me out the whole time? What about the pimp in the green suit who took two million dollars off my hands for supposedly leaving the Khaleed brothers' money with Ivan's buddies? He dropped out of the sky to fuck with me. Why?

I'm questioning everything now. Shit's starting to smell mighty fishy.

Why'd I end up in Dubai by myself in the first place, where these Khaleed brothers handed me two hundred and thirty million in cash?

And this Jargons cat and all his Yemen bullshit. Now the Nova Terra deal pops up, again. My money's been stolen, and I've been left for dead.

The common denominator in all this is Mikale.

When the Feds picked me up for the arms deal in Yemen, Mikale must've surely thought my goose was cooked. He couldn't catch me or put me down...my dumb luck with The Count did. I bet Mikale started countin' his chickens almost immediately after that. Went to grabbing everything he could put his grimy little hands on. He must've shit all over himself the day the judge let me off the hook.

It suddenly dawns on me that I just keep getting away.

Sometimes by the skin of my teeth.

Dating all the way back to Dubai.

"Ready or not, Mikale, I'm comin'."

I've sunk all the way into the seat now, but at the same time I feel weightless. The heroin has slowed my mind all the way down. Memories of my family start rotating on a screen, dating all the way back to the beginning—to the point I can now "feel" the memories. There's a sound in the background. Like the wind's moving and shifting in one big sheet.

Whoosh…whoosh…whoosh.

The images start to ripple as the memories speed up. Almost to the rhythm of the *whoosh, whoosh, whoosh*. It takes me a second to understand what the whoosh is….*a helicopter.*

I open my eyes.

Fuck! Fuck! Fuck!

Cops are coming at me from all directions. A SWAT team just rolled up, and they are filing out of the vehicle. I cannot tell you how many guns are pointed at me right now. *Has to be the bank job, right? What else could it be?* Immediately, I realize Paper's money is not in a lead-lined bag. There must be a tracker in one of the bills.

Fuck, David, how stupid could you be?

I'm screwed. Not to mention, I've got a needle hanging out of my arm and a gun under the seat with the serial number scratched off.

Always a cop's wet dream.

The cops have moved all the way in. They're crouched behind their car doors with their service weapons drawn. Radios are going off everywhere. I need more time. I reach under the passenger seat nice and easy and grip the handgun. Then I aim it at my head.

Everyone's screaming at me to put the weapon down.

This gives the cops pause and me time to scroll through the contacts on my phone with my free hand. I'm calling Ocean. She's the only person who can get the cash from my garage and get Kennedy to London for her final round of treatment.

I find Ocean's number, hit dial, and put it on speaker.

The cops are screamin' again to put the weapon down.

C'mon, pick up. Pick up. Please.

"Hello…."

"Listen to me. I have no time. I'm going to prison for robbing banks in about five seconds. The final payoff for Kennedy's treatment to this London doctor is in the ceiling above the garage. Be careful, the cops will be snoopin' all over the house. The money's hidden well, though. In the far northwest corner, pull up the insulation. You'll find the lead bag. The entire three-hundred and fifty thousand dollars is in it. The bills are marked. Take a boat over to the Bahamas. Do not open the bag until you get there."

"Are the cops there now?" Ocean asks.

"If not, they will be. And do not hand over the money until this doctor gives Kennedy the shot."

The cops have moved the rest of the way in. They are now next to my window, screaming with their guns zeroed in on my head.

"I will be in contact, but not until I know you're back in London. Please, tell Kennedy I love her and why I did it. I have to go."

"I will take care of everything, *Da-veed*. When I am done, I will immediately come back here and start working on getting you out. We love you, Boss."

And just like that….

TO MY READERS

Thank you so much for reading *SNIFF*. I hope you enjoyed it and are looking forward to Book 2: *SMOKE*, and Book 3: *SHOOT*. Please, leave a review! In the meantime, turn the page for a sneak peek of *Taken by Storm*: Book 1 in my Mason Storm crime series—due out in March of '25.

I know, I know, I'm told by my reps that I'm not supposed to release two different series simultaneously. "Stick with one." But, hey, we're charting new territory here. Not to mention, I was in the clink, and no one gave me the memo.

—GC Brown

TAKEN BY STORM

1

LOCA MOCA

It's hot outside.

Like, "die already!" hot.

I'm not going to beat around the bush, my balls are stuck to the inside of my leg. And they won't unstick 'til about the middle of October. You want dry balls, you buy a place up north. You don't live in South Florida during the summer months. Me, I happen to like the heat and humidity.

Hot and sticky balls come with it.

Here's something else to chew on.

I just walked out of the Mental Wellness Group of the Palm Beaches. Rich people are fucked up too. Makes you think maybe the grass isn't greener. Once you have money, you realize it doesn't fix shit. Trust me, I know. I'm not Bezos, but I don't have to work either.

Before I became a cop, I was a professional MMA fighter. Back before the UFC turned into a bunch of Hollywood pussies, I was the Heavyweight Champion. I got hurt. The money stopped.

I now drive an American classic.

I bought a behind-the-garage, rusted-out '69 Camaro SS for a song from a woman nearing ninety. I rebuilt it from the ground up. I call her Loca Moca after the ex-girlfriend I dated during the rebuild. Her name was Monica. She's a Cuban, who sometimes went a little crazy.

The name stuck.

She did not.

Loca Moca runs hot and the air-conditioning sucks. Most people don't want to ride with me, Suits me perfectly.

I'd parked Loca Moca under a ficus tree at the back of the parking lot. As I'm unlocking the door, I hear my phone ringing from inside. I lean in and grab it but miss the call. And apparently seven others. I'd love to know from whom, but I'm simple.

My phone is not.

A gift from another ex-girlfriend.

I'd always had the Plain Jane Nokia. With actual buttons you pressed. Green for *speak*. Red for *go away*. No touch screen. No camera. No apps. A simple phone, made for the simple man. This girlfriend, this ex, called me a dinosaur. She wanted me to trade up. I didn't. She eventually did.

Married a defense attorney if you call that a trade-up.

Anyway, she sent me this "smart" phone a year and a half post-breakup for Valentine's Day. Had to be a gag gift. I mean, it was more than a decade old at the time. She wrote her new number inside the card and told me to call. I threw the phone and her card in the back of a cabinet. Later that same week, I dropped my Nokia in the toilet.

I took it as a sign.

Hooked up the First-Generation iPhone.

The fucking thing is a mess now. It's constantly either beeping, vibrating, or flashing with *SYSTEM ERROR* messages. Every time I try to use the device, I have to *X* my way through a thicket of shit.

Hi, by the way. My name is Mason Storm, and I'm an alcoholic. Not really, but I've always wanted to say that. I am—or was—a homicide detective for the Palm Beach County Sheriff's Office. Now I'm in limbo…detective, not a detective, detective.

Well, fuck, you get the point.

I finally make it to my missed calls. Right as I do, the fucking thing rings.

Mia Zorrillo.

She's my partner—or, well, my partner before the suspension.

"What?"

"I've been calling you all morning, Storm."

"How many times?"

"How many times what?"

"I have eight missed calls. I'm trying to figure out from whom."

"Both you and that phone have a mental disorder."

"My new hot doctor doesn't seem to think so."

"Give her time. And change your voicemail. It's offensive."

"It's Will Smith…from the Oscars."

"I'm well aware who it is, Storm."

"Do you actually want something?"

She pauses. "We just pulled a Jane Doe from the water in front of Singer Island—"

"I'm suspended. Beat it."

"Let me finish. Last week, while you were in the Keys fishing, we pulled the first Jane Doe out of the water, right in front of the Breakers Hotel. Today's number two."

"Coincidence?"

"Not on your chinny, chin, chin. The killer left behind a riddle."

"Wish I could help. Send the chief my love."

"He's been trying to reach you too."

"He sus-pen-ded me! Tell him I'm nowhere to be found."

"Negative. I just sent him a text. Told him you're on your way in."

2

DIFFERENT WOKES FOR DIFFERENT FOLKS

Out on the west side of Boca Raton, I turn out of the parking lot and make my way back to I-95. At the highway, I hit the northbound ramp and mash the gas. So much has changed in Palm Beach County over the last fifteen to twenty years, especially on the east side. If you're headed north, the first city over the county line is Boca Raton.

Everyone's heard of it.

If you haven't, let me tell you about the place. In Spanish, *boca de ratones* translates to *mouth of the rat*. Quite ironic considering the lack of Hispanic *residentes* in the area. It's the high-rent district. The city of three Ps, I call it: pompous, prissy, pretentious. Every cliché you can dream up. Lots of Karens and Kens, all ignoring "woke," sporting sweaters tied around their necks, khakis paired with pink Polos.

It's far-right, lily-white crackers—mostly Matzah.

A short jog north is Lake Worth. No Spanish translation. Meanwhile, the place is flooded with Mexicans of all walks of life. A seeming contradiction considering none of them can surf, and Lake Worth is Surf Town, USA. There's high rent, low rent, and for the homeless, no rent. It's gluten-free pizzas and almond milk lattes and almost everyone's woke. Still the sweater around the neck, only sometimes nothing else. Trust me when I tell ya.

It's leather chaps, body paint, bondage.

A big fruit salad, hold the melons.

A little farther north and you can smell the opulence in the salty air. From the city of Manalapan all the way up through the island of Palm Beach. Big, big money. Private jets. Mega-mansions. Rolls Royces. Names like Trump, Fitzgerald, Rothschild. No sweaters. No body paint. Not woke. Maybe some bondage.

Definitely black tie and silver spoons.

It's truffles, soufflés, and caviar—all served by the help.

Over the bridge and through the city we go to West Palm Beach. It's different folks with different wokes. White, black, brown, and a few Asians. If we were to stick with the food groups, West Palm Beach would be Ruth's Chris, Tom's BBQ, Cuban sandwiches, and egg drop soup.

All served on the same corner.

I exit I-95 at Southern Boulevard and head west. This is one of the gritty neighborhoods of West Palm. Lots of pawn, skin, and smoke shops. The light turns green, and I make a right. Up on the left is me.

Palm Beach County Sheriff's Office.

The parking lot is full of Chevys, Toyotas, Fords, and one Hummer. The building is full of high school bullies wearing uniforms and guns, middle-aged housewives in need of the second income, and a slew of detectives running around chasin' a caseload they can't manage.

I park Loca Moca at the far end of the lot all by herself. She's not a fan of door dings. I unlock the trunk and grab my service weapon from the lockbox. I stick the piece in my waistband, just like the bad guys. I carry a 9mm Glock.

Nothing fancy, but it stops 'em in their tracks.

I know, you've watched a lot of TV. The detectives always sport five o'clock shadows and those nifty shoulder holsters, under their suit jackets. That's Hollywood. Why do you think the bad guys keep their heat in their waistbands? It's faster. Plus, I'm not wearing a suit. I'm a pair of Tommy Bahama drawstring pants with a designer T-shirt and Mark Nason slip-ons.

Again, nothing fancy, but it stops 'em in their tracks.

I'm going to let you in on something. Not everyone around here considers me a bursting ray of sunshine. They think I'm an egomaniac, looking to get my name in the papers. Which is fucking hilarious because I hate the media. But when the chief calls me in to save the day on all the big cases, it makes me look like a glory hound and a suck-up.

I've had run-ins with some of the guys over it.

I've never lost and that only makes it worse.

I gaze at the front doors, covered in reflective tint, and know my fellow officers are staring back at me. They all know I was suspended. And now there are rumors of a new monster out there floating around, and in walks me.

Even these halfwits can put two and two together.

I square my shoulders, open the door and walk in. Right away, I'm hit with cool air and judgment. I feign indifference and move toward the back stairwell. The room's a sardine can of the usual scum: hookers, johns, pimps, druggies, dealers, and drunks. Most of them repeat offenders. I nod toward Michael Rubin, Palm Beaches' slickest defense attorney, and wonder whose cage he's rattling now. He nods back with a look that says, *I'll have him out in an hour,* and he probably will.

I keep moving up the stairs, two at a time, to the homicide department.

This is my first time back since the suspension. I kick open the door and flick the lights on. It smells like wet towel. The place still resembles a shrine. The back wall is covered with pictures of children between the ages of seven and fifteen. All of them dead. All victims of the child molester I'm currently in hot water over. The public dubbed him "the Peddler." There's a local newspaper from three weeks back on top of my desk with a Post-it note: *Nice job, asshole!*

I've made the front page...again.

"The Peddler Meets the Imperfect Storm!"

I'm leading a cuffed Levin Rubenstein into the FBI building in downtown West Palm Beach. He appears to have been roughed up a bit. A thick and dark streak is running down his cheek, pooled-up on his shirt collar.

The article goes on to explain that because of my actions, past and present, the perv might walk.

He won't, but this is what the press does.

3

BRUISED EGOS AND BUSTED FINGERS

I'm still at my desk when I hear Mia coming from down the hall. The door smacks against the opposing wall for the millionth time. She looks around the office, sniffing the air.

"Wow, I thought the time off might do you some good, but you look like crap...and it smells like a gym sock in here."

She plops down in a chair and throws her feet up on the corner of my desk. "One of the other detectives has been working the case. That's part of the file on last week's Jane Doe," she says, handing me the folder she came in with. "The rest is being copied as we speak. I gotta warn you, it's not pretty."

"Never is. What do we know about today's body?"

She hits the high points. A couple of lovers on their honeymoon were strolling for seashells and found the body instead.

The first thing I notice is the autopsy report is missing. I give her a look.

"Well, that's the part I haven't told you. How we concluded it's a serial case. We have an appointment with the medical examiner tomorrow morning. We'll be given the report at that time."

On the third page, down about the middle, some digits catch my eye, branded across the forehead of the body: *66 20 28 17*.

"Branded with what?" I say, more to myself.

Mia pulls out a crumpled piece of paper and sets it on the desk. It has the numbers *66 23 24 18* scribbled on it. "Look at the pictures first, then I'll explain."

There's a stack of photos a half inch thick, numbered in the upper-right-hand corner. I start from the beginning and make my way to the back. The body is free of any clothing, bruised, mutilated, and obviously branded. I stare at the pictures where the branded numbers are most clear, wondering what sick riddle they represent.

I look back at Mia.

"Yes, the branding is on today's body too. Only it's the numbers I just gave you, which the M.E. found on a note in a plastic baggie inside victim number one's throat."

"Let me get this straight. Today's body, victim two, has the numbers from the back of victim one's throat branded onto her forehead."

She nods. "We got a call a short time ago and, as you may have already concluded, there's a baggie in the back of her throat too. Smart money says there'll be a new set of numbers. We'll know for sure when the M.E. pulls it out."

This is us against Death. Round one.

My desk phone rings.

"Storm," I answer, loud and coarse.

I hear the raspy, cigarette-tainted voice of the chief's secretary, beckoning us to his office. She finishes in a sing-song voice, "Oh yeah, the governor's with him."

Great! I hang up and let Mia know the chief has summoned us and that the Cocky Little Twit is there.

We make our way through the hallways of background chatter to the chief's office, which is at the absolute farthest point from mine, and I wonder sometimes if there's something to that.

His sentry...err...secretary, Beverly—*no one calls her Bev*—is holding point at her desk.

Beverly's twice as mean as sin. Saggy boobs, dirty teeth, deep frown lines, and about as cheery as an unkind word at a funeral. She informs us that he'll be another minute or two. "Coffee or bottled water?" she spats.

We pass, sit, and the seconds tick by.

Through a thick cloud of smoky resentment, she tells us the chief's off the phone and to go in.

I open his door, and the air's drenched with the stench of a pissing contest.

I nod to the chief.

He's standing behind his desk, the governor's fifteen paces away, looking out the window with his back to us. He's a faint little man, paunchy middle, snake eyes, and a crooked politician's smile. He's Daddy's Daddy's money polished to an edge, and I'm definitely not his top cop. He and I have gone our rounds, the most recent a few weeks ago.

The Cocky Little Twit poked me in the chest. Twice! In public! I warned him the first time. The second time, I bent his finger backward until it snapped.

"How's the finga, Gov'nah?" I say in my best British accent.

The chief gives me a look, begging for a break, and I think I hear Mia chuckle.

The governor pivots his body on hellfire to face me.

"I'm warning you, Storm!" he screams with no bass in his voice. "Don't mess with me today, or I'll have you handing out parking tickets downtown until you retire!"

Could he be any more 1984?

Then at about four hundred decibels, he yells, "Do you understand me?"

"Got it. Parking tickets. Downtown. Until I'm your age. All clear."

The governor must realize that he's getting nowhere, fast, and decides to let it pass.

I used to be somewhat of an icon in this town...outside the ring. I was given the Key to the City of West Palm Beach a few years back by the previous mayor. We met after I'd just solved a very public murder, ending in a shootout. I took one in the leg, and she stopped by the local hospital to thank me.

One thing led to another and, well, you know...eventually she slept over.

Then, almost two years later, on the *Six O'clock News* the Cocky Little Twit took the key back, claiming insubordination among a host of other things they were never able to prove. It's long story for another time.

The governor turns to the chief and says, "I expect you to put everything you have on this! And I expect you to keep this madman on a short leash," and he's gone.

The chief turns to me. "I don't know why you can't try to get along with him, Storm. It sure would make my life a hell of a lot easier."

"Chief, I asked how his finger was. What does he want, balloons?"

He just shakes his head as he takes a seat at the desk. He looks nervous. There's something below the surface.

"What aren't you telling us?"

"The body from last week is no longer a Jane Doe." He pauses. "It's Sophia Pennington."

It takes me a second to place the name. "As in Arthur Pennington?"

"The very one. I need you two to go there now. They don't even know their daughter's dead, and it's going to make the news soon."

This explains why the governor was just here instead of the mayor.

Arthur Pennington is the proverbial man. Top One Hundred Wealthiest People in America. Founder and CEO of some publicly traded software company.

And just as my luck would have it, his BFF is the Cocky Little Twit.

ACKNOWLEDGMENTS

God first. Right behind him are a bunch more people. So many that I know I will forget some. I'm sorry.

To my Family from top to bottom, right to left. To Jim and Sis…Wow! Who'd have thunk it? Thank you for the reboot. To the two li'l Girls I left behind. To their amazing Mothers, who were so much more than I ever was.

To my two li'l Bonus Boys and their look-alike brothers.

To the Men Behind Bars. To the characters I've written about. To the Homerun King, the Doc, to when in Rome, all the way to the Downunder, and all the Paper along the way. To all those in between and to the Matchmaker at the end. Stay strong!

To the Hollywood Movie Guy and his killer Editor. To the Beverly Hills PR Firm with the best Press, all the way over to the Texas Two-Step handlin' Social Media.

Can't forget the hot shot LA Entertainment Attorney…let's do lunch.

At last, to my Kennedy, my fascinating wife, Carla. Unbelievable, Babe! Are you fucking kidding me? Dude, we talked about this shit. *"From the worst of places to the best of intentions."* In all those written words, we found Our Love Story. You are absolutely wrapped around my heart.

I will see ya at the swing.

Bring all the kids….

ABOUT THE AUTHOR

From a farm in small-town Indiana to the diamond fields of Africa to federal prison back in the states and everywhere in between, GC Brown has surfed some big waves in the ocean of life's adventures. Now, from his home in California, where he lives with his wife and brand-spanking-new identical twin boys, he's writing all about it. *SNIFF*: Book 1 in The SNIFF, SMOKE, SHOOT Series is his debut novel. *Taken by Storm*: Book 1 in The *Mason Storm Series,* about a champion MMA fighter turned West Palm Beach homicide detective, is due out next. Check it all out at gcbrownbooks.com.

SNIFF

Made in the USA
Middletown, DE
23 October 2024